The Prodigal Nun

Also by Aimée and David Thurlo

The Sister Agatha Series

The Ella Clah Series

The Prodigal Nun

AIMÉE AND DAVID THURLO

St. Martin's Minotaur ⚞ New York

THE PRODIGAL NUN. Copyright © 2008 by Aimée and David Thurlo. All rights reserved. Printed in the United States of America. For information, address St. Martin's Press, 175 Fifth Avenue, New York, N.Y. 10010.

www.minotaurbooks.com

Design by Dylan Greif

Library of Congress Cataloging-in-Publication Data

Thurlo, Aimée.
    The prodigal nun : a Sister Agatha mystery / Aimee and David Thurlo.—1st ed.
        p.   cm.
    ISBN-13: 978-0-312-36731-2
    ISBN-10: 0-312-36731-7
    1. Agatha, Sister (Fictitious character)—Fiction.   2. Nuns—Fiction.
3. Catholics—Fiction.   4. New Mexico—Fiction.   5. Monasteries—
Fiction.   I. Thurlo, David.   II. Title.
    PS3570.H82P76 2008
    813'.54—dc22

                                                    2008011561

First Edition: July 2008

10 9 8 7 6 5 4 3 2 1

To Laura, who helped us find our faithful office companion, Gabriel, and to the Carolina Poodle Rescue folks, who helped us bring him to New Mexico. Thank you all for bringing Gabriel into our lives.

Acknowledgments

With special thanks to Phillip and Diane Uzdawinis for sharing their time and knowledge with us whenever we needed them. Job had nothing on you guys!

The Prodigal
Nun

I

IN THIS CORNER OF NEW MEXICO, ONLY NUNS AND FARMERS got up before sunrise *every* day of the week. Sister Agatha took her customary place in the last pew of the old adobe chapel at Our Lady of Hope Monastery. The voices of her cloistered sisters behind the partition rose in an angelic blend of altos and sopranos, praising God with one heart.

Extern nuns like Sister Agatha were the monastery's lifeblood. Sisters who had not taken a vow of enclosure, they kept the monastery running smoothly by handling necessary duties like shopping and greeting visitors.

The externs worshiped in the public section of the chapel where she was this morning. Looking around, Sister Agatha noted that the uncloistered section of the chapel was nearly empty. Only five of their regulars from town had come to six-thirty Mass this Sunday. Masses in town started at eight—practically midmorning to Sister Agatha—and those services were far more appealing to those who wanted a leisurely breakfast before venturing out.

Sister Agatha made the sign of the cross and whispered "Amen" as Father Rick Mahoney ended his greeting. Knowing that one of their regulars was missing but would soon arrive, Sister Agatha glanced back at the tall entrance doors. One thing that could be said about Jane Sanchez was that she had perfect timing. The woman always came in right before the first reading—the last possible minute that still allowed her to meet her Sunday obligation.

In her midfifties, hardworking, and devout, Jane seemed to be a good wife to her husband, Louis. Although they were usually together whenever Sister Agatha met them in town, Jane normally came to Mass alone.

As the reading from Acts began—Jane had cut it too close today—Sister Agatha heard a car outside, then a door slam. She listened for the sound of heels on the steps outside but instead heard a hollow snap, like someone with gum blowing a bubble.

Last Friday, Jane had called the monastery and spoken to Sister Agatha briefly. Something had disturbed her deeply, but she'd been reluctant to discuss it on the phone, afraid she'd be overheard. Too busy to meet with her that day, Sister Agatha had convinced her to stop by the parlor on Saturday, but Jane hadn't shown up.

A former journalist, Sister Agatha was always energized by cryptic calls, and she was *really* curious now. Jane's problem probably had something to do with her relatives. She didn't get along with her daughter or son-in-law and had recently sought out counseling from Father Mahoney. Sister Agatha had speculated that Jane had been dissatisfied with Father's take on whatever had happened and now wanted a woman's perspective.

Sister Agatha glanced back at the doors. She was looking forward to finally resolving the mystery of what Jane had seen. With effort, Sister Agatha pushed all distractions from her mind, faced front, and focused on the Eucharistic celebration. Soon Jane faded from her thoughts.

Early morning Mass tended to have very short sermons, and Father Mahoney used shorter Eucharistic prayers then, too. Since there were few at Communion besides the nuns, Mass usually lasted forty-five to fifty minutes.

Once Mass had ended, Sister Agatha stepped outside, and as she stood on the front steps, Mrs. Lenzi joined her.

"Good morning, Sister Agatha. I just wanted to say good-bye. I'll be returning to Italy with my daughter this week, so I won't be coming back to Mass at Our Lady of Hope."

Mrs. Lenzi had been a regular for the past year, and she'd be missed. Sister Agatha was about to say so when a shrill scream pierced the air. Her heart hammering wildly, Sister Agatha looked around quickly for the source.

Before she'd even taken a step, Sister Bernarda shot past her and ran across the parking lot toward the cries. As an ex-marine, her soldier's instincts always gave her the edge in emergencies.

Sister Agatha struggled to catch up to her fellow extern. Drawing near, she saw Mrs. Brown, who'd been the first to leave chapel, on her knees, sobbing. A figure was lying on the ground beside her.

Hearing running footsteps behind her, Sister Agatha turned and saw Sister Jo rushing up. "Go back and call the paramedics. Someone has been injured."

"Right away, Sister Agatha!" Sister Jo turned around and raced toward the parlor.

Uncertain if the parking lot was now a danger zone, Sister

Agatha realized that the best place for the worshipers was inside.

"Everyone, please return to the chapel now, for your own safety." She watched as Mrs. Lenzi and the rest stopped, saw that something was wrong, then complied.

Sister Bernarda glanced back at Sister Agatha and shook her head imperceptibly. She then focused on eighty-two-year-old Mrs. Brown and led her away, speaking calmly.

Sister Agatha took an unsteady breath. Based on Sister Bernarda's cue, the person sprawled on the graveled parking lot was beyond help. Taking a step closer, Sister Agatha realized that the body belonged to Jane Sanchez.

Sister Agatha made the sign of the cross. Shock numbed her senses, and for a moment she stood frozen to the spot. Their monastery was dedicated to the Lord, and a sin of this magnitude was an affront to everything they stood for—charity and love, based on a deep reverence for all of God's commandments. Reaching out to God for courage and the wisdom to accept what she couldn't change, she said a prayer for the repose of Jane's soul.

When she opened her eyes again, her gaze fell on the earthly remains of the woman they'd all known. Sister Agatha forced herself to study the scene with the practiced eye of an investigative reporter. Though that had been a lifetime ago, those skills would remain with her forever.

She crouched beside the body and, making sure not to touch anything, blinked back a tear. There was blood—Jane had either been shot or stabbed, and her purse lay open on the ground beside her. Scattered about were her keys, an empty-looking billfold, an embroidered handkerchief, a ballpoint pen, and her prayer book. She had been robbed and killed . . . or vice versa.

Sister Agatha took a deep breath, tearing her gaze from the body. She glanced around to avoid having to look at it again. It was then she realized that the doors of at least two of the cars in the parking lot were open. Maybe Jane had caught the robber riffling through the vehicles and confronted him. Robbery had then turned into murder.

Sister Agatha suddenly noticed that the driver's door of the monastery's old station wagon, the car they jokingly referred to as the Antichrysler, was also open. It had been vandalized with big scratches.

Hearing running footsteps coming toward her again, Sister Agatha turned her head. Sister Jo could have been her twin in size and shape, though there was a lot more bounce in the younger nun's step. Sister Jo, the latest addition to their family, was gifted with a sharp mind and immeasurable amounts of energy. Pax, the monastery's large white German shepherd, had followed but now rushed out in front of her.

"Pax, wait!" Sister Jo ordered, grabbing the dog's collar.

Pax dropped his haunches into an immediate sit but slid several inches. Sister Jo wrapped her arms around the dog's neck, making sure he went no farther.

"No need for that, he'll stay," Sister Agatha said. "Did you make the call?"

"Yes, but Sister Bernarda said I should call the sheriff as well. She said that Mrs. Sanchez had either been shot or stabbed and was already dead. So I called the sheriff and told him what had happened. He said to keep everyone away from the scene and make sure no one touched anything. He also asked that everyone stay inside the chapel until he and his team get here."

"All right," Sister Agatha said. "Do as he asked and make sure everyone remains inside. I'll stay out here, guard the area, and make sure no one approaches."

"What if the killer comes back?" Sister Jo asked, standing on tiptoes, trying to look past Sister Agatha to get a glimpse of the body.

"That's not likely, but Pax will protect me," Sister Agatha answered, moving to block her view. "Go back and help Sister Bernarda and Sister de Lourdes keep everyone calm. Nobody can be allowed to leave until the sheriff says it's okay."

Just then Sister Bernarda come down the chapel's steps and strode briskly toward them. "The paramedics are on their way. As soon as they arrive, please send them inside. They need to check out Mrs. Brown," she said. "She's as pale as a ghost, and I think she's going into shock."

"Poor woman," Sister Agatha murmured.

"I know the sheriff will want to speak to her, but I have a feeling he's going to have to wait," Sister Bernarda said softly. "She's barely coherent at the moment."

"Did Mrs. Brown mention having seen someone leaving the parking lot in a hurry?"

Sister Bernarda shook her head. "She just rambled on about how nice Jane had been to her. She'd always make sure that Mrs. Brown had a hot dinner. That was before the Good News Meal Program got started."

"Jane always said that no one in her neighborhood would ever go hungry while her two hands still worked," Sister Agatha said quietly.

"There's something I need you to pass on to the sheriff," Sister Bernarda said. "When Mrs. Brown saw Jane on the ground, she hurried right over to help. There's no telling what she might have touched."

"Of course. Sheriff Green will go easy when he talks to her. He's a good man," Sister Agatha said.

As Sister Bernarda left with Sister Jo, Sister Agatha

confronted the knowledge that Jane had needed to talk to her about something and she hadn't made time to help. She'd allowed other concerns to overrule the second great commandment—to love thy neighbor as thyself. Guilt made her chest tighten. Was Jane's problem somehow related to her death, or was it just an unfortunate coincidence?

Sister Agatha had no time to ponder the question. Sirens filled the air.

The paramedics, despite being called last, pulled up first. After taking a quick look at Jane's body, the three-person team rushed toward Sister Bernarda, who was standing at the entrance to the chapel.

Sheriff Tom Green arrived next, with the crime scene van and another squad car trailing behind. Sheriff Green, a tall former college track star with thinning hair and a slender waist, joined her a moment later. As he adjusted the latex gloves required for his work, she noticed that his pale blue eyes were bloodshot and his face was drawn with fatigue.

"Before you say anything, no, I'm not sick or hungover. We had a long night at the station. I'd be home in bed right now if I hadn't been in the area when the call came through," he said. "Now tell me everything you saw and heard. Sister Jo said that the victim may have been shot."

Sister Agatha recounted the sequence of events, including the sound of the car door, the pop, and finally how Mrs. Brown had discovered the body. She then pointed out the car break-ins and the way the Antichrysler had been vandalized.

"Doesn't anyone lock their car doors?" Sheriff Green muttered.

"Maybe at St. Augustine's in Bernalillo. But out here, we all feel—felt—safe," she answered.

"You mentioned a pop. That had to have been the gunshot.

It makes sense that the killer would use a small caliber—less noisy," he said.

"My brother and I used to shoot tin cans with his .22, so I've heard gunshots plenty of times. But the noise I heard was more of a pop—or more precisely, a plop—not quite like a gunshot, really. It reminded me of a bubble of chewing gum being popped, only a little softer, I guess. I didn't give it much thought at the time." She took an unsteady breath, then added, in a voice that didn't sound like her own, "I should have gone outside to check when she didn't come into the chapel."

"I hope you're not blaming yourself. If you'd come out to look, you would have undoubtedly interrupted the killer while he was going through her purse or through the other vehicles. You might have become his second victim."

"Maybe so," she answered in a whisper.

"It's possible, from what you said, that the gun had a silencer. Did you hear any other noises outside?" Tom pressed.

"No."

They both looked over as a black car roared up and slid to a stop beside Tom's vehicle, raising a small cloud of dust. A red-haired man in an expensive gray suit, turquoise bolo tie, and black Western boots climbed out. He took a step toward them, but Tom intercepted him before he could come closer.

"Stay put, Albrecht. Crime scene here," he said, gesturing to the deputy who was working quickly to put up the yellow tape.

"Understood," the man said, moving back and bringing out a BlackBerry.

"What's Fritz Albrecht doing here?" Sister Agatha asked Tom softly. "The last I knew, he was working for Channel 7 in Albuquerque."

"He's on Mayor Garcia's staff now. His official title is law enforcement liaison, but he's more of a pain in the . . . neck, or thereabouts."

"Back when I was a journalist, the word was that he was a real lightweight as a reporter. He was more of the press conference type."

"Word has come down from above—Mayor Garcia, not God—that our department needs to improve our image, and we've been told to pay particular attention to community relations. Fritz is supposed to help us out on that. If we look good, Garcia looks good," Tom said in a taut voice.

"And what else, Tom?" she pressed, reading his tone correctly.

"I've been told to make sure civilians don't get involved in our criminal cases. When citizens uncover vital evidence, it makes us look incompetent, according to Garcia."

"I guess that means me, but this time the monastery has a vital interest in what's going on. My old journalism skills can be an asset to you now. I'm not after credit. Your department can take it all."

"This is a murder investigation, Sister, and you need to stand back and go about your own . . . calling," he said as the tape was placed between them.

"That's kinda hard to do, Tom. One of our own parishioners just got killed outside our chapel."

"Yeah, and let's hope this leads away from the monastery, not toward it." Seeing Albrecht staring at both of them, he looked back at Sister Agatha. "I better get to it."

He went to look at the black beaded handbag lying on the ground. Less than a foot away was the victim's wallet. He picked that up, taking a closer look. "No money, but he left a credit card, her driver's license, and a voter ID card," he said, just loud enough for Sister Agatha to hear.

"She has her watch and rings, too, and a pearl necklace that looks expensive," Sister Agatha said after making sure Fritz wasn't within hearing distance.

"That kind of thing is hard to get rid of around here," he answered. "I'll check and see if she carried more credit cards and a checkbook. Did she normally make her offering with cash or a check?"

"Our cellarer would know. I'll ask her," she answered, then added, "Where's her cell phone? I know she carried one."

Tom looked in the purse and around the area, then stood. "It might be in a pocket, or her car. Thanks for the tip. Anything else you might want to add?"

"Yeah," she admitted reluctantly, guilt forming a lump at the back of her throat. "Jane called me on Friday. Something she'd seen was really bothering her, but I was too busy at the time to meet with her. I asked her to come to the parlor the next day, but she never did."

"Interesting. I'll check it out with her husband and see if he can tell me what that was about, but it may be totally unrelated."

She swallowed hard but didn't comment. "I know Father Mahoney had been counseling her regularly, but I don't know the details. You'll have to ask him about that yourself."

"I'll do that. I'll be interviewing everyone—and you again as well—before I leave." Tom motioned to some officers who'd been hovering near the scene.

As two members of the crime scene unit walked up with their cameras and gear, Sister Agatha stepped back. A third deputy, female, started attaching yellow crime scene tape to a vehicle aerial.

Sister Agatha said another prayer for the soul of the departed. For now, Father Mahoney would be prevented from administering Last Rites. Access to homicide victims was restricted to police personnel taking part in the investigation.

As one of the women deputies, wearing latex gloves, inventoried the contents of Jane Sanchez's purse, Sister Agatha glanced away. That was when she noticed what looked like the letter Y on the door of the Antichrysler. Sister Agatha moved to her left, realizing that she might have been premature when she'd assumed what she'd seen there was only scratches. Positioning herself to see the entire door, she read the message, and it brought chills to her blood.

Etched in crude block letters at least a foot high was YOU'RE NEXT, NUN.

2

HER HANDS SHAKING, SISTER AGATHA LOOKED AT THOSE gathered there. The only person who seemed to be looking in her direction at the moment was Fritz Albrecht. He nodded, and she nodded back.

Sister Agatha moved around until she caught Tom's eye; then she pointed toward the old station wagon.

"You didn't leave anything valuable in that old rust bucket, did you?" Tom asked, coming over.

"No, but I just realized what was scratched into the door. Take a look for yourself," she said, pointing.

"Oh, crap," Tom muttered once he was at the proper angle to see the entire message. "It wasn't there last night?"

"No, and we wouldn't have left the door open like that either. So what now? This is either the work of a very sick person or a direct threat to our monastery," she said. She swallowed, but her mouth remained infernally dry.

"Maybe not the entire monastery. It could be directed at you or one of the other externs who drive this car. This is the vehicle you use to deliver the Good News meals to people all over the community, correct?"

"Yes. Sister Jo usually handles the details and makes most of the deliveries. Sister Bernarda and I help when needed. Did you know that Sister Jo did all the paperwork that resulted in the county handing the contract to us and St. Augustine Church? This is the first faith-based initiative in our area. Of course, we don't make any profit from it, but it's now a better and more reliable service to the community."

"However, I remember some people were upset about a state-funded program being awarded to religious groups. Have you caught any flak over it?"

"Only from Peter Aragon, but he's just a city councilman using the program to promote his own agenda. Some nonsense about us using the program to try to push religion down the throats of senior citizens. He's a political hack, not a killer."

"Probably, but this threat's real, and I have to check out all the possibilities. Make sure everyone at this monastery stays alert, the externs in particular."

"I'll pass the word."

"Which car is Jane Sanchez's?" he asked.

Sister Agatha pointed to the maroon sedan, an older model with faded paint. "That's hers."

Crime scene officers were already inspecting the cars, which would be dusted for prints. Leaving Sister Agatha outside the tape, Sheriff Green began searching the ground around Jane's car, moving outward from the parking area toward the opened gates and the driveway beyond.

Except for the rose bed in the circular planter at the center, and some lilac bushes beside the walls, the parking lot was covered with a thin layer of gravel. Over time, activity and the elements had shifted the rocks, creating areas where there was more sand and soil than stone.

Tom looked up. "Someone walked in," he said, pointing at what appeared to be large footprints. "Those impressions lead right up to the body. Any idea who arrived on foot?"

Sister Agatha shook her head. "Why would the killer come in on foot this close to where Mass was being celebrated? If he'd been seen, his only option would have been to run for it."

"Wait there. I'm going to check outside the grounds." He continued on, studying the ground all the way outside the monastery's property line. He stopped beside the wall, looked down and toward the road, then came back.

"Anyone come to church on a bike recently, like today?" he asked.

"Not that I know about."

"Someone rode up on a bicycle, leaned it against the wall, then came back for it and took off. The tracks are fresh, and there isn't any gravel to confuse the markings. The size of the footprints rules out a child. So let's say that it was our killer on that bicycle," he said in a soft, thoughtful tone. "Providing he was in shape, that would have given him a way to make a fast exit. He could ride down this road about a hundred yards, then cut across into the bosque, out of sight, taking a route most cars couldn't access. And on a bicycle, he would have been virtually silent. All things considered, it may have been a very good strategy."

"So is this a burglary that escalated to robbery and then murder, or was murder the intent all along?" Sister Agatha asked him, making sure Fritz was still out of earshot. "Was Jane the unfortunate target because she happened to show up alone at just the wrong time?"

"It's hard to say at this point, but if the killer did indeed bring a silenced weapon that would imply premeditation. Now here's the critical question—was Jane *always* the last person to arrive?"

Sister Agatha nodded. "Without fail. Our list of regulars is small and well established, and you could almost set your watch by Jane's arrival."

"So my guess is that the shooter knew exactly who his target was going to be. Whether her selection as the victim was circumstantial or personal—that, I don't know. He may have been watching Jane in her own neighborhood as well and learned her routines."

"How does the warning on the monastery's station wagon fit in with all that? Are we next on the killer's list?" she asked.

"If Jane was the intended target, then the robbery and the message on the monastery's car could be just a smoke screen."

"If Jane *was* the target, could it have something to do with what she wanted to talk to me about? Could that have been important enough for someone to kill her?" Sister Agatha asked in a strangled voice.

"Do you think Jane might have had something she wanted to show you, too? Something that may have motivated the killer to go through her purse to remove it?"

"And then take the money and rummage through the other cars just to hide that? I can't answer that, Tom. I'm sorry," she said in a strained voice. "I have no idea what she wanted to talk to me about. I wish I'd taken time to talk to Jane when she called. I failed her—and God."

"No matter what the investigation uncovers, you're not responsible for what other people do."

"A sin of omission is still a sin," she said.

"The killer is the only one who should be feeling guilty,"

Tom answered. "Now you'll have to excuse me while I get back to the crime scene," he added for Fritz's benefit, seeing that he'd ventured closer.

As Tom walked off, Sister Agatha gave Fritz a nod and decided to go inside to see if she could help there. She was a few feet from the doors when Tom caught up to her again.

"No cell phone anywhere. Either she left it at home, or the killer took it. I'm going to question the people who were in the chapel. It might help keep them calm if you sit in," Tom said.

"I appreciate the offer. Most of them are elderly, and they've been through quite a shock." Sister Agatha led the way to the entrance. "What I still can't understand is why Jane didn't scream for help. We *would* have heard her." Sister Agatha stopped in midstride as a thought suddenly occurred to her. "Do you think Jane knew her killer?"

"Maybe so. That might mean it's someone people would ordinarily trust, so you better warn the other nuns right away."

"When it comes to defending ourselves, we have very few options," Sister Agatha said.

"I'll increase patrols in the area and assign a deputy to keep an eye on the monastery. You have Pax, too. Keep him outside at night for the time being. If there's a problem, he'll bark—and be one heckuva deterrent."

Whispering a soft prayer that God would also send His angels to watch over them, Sister Agatha led Sheriff Green through the chapel doors.

3

WHILE THE EXTERNS SERVED TEA AND SISTER Clothilde's Cloister Cluster Cookies in the chapel foyer, Sister Agatha and Sheriff Green questioned people individually in the parlor.

Simplicity defined the decor here. A crucifix made of pine stained a dark brown had been placed on the whitewashed wall. A wooden desk stood toward the back and, thanks to the extremely prolific lilac bushes outside, there was a vase filled with blossoms on it. A small quilted wall hanging depicting the Annunciation, crafted by Sister Maria Victoria, their resident seamstress, was hung on the right wall.

The townspeople who'd attended their early morning Mass hadn't been very helpful so far. They'd neither seen nor heard anything outside during the service. Although she'd hoped things would turn out differently, Sister Agatha wasn't surprised.

Mrs. Brown was the last churchgoer Sheriff Green questioned. The paramedics had, at long last, pronounced her in good shape. Despite her age and the shock she'd received, Mrs. Brown seemed more angry than frightened now. Although she'd willingly answered all the sheriff's questions, she was now demanding answers from him.

"Jane cared about everyone. She didn't deserve this," Mrs. Brown said. "Why was she attacked? Was it a robber? I saw the open car doors. Was my car broken into?"

"We've just started to work this case, Mrs. Brown," Sheriff Green said. "It's much too early for us to have definitive answers on anything. That's why we need your help. Can you tell me if Mrs. Sanchez had any enemies?"

"That woman helped anyone who needed her. I don't know why anyone would want to harm her." She wiped a tear away with her white linen handkerchief.

After a few more questions that got him nowhere, Tom stood and signaled Sister Bernarda. She'd help Mrs. Brown back outside, where a deputy would try to find out if anything was missing from her vehicle.

As the two left, Sheriff Green glanced at Sister Agatha. "Who's next?"

"Father Mahoney."

Their priest, a former professional wrestler, came in a moment later. As he sat down they could see the lines of tension around his eyes and mouth.

"I've done my best to keep everyone calm as you asked, Sheriff Green, but I was scheduled to celebrate other Masses today. Is it possible for us to talk this afternoon?"

Tom shook his head, then held out his cell phone. "Call whomever you need to take over those duties for you, Father. I have no idea how long this is going to take."

"Thanks, but that's not necessary," he said, exhaling softly. "I had a feeling you'd say that, so I already called to make arrangements."

"Good," Sheriff Green said, placing the cell back in his pocket. "How well did you know Jane Sanchez, Father?"

"For the past three months she and her husband have been coming to my office for counseling."

"Was their marriage in trouble?" the sheriff asked instantly.

Father Mahoney hesitated.

"I'm assuming this isn't covered by the seal of the confessional," the sheriff pressed.

"No, it isn't, but I'm a licensed psychologist, and doctor/patient confidentiality survives death."

"Father, with all due respect, let me remind you that Jane Sanchez was a *murder* victim."

"I understand, Sheriff Green, but there are certain things I can't discuss with you. What I *can* tell you is that they were both committed to making their marriage strong. So if you're thinking that her husband may have had something to do with her murder, you're way off the mark. They had problems, like most couples, but Louis loves . . . loved . . . that woman."

"Generally, what kind of problems were they facing?" When Father Mahoney hesitated, Sheriff Green added, "If you don't think her husband's responsible, then help me eliminate him from my suspect list so we can move on in the investigation."

Father Mahoney considered it, then at last nodded. "I can only tell you what's already public knowledge. Louis has a heart condition, and Jane was terrified of losing him. They were constantly at odds because Louis had his own outlook on how to deal with those health issues. He wanted to live his life to the fullest—rejecting the idea of diet and exercise. Jane was doing her best to keep him on a saner course of action."

"Is there anything else you can tell me about the couple? Was there any reason for jealousy—perhaps a third person in their relationship?"

"I've already told you all I can, Sheriff."

"I appreciate your help," Tom said, shaking his hand.

Once Father left, Tom glanced over at Sister Agatha. "I'm through here for now. I'm going to pay Louis Sanchez a visit."

"Take me along," she said. "The news of his wife's death may be easier to take from me—a nun who knew her—than from you. Since you'll need to get clear answers, having a calming influence there will help you."

"Good idea."

"Oh, wait. I just remembered. Do you suppose Fritz Albrecht will tell his boss about you taking me along—me, a member of the public?"

"Mayor Garcia wouldn't want my job today. Let me deal with Fritz. You ready to go?"

"I'll get Reverend Mother's permission, then meet you at your car."

As Sister Agatha went through the inner door and entered the cloister, Reverend Mother was coming down the hall. Reverend Mother Margaret Mary was a tall woman with rich, dark brown eyes and gentle lines around her face. There was a serenity about her that conveyed a sense of peace, no matter how dire the situation.

Sister Agatha updated her quickly, then asked for permission to leave the monastery.

"Go with my blessing, child." Reverend Mother called all of them "child," as was their monastic custom.

Sister Agatha knelt, and Reverend Mother reached for a vial of holy water deep inside the pocket of her habit. Moistening her finger, she made the sign of the cross on Sister Agatha's forehead.

A short time later, Sister Agatha was walking across the grounds. Seeing her, Pax came running up. Sister Agatha crouched down and patted the dog. "Not this time, Pax. You're needed here to take care of the monastery."

Almost as if he'd understood, the dog ambled off and lay down at the bottom of the shaded steps leading to the parlor.

Sister Agatha joined Sheriff Green, then glanced back at Pax. "He's really a great dog."

"As a monastery pet, he's perfect. As a police dog, he drove his handlers crazy. He has a mind of his own."

As soon as they were under way, Sheriff Green turned to her and asked, "Is there anything else you've remembered about the victim? Maybe something about that last conversation you had with her? I'd really like to get some insight into this woman."

"We really didn't speak that often. She asked me to pray for her and Louis a few times, but that's about it."

"Yet she called to confide in you?"

"It's not that surprising. As an extern, I'm one of the nuns she sees most, and people in trouble often find it easier to talk to a nun," she said, then with a sigh added, "I just wish I'd done more to help her." She'd be praying for forgiveness for a long time on this.

They arrived at a modest residential neighborhood in northern Bernalillo a short time later. The midsized pueblo-style houses dated back to the fifties and sixties. Cars and pickups, most of them older models with faded paint and small dings, filled the driveways. Several of the low block walls around the houses had been spray-painted with graffiti, painted over, then vandalized a second or third time. The owners were obviously unable to keep up with the taggers.

"A working-class neighborhood," Sister Agatha said, mirroring what she was sure he was thinking.

"Help me out. I'm looking for 4432 Calle de Lupe. The street numbers defy logic in this old development."

"I think it's the white stucco house with the Taos blue trim," she said, pointing ahead. "Sister Bernarda came to visit a few months ago, and I remember her mentioning the Taos blue paint."

"So Sister Bernarda knows them?"

"Yes, but she hasn't spoken to Jane as much as I have. As I recall, she only stopped by that one time to deliver a prayer book to them."

They parked in the empty driveway, and Tom went up to the front door, Sister Agatha a few steps behind him. Tom knocked hard, but there was no answer. He tried the doorbell, too, but it didn't seem to work.

"I'll check out back. It's a warm day. Maybe he's on the patio," she said.

Stepping off the porch, she walked around the corner. The backyard had an elliptical terra-cotta concrete patio, a gas barbecue, and a small café table with four metal chairs—but no Louis.

Sister Agatha stepped up onto the porch and knocked on the metal and glass screen door. She could make out someone moving through the kitchen.

"Louis?" she called.

Suddenly the door flew open, catching her hard on the left shoulder.

"Help!" she cried out, tumbling off the porch. As she fell, the man raced past her, and she caught the strong smell of sweat. A figure in a gray hooded sweatshirt and sunglasses raced around the corner of the detached garage and disappeared down the alley.

"Tom!" Sister Agatha struggled to untangle her legs from the folds of her habit and scramble to her feet.

Tom came rushing around the corner of the house. "What the . . . ?"

She pointed toward the alley. "Burglar, gray sweatshirt. Big guy."

"You okay?"

"Yes, go! He's getting away!"

Tom sprinted across the yard, then around the garage.

The sound of his footsteps soon faded, and by then she was on her feet, rubbing her aching shoulder. At least nothing was broken—except the glass on the back door.

4

SEEING A NEIGHBOR PEERING AT HER FROM A SIDE WIN-dow, Sister Agatha waved frantically and hurried around the low wall to the identically styled pale green house on the next lot. Sheriff Green needed help, and she didn't have the monastery's cell phone with her.

As Sister Agatha approached the neighbor's porch, the door swung open. "Sister, what's going on over at the Sanchezes'? I heard a loud bang, walked to the window for a look, and saw you on the ground. Did you fall off the porch?"

"I was pushed. A man rushed out of the house and slammed into me. Unless Louis has grown a foot in height since I last saw him, I just surprised a burglar. Sheriff Green chased after him, but I'd like to call the police and get more help."

The woman nodded and pointed to the phone on the side table. Sister Agatha immediately called 911, but before she'd said more than a few words she learned that Tom had already called for backup. Deputies were on their way.

"Thank God the Sanchezes weren't home," The woman said to Sister Agatha, her eyes big with concern. "But what were you and the sheriff doing there, Sister . . . ?"

"I'm Sister Agatha, and we were looking for Louis," she said, then quickly added, "How do you know Louis isn't home?"

"I'm Betty Malone," she said, introducing herself.

"Louis usually leaves right after Jane goes to church. I haven't seen him pass by, so I don't think he's back yet."

Sister Agatha looked out the living room window, praying that Betty was right. If Louis was at home, there was a chance he'd been hurt, even killed. She brushed the possibility out of her mind, finding it too horrible to contemplate. "Do you happen to know where Louis goes while Jane's at Mass?"

"Not really, Sister Agatha."

Before she could ask anything else, Sister Agatha saw Tom come around the corner, walking toward the house. He looked up, saw her, and shook his head.

"They have just the one car," Betty continued, unaware of the sheriff's return. "After Jane leaves, Louis goes out on foot. He comes back an hour or two later, which is usually long before Jane gets back. She likes to run errands by herself on Sunday."

Betty joined Sister Agatha at the window and pointed farther down the street. "There's Louis now. Right on time. And that must be the sheriff over there by the house," she said, looking in the opposite direction. "Guess he didn't catch the burglar. That's too bad."

Sister Agatha looked at Louis, recognizing the overweight, middle-aged man with the slicked-back hair. He was obviously not the man who'd fled the Sanchez home. The burglar had been taller and less . . . robust.

Catching Tom's attention, she signaled to him and pointed. Tom caught on quickly and walked to meet Louis, who'd stopped to stare at Tom's unmarked department vehicle.

"Do you suppose that Jane talked Louis into taking those walks so he'd exercise?" she asked, heading to the door.

Betty followed. "I really can't say. It's been a long time since Jane and I had time for anything more than a quick hello. She's always rushing to her job during the week. On weekends, she's got her hands full catching up on all the things she didn't have time to do during the workweek. Louis usually has the car and drives her to work, so she's stuck until he picks her up in the afternoons. I think that's why she enjoys her Sunday errands so much."

"Thanks for letting me use your phone, Betty," Sister Agatha said, walking out onto the porch.

"Sister, I hope you don't mind me asking, but it seems a little odd, you and Sheriff Green showing up out of the blue," she said, waving at Tom. "How did you know that a man had broken into the Sanchez home?"

Sister Agatha hesitated. Though Louis was bound to need the support of friends and neighbors, there was probably a connection between the break-in and Jane's death. Not wanting to give too much away, she measured her words carefully.

"The burglary attempt might have been unrelated to our business with him," she finally answered. "We actually came to give him some very bad news. That's all I can tell you, but I'm sure he'll appreciate your visit later."

Betty nodded, understanding reflected in her eyes. "I hear you."

Sister Agatha hurried to join Tom. After telling Louis about the intruder, Sister Agatha gave Tom the few details she remembered about the man. Soon they went inside. After Sheriff

Green cautioned Louis not to touch anything, he and Sister Agatha followed Louis as he searched for anything that might be missing, but he didn't notice anything.

Louis led them into the kitchen, since it clearly hadn't been disturbed by the burglar, and joined them at the table. The first thing that struck Sister Agatha was the host of handwritten memos in bright pink that were stuck on the refrigerator. Through the doorway, she could also see dozens more on a cork bulletin board above the desk in the living room.

Louis stood and began to pace nervously. He was wearing neatly polished brown loafers, tan slacks, and a Hawaiian print shirt with a squared-off hem. He wasn't wearing cologne—or maybe that was masked by the pronounced garlic scent on his breath.

"What's happening, Sheriff?" he asked, his words rushing out.

"We didn't come to catch a burglar," Tom started, then looked at Sister Agatha.

"I'm here for a different reason, Louis," Sister Agatha answered. She broke the news to Louis as gently as she could.

When she finished, Louis stared at her in shock and confusion. "Jane was shot? No, that can't be right. She was heading to Mass, then she was going to drive to the Farmer's Market in Alameda for some spaghetti squash. She'll be turning into the driveway any minute now, you'll see."

"There's no mistake, Louis," Sister Agatha said softly. "I'm so very sorry."

There was a sickly pallor on his face, and his eyes were brimming with tears. "Murdered? My Jane? I bet it was one of those gangs, wasn't it? A drive-by and she got in the way! Then, since they knew she wouldn't be at home, they sent someone to rob our house." His voice rose sharply in anger, and he shook his head. "No. This isn't happening."

"We don't know who's responsible yet, or if both incidents—the burglary and Jane's murder—are related. I have to ask you some very tough questions now, so you have to try to focus," Tom said, his voice firm. "First of all, your wife was apparently robbed. How much money did she usually carry?"

"On Sundays, around a hundred dollars in cash. She buys some groceries after church. She also carries a credit card. Is that gone, too?" he asked, trying to keep his voice steady but failing.

Tom shook his head. "The credit card was still there, but no money. I understand she usually carried a cell phone, too, but we didn't find one. Do you know where it might be?"

He shook his head. "She . . . always took it with her."

"We'll check to see if anyone uses it. Can you give us the carrier and the phone number?" He handed Louis a small notebook and a pen, and Louis took a credit card out of his own wallet and wrote down the information.

"Do you know if your wife had any enemies?" Tom continued.

"Enemies?" Louis shook his head in confusion. "Jane ticks people off from time to time. She's a strong woman with a mouth on her. But so what? Who's perfect?"

"*Think,*" Tom said. "Maybe there's a neighbor who hates her, or someone at work."

Louis shook his head, bewildered.

"Sister Agatha received a call from Jane a couple of days ago. Jane was troubled about something she'd seen. Any idea what that was?" Tom pressed.

"Jane seemed a little nervous as she got ready for church today, but I didn't ask about it, because I didn't want to get into another argument with her. She's been upset about my health, and of course the fact that she doesn't like our daughter's husband at all."

Louis brushed a hand through his hair, a quiet desperation in his eyes. "Maybe I should have gone to church with her today. If I had, she might still be—" Horrified by the thought, he suddenly sagged back, his hands over his face. "Oh God, oh God," he moaned, his face buried in his hands.

To Sister Agatha's surprise, Betty Malone suddenly appeared at the door. She walked over, sat beside Louis, and placed her hand on his shoulder.

"You'll get through this, Louis," she said with absolute conviction. "You're not alone. You've got family, friends, and neighbors who'll be right here for you."

Betty looked at Sheriff Green, then at Sister Agatha, and shook her head. "I know you want answers, but he won't be able to help anyone right now. He needs time. Maybe this afternoon."

Sister Agatha knew that Sheriff Green couldn't wait that long. Wanting to give him a chance to speak to Louis one-on-one, she motioned for Betty to step into the kitchen with her. Once there, Sister Agatha told her about Louis's heart problems.

Betty nodded. "I know all about that, and I'll watch him, don't worry. His daughter will be here shortly, too. I took the liberty of phoning her before I came over. She'd been staying away because of family issues, but I told her that her father needed her now. I'll tell her the rest when she arrives."

When Sister Agatha returned to the living room, Tom looked at her, then focused back on Louis. "I'll be back in a few hours, Louis, but before I go, I need to know where you were earlier today. You didn't just go out for a walk, did you?"

Louis blinked and stared at him, no sign of comprehension on his face. It was as if the sheriff had just spoken in Chinese. Tom repeated the question.

"I usually catch a ride with my other neighbor, Christy White, when she goes to work Sunday mornings at Rio Casino. Afterward, I walk home."

"You go gambling every Sunday, then?" Tom asked. "Doesn't that add to those family problems you mentioned?"

Sister Agatha waited for Louis's answer. Rio Casino was only a few miles away, just inside pueblo land.

"Gamble?" Louis looked at Tom in confusion. "Gambling's for rich people, not me."

"Then what do you do at Rio Casino? Socialize? Meet someone?" Tom pressed.

"Meet who? Hell, no—excuse me, Sister—I go there to *eat*. All Jane lets me have around here is the low-fat, low-taste rabbit food she and my doctor keep harping about. Then she insists I ride a stupid bicycle up and down the street like some paper boy." He rubbed his eyes, and when he looked up at last, love, grief, and even hate were mirrored there. "If God had intended me to eat alfalfa, he would have given me hooves. I like *real* food like lasagna, and steak and potatoes with thick gravy. The casino's Sunday brunch is great, and it's all you can eat for less than Jane puts in the offering basket." His jaw fell open as he realized what he'd just said. "Not that I cared how much she donates . . . donated," Louis added, his voice catching.

"So you've been sneaking out on Sunday just to eat?" Sister Agatha confirmed.

He nodded. "I go while she's at church, then work some of it off by walking back."

"How many people know that your house is empty for a few hours every Sunday morning?" Sheriff Green asked next.

"I'm not sure. I guess anyone in the neighborhood who has seen me walking back."

"The man who knocked Sister Agatha down was a big guy. How many men in the neighborhood fit that description?"

"None of the men. Miss Herring, a block down, is about six foot two, but she's a retired math teacher who's around sixty years old. Anyway, none of my neighbors would break into my house. You think the burglar might be the same man who killed my wife?"

"I can't rule that out, not yet," Sheriff Green replied. "A deputy will be by shortly to check your home for trace evidence and examine the back door for fingerprints."

"Gloves, Sheriff," Sister Agatha suddenly interrupted. "I just remembered catching a glimpse of brown work gloves on the man's hands."

"Then fingerprints are out. There's one more thing, Mr. Sanchez. You mentioned owning a bicycle?" the sheriff asked.

He nodded miserably. "Jane bought me one so I'd exercise. It's got big, knobby tires—one of those mountain bikes. I hate the danged thing. I got lucky when someone stole it a few days ago. I didn't report it missing 'cause I'm hoping it doesn't find its way back."

"Thanks for your help, Louis, and I'm truly sorry for your loss," Sheriff Green said, standing.

As they walked to the car, a sheriff's department vehicle pulled up behind Tom's vehicle. Tom took a few minutes to speak to the deputy, then joined Sister Agatha.

"The casinos have cameras all over the place, and they're bound to have picked up Louis Sanchez in that flashy shirt of his. I'll be able to verify his alibi easily enough," Tom said as he drove down the street. "For a while there, after he told us he was sneaking out, I was sure we were about to uncover a motive. Then it went up in a puff of smoke."

"No man could have wanted to eat pasta badly enough to

take out a contract on his wife, Tom," Sister Agatha said. "Louis's grief is real."

"I'm guessing you're right about that, but I'm still going to have to confirm his alibi. Jane may have thought he was having an affair—and maybe he was, and not just with the potatoes and gravy. That could explain why she was worried about something she'd seen and why she didn't want to discuss it on the phone."

"It's possible, but I think someone was after Jane," Sister Agatha said. "That person studied her habits and was able to make the hit at just the right time. I think the killer rushed over to burglarize Jane's home, knowing Louis wasn't home and she wasn't coming back. The break-in today is just too coincidental."

"The killer was probably searching for something specific— something Jane left behind that was important to him. He tried searching through her purse after he killed her, then covered for it by trying to make it look like a simple robbery."

Sister Agatha nodded. "Jane *was* going to tell me something but was afraid of being overheard. That opens up a lot of options now that I think of it, like maybe even phone taps."

"I thought of that, too, and told the deputy to look around the house for bugs. Maybe she planted them herself to keep tabs on her husband and didn't want her conversation with you to be recorded." Tom paused, then added, "Did you notice all the bright pink memos stuck on the refrigerator and on the corkboard?"

She nodded. "Jane always kept a memo pad with her, the brightly colored sticky kind. She sometimes used them to mark places in her prayer book. I've even seen her taking notes in church during the epistle." She had a sudden thought. "Did you find a memo pad in her purse?"

"No. There wasn't even a grocery list, which I'd expect to find if she was going shopping after church. I didn't see any pads on the counter, the tabletops, or the desk at their home either. So what happened to her memo pad? Did Jane just run out, or did the killer take it with him? Was that what the burglar came to retrieve?" Tom muttered, not expecting an answer.

"Jane would have written down a reminder to herself to come talk to me, and maybe even what she intended to say," Sister Agatha said. "And there *would* have been a grocery list in her purse. She wrote everything down."

"I'll double-check with the crime scene team and see if they found the missing notepad. I'll have the deputy at the Sanchez home search for one as well."

She nodded.

Tom called it in, then continued, "Let's be careful about making premature assumptions, too. I keep thinking of the message scratched on the Antichrysler. It's possible that we're dealing with a psycho."

A shiver touched her spine. The danger hadn't passed. She could feel it surrounding them, drawing closer. What she needed to do more than ever now was trust God completely. Perfect charity casteth out fear. St. John had said so. She was all too human, though, and fear came with the territory.

5

WHEN SHERIFF GREEN AND SISTER AGATHA RE-
turned to the monastery, the crime scene team was
still working. Sister Agatha relieved Sister Bernarda,
who'd been outside observing the monastery's law enforcement
visitors.

Since the mayor's aide had already left, Sister Agatha felt
less pressured to hold back. Knowing that the sisters had a
personal stake in finding the killer's identity—they'd been threatened as well—gave her all the impetus she needed. She drew
closer to the officers and listened.

Tom was reading a report when one of the crime scene
techs came up to him.

"We found some footprints, Sheriff, from a size eleven running shoe," the officer said. "Once we're back at the lab, we'll
try to get a brand from the imprint. One last thing, the bicycle
tracks led to a trail that goes along the river."

"How far were you able to follow the tracks?" Tom asked the man.

"A half mile south. There were two sets, one coming, the other going. They ended just past the stand of cottonwoods near the Rio Grande Conservancy marker. I found vehicle tracks, and the overlapping pattern indicates that the killer left his pickup parked there while he rode here on the bike. After the shooting, he returned to his vehicle, loaded up the bike, and drove off."

"What can you tell me about the vehicle's tire tracks?" Tom asked.

"The pattern isn't too clear, but the size indicates a big pickup or an SUV."

As the deputy walked away, Sister Agatha glanced at Tom and said, "It's too bad you don't have access to Louis's bike. A tread comparison would have been helpful."

"Maybe we can find some around his home," Tom answered. "Are you sure you never heard a scream or a shout of any kind while Mass was going on? One of the reports I just skimmed suggests the shot was taken at nearly contact range."

"All I heard was the popping sound I mentioned."

"Then it's clear that the killer was able to get close without alarming her."

"That lack of surprise is what would have made Louis the ideal suspect, but I bet his alibi will hold," Sister Agatha said.

"I've got to check on gang activity in this area. This could be the work of some kid being ranked in."

"A *big* kid, with size elevens. You're right, though. Jane wouldn't necessarily have been concerned about a kid who'd come up on a bicycle."

"The problem with the gangbanger theory is that it doesn't fit in with some of the other evidence," Tom said slowly. "The target was selected carefully, and the crime itself appears to have been well planned. The killer only took one shot at point-blank range—not like typical gangbangers. They blast away with the entire magazine, and they don't bother with sound suppressors."

Sister Agatha turned and watched as Sister Jo came out of the parlor entrance with a small camera and took a few photos of the door of the Antichrysler.

Seeing Sister Agatha watching her, Sister Jo waved. "Insurance. If we have any." Then the young nun hurried back inside.

"That was Sister Jo, right, the new nun?"

"That's right. Sister Jo's from a different order, the Incarnate Word. She was at the convent that closed down in Santa Fe. Incarnate Word is a teaching order, and the Archbishop wanted Sister Jo to relocate here instead of going out of state with the elderly sisters."

"How did Sister Jo end up living at a cloistered monastery, of all places?"

"We're always in need of externs, and St. Charles needed a nun who could substitute teach regularly, so it worked out for everyone. To help cover our expenses, the diocese paid for our new well. We got the best of the deal, because Sister Jo's been doing a lot of good work for the parishioners since she arrived. She's the one in charge of the Good News Meal Program, though because of our duties here, we only deliver to about fifteen people. St. Augustine's in town has a committee that takes care of the rest. Also, we make our meal deliveries at noon because that's what fits with our schedule."

"Worked out for everyone, I see. So how long will Sister Jo be staying?"

"That's up to the Archbishop, but from what I can tell, she'll be with us for the foreseeable future."

"You like her," he observed.

"Sister Jo's hard not to like," she said with a smile. "Did you want to speak to her?"

"Yes. I saw in the report that the other externs have already been questioned. She's the only one that was missed. I need to talk to her about Jane, and also about the people she's met while delivering meals or running errands for the monastery."

Once they entered the parlor, Sister Agatha sent Sister Bernarda to find the young nun. A few minutes later, Sister Jo rushed in, Pax at her heels. Her cheeks were flushed, and from Pax's panting grin, it didn't take much to guess she'd been out exercising him.

"Please sit down, Sister," Sheriff Green said.

As soon as she'd complied, he began. "How well did you know Jane Sanchez?"

"Not very. I haven't been here for very long, but Mrs. Sanchez and I hit it off really well the few times we spoke after Mass. She wanted to help the monastery with our Good News Meal deliveries, but with her day job and all, she could only help on weekends. She made a few deliveries for us last Sunday after Mass, and those came out well, I think. I mean, nobody complained, and that's always a good sign."

Tom bit back a smile. "Has anyone in town shown any particular interest in either you or the monastery?"

Sister Agatha expected a quick no, but Sister Jo paused, considering. "It's strange that you should ask me that," she said at last.

Sister Agatha's attention was riveted on the young nun as they waited for an answer.

"I'm the new nun in town, and a lot of people want to know who I am and if I'll be staying, but it was all normal curiosity—that is, until this last Friday when I substituted at St. Charles. While I was out front after school waiting for Sister Bernarda to come pick me up, I had the strangest feeling I was being watched. At first I didn't see anyone paying particular attention to me. Then I caught a glimpse of a man on the other side of the cars looking through the windows in my direction. It was . . . creepy. We're always careful about people hanging around the school, so I went inside to get the security guard. By the time we came back out, the guy was gone. The guard promised he'd notify the office and have them alert the teachers, too, just in case."

"Was this man tall, short, or average? And what was he wearing, do you recall?" Tom asked.

"He was stooped so he could see through the windows, so I can't tell you how tall he was. He was wearing some kind of gray top. I think it was a sweatshirt with a hood."

"And sunglasses?" Sister Agatha asked.

"Yes, I remember that now. Not the shiny mirror kind, dark ones."

Tom and Sister Agatha exchanged glances.

"You didn't mention this to Sister Bernarda?" Sister Agatha asked.

"It seemed like a school issue, though I know nuns can be a source of curiosity. I didn't think it was important except to St. Charles—until now."

The Maria bell rang for None, the midafternoon prayer commemorating the ninth hour, when Christ died, and Sister Jo stood up. "I need to go to chapel, Sheriff Green. Well, no, that's not exactly true. I'm an acting extern, so I don't *have* to go, but I'd like to. Are you done with me for now?"

"Go ahead. I know where to find you if I need anything else," Sheriff Green said.

Sister Jo hurried into the enclosure.

Sister Agatha studied the sheriff's expression. What she saw there worried her. "What's bothering you, Tom?"

"Sister Jo's comments about the Good News Meal Program reminded me again of the big ruckus Aragon made in the council about faith-based initiatives mixing religious organizations and government funds."

"Aragon has always used public employee positions as rewards and payoffs for those who support him. At least we've taken away some of his power to corrupt others. Did you know that the director of the public meals program was making more money than even you, our county sheriff? The program has saved thousands of dollars by turning the work over to Our Lady of Hope and St. Augustine."

"You're on Aragon's enemies list now. When your contract expires next year, expect a fight."

"We were really sorry that some people were against our involvement, but the thing is that the Church *should* serve the public, and this is one way we can do that. As an added bonus, we're saving taxpayers some money."

"No need to get defensive. On that issue, I'm on your side."

"Do you think the negative reaction to the Good News Meal Program might be connected to what happened today?" She paused, then added, "One thing's for sure. Peter Aragon isn't our burglar. He's barely five foot four."

"It's probably not connected. What's worrying me is the killer's threat to the monastery, particularly in light of what Sister Jo mentioned about being watched."

"Sister Jo's sharp and capable. If she said someone was watching her, you can bank on it."

"Now that we know he's out there, we'll be watching for his next move." Seeing Sister Agatha's horrified expression, Tom quickly added, "Stay calm. We don't know if he really intends to carry out the threat. All we have is conjecture and speculation. That's it."

"How do we protect Sister Jo and the other externs?"

"I'll have officers watching the monastery, but *everyone* here has to be very careful now. Sister Jo especially needs to stay alert, since she's the one we know was being watched, but that doesn't mean the other externs haven't been under surveillance, too." He paused. "Talk to Sister Jo after I leave. People have a tendency to remember things after they've been questioned, maybe just a detail or two they'll dismiss because they think it's not important. If you get anything from her, let me know. Don't come to the station—just call."

"All right." Sister Agatha knew he didn't want her to run into the mayor's man, Fritz Albrecht.

"Also please let Reverend Mother know how much we appreciated the cooperation we got from the sisters. They really helped keep the parishioners calm and out of our way."

When Tom opened the parlor door, they spotted a handful of reporters. Some were shooting video of the crime scene team while others took photos of the front of the chapel and of the monastery.

"I kept the lid on as long as I could, but the story was bound to break," Tom muttered. "After the morning worshipers finally got home, they all had stories to tell."

"I better get out there," Sister Agatha said, hurrying past him. "They can take all the pictures they want from the public road, but once they come through our gate they're on private property."

"If I were you, I wouldn't interfere with them right now. They'll just use their telephoto lenses and take photos anyway. You might be better off if you're seen as trying to cooperate with them. Just control what they have access to, and consider keeping Pax at heel. You're more likely to get and keep their attention with him by your side."

He started toward his police unit, stopped, and glanced back at her. "Remember that there'll be a deputy on duty here 24/7 until we have a handle on what's happening."

"Thanks."

Sister Agatha whistled for Pax, who came running instantly, then went to talk to the reporters. Chuck Moody from the *Chronicle* was a friend, one she could rely on. He and a cameraman from an Albuquerque TV station were just outside the perimeter of yellow tape. Although the police had released the scene, the tape had remained in place, and the reporters seemed to want shots from every angle.

"Hey, Sister, how about a few photos of you standing next to the tape?" a reporter she didn't recognize called out to her. "And how about a shot from inside the chapel, looking out into the parking area?"

"The chapel is off-limits to everyone until the next Mass, and no cameras are allowed inside in any case. Just so you're clear on this, the crime happened out here."

"Thanks for the heads-up, Sister," Chuck said, then helped her divert the other reporter by calling his attention to an approaching vehicle.

The red SUV stopped just inside the gate. Moments later Sister Agatha sighed, recognizing their local state senator, Dwight Holman, as he stepped out of the passenger side. She should have expected this. Wherever reporters gathered, Dwight Holman was sure to be.

He made a show of coming toward Sister Agatha with a somber, concerned expression on his face and then shook her hand. Shifting slightly so the cameras could have a better angle, he gave her his most sympathetic smile.

"I heard what happened, and rest assured that all the sisters here at Our Lady of Hope have the support of my state office behind them," he said in a voice loud enough to be picked up easily by the microphones. "My prayers are also with the family and friends of the victim of this senseless act. This community is my community . . . the people, my people. We'll stand as one and bring whoever did this to justice."

The photographers went crazy for several seconds. At long last Sister Agatha gently extricated her hand from Senator Holman's cold, dry grip. The man never missed a photo op and the chance to land a sound bite on the evening news, but she didn't want to be part of his reelection campaign.

"We're a community of law-abiding citizens," he said, facing the reporters and stepping away from her so he could command their attention exclusively. "Attacks on our centers of worship, the very heart of our religious freedoms, will *not* be tolerated. We *will* find the person who committed this crime, and he will be prosecuted to the full extent of the law."

She wasn't needed here now, so Sister Agatha walked back toward the parlor entrance. Holman was welcome to the media attention. She wanted no part of it.

Before she could get far, a reporter shouted a question at her. "Sister Agatha, in your own words, what happened here earlier this morning?"

She recognized the man as a reporter from the Albuquerque morning paper. Years ago, he'd taken one of her journalism classes. "You'll have to get the details from the sheriff's department. It's their investigation," she answered.

"Do you believe that the monastery is a target now?" another reporter asked.

"As I said, you'll have to speak to Sheriff Green about all that. But let me offer one word of caution. Be *very* careful about printing any speculation that may be in conflict with the facts."

Of course, the nuns didn't have the funds to sue anyone for anything, nor would they. Still, it couldn't hurt to give the media a little wake-up call. Almost as if to emphasize what she'd said, Pax stood, edging closer to Sister Agatha, and growled.

"Maybe you should put that dog inside your compound," one of the reporters said.

"It's a monastery, not a compound, and absolutely not. This is *his* home. He goes where he will," she said, deliberately sending out the one message she hoped they'd print. "Just be aware that he's a former police dog and very protective of our monastery."

The man moved away from her, then started taking photos of the Antichrysler's door.

Several moments later Sister Bernarda came out to join her. "Everything under control?" she asked in a whisper.

Sister Agatha nodded and filled her in quickly on Sister Jo's experience at St. Charles. "We'll have to keep an eye on her. Sister Jo is nothing if not high profile in town. Her energy and enthusiasm always draw people to her."

"We should start traveling in pairs while making the meal deliveries," Sister Bernarda said.

"That's a good idea. I'll also be sure to tell the principal about our concern for her safety. He'll probably hear about the threat soon enough." Sister Agatha pointed to the door of the Antichrysler.

Sister Bernarda nodded.

The reporters' attention shifted once again as yet another car pulled up. A heartbeat later, Louis Sanchez stepped out. The driver, a woman in her twenties, followed.

"Family?" Sister Bernarda whispered to Sister Agatha.

"Jane's husband, and maybe their daughter," she said and went over to meet them.

"How may we help you, Mr. Sanchez?" Sister Agatha asked

gently. Louis still looked dazed and disoriented, as if he hadn't been able to fully take in what had happened.

The young woman with him, her tanned face showing only a trace of lipstick, was wearing a black blouse and a long, pleated dark blue skirt. She stepped forward and immediately introduced herself.

"I'm Evelyn Sanchez-Bennett," she said, shaking Sister Agatha's hand. "We've come to ask permission to set up a *descanso*, a small memorial where my mother—" Her voice broke, and she swallowed hard. "Where my mother passed away," she finished at last. "Just a few candles, a cross, and some flowers."

Sister Agatha knew the New Mexican custom well, having seen countless of the small, makeshift roadside shrines at scenes of fatal accidents.

"We are so very sorry for your loss," Sister Agatha said. "If you'll excuse me, I'll go ask Reverend Mother for permission to set up a *descanso*."

"I'll go, Your Charity," replied Sister Bernarda, who was standing a few feet behind her.

Sister Agatha shook her head. "I need to speak to Mother on another urgent matter."

As Sister Agatha hurried inside, she turned and saw Sister Bernarda comforting the grieving family. Though normally a gruff woman, Sister Bernarda had a wellspring of gentleness inside her that always came to the surface in situations like this. Jane's family couldn't have been in more caring hands.

6

SISTER AGATHA KNOCKED ON THE PRIORESS'S OPEN DOOR. Reverend Mother was facing the small statue of St. Joseph in the far corner, lost in prayer.

As Sister Agatha silently waited for her to finish, she could hear the sounds of Sister Maria Victoria at the sewing machine farther down the hall. She could also see Sister Ignatius busy with an arrangement of flowers placed at the feet of the large statue of the Blessed Mother by their library's entrance.

"Praised be Jesus Christ," Reverend Mother said at last, turning around.

"Now and forever," Sister Agatha answered, coming in.

Sister Agatha quickly updated Reverend Mother on what was happening with the sheriff's investigation, the incident with the intruder at the Sanchez home, and the apparent threats to the sisters. Last, she told her about the request they'd received from the victim's daughter.

"It's an old New Mexican custom to erect a small shrine near the place where a loved one has died. We'd have her place the *descanso* off to one side, of course, out of the flow of traffic, maybe among the lilacs," Sister Agatha added.

"All right. Tell them to go ahead. It's the least we can do for the family."

"Thank you, Mother."

Sister Agatha excused herself, then hurried back outside to join the others.

Sister Bernarda came up to meet her. "Jane's son-in-law is a deputy, one of Sheriff Green's men," Sister Bernarda whispered, then gestured to a white and brown department vehicle. "That's Deputy Gerry Bennett's patrol car."

"It's understandable he'd want to be with his family at a time like this," Sister Agatha said, "but that's probably as close as Deputy Bennett's going to get to this case. Tom won't allow him to take an active part in this investigation, for obvious reasons."

When Louis and Evelyn went inside the chapel, Sister Agatha followed. Sister Bernarda, a half step behind her, moved to intercept the photographers.

"Show some respect, please," she said, then faced them, arms crossed in front of her chest. "This is God's house. You will *not* turn it into a photo gallery."

Knowing things were being handled outside, Sister Agatha closed the chapel door and followed the mourning family down the center aisle. Evelyn genuflected, crossed herself, and knelt at the altar railing. Louis stood behind her, his shoulders sagging.

Sister Agatha's heart went out to them, and she stood back, giving them their moment of prayer.

Hearing the door behind her open, Sister Agatha turned her head and saw a tall, slender deputy standing there, billed uniform cap in hand. A glance at his name tag told her who he was, and she went to meet him. He'd chosen to remain in the foyer instead of entering the chapel.

"Would you like to come in, Deputy Bennett?" she asked him.

He shook his head. "Not while I'm armed. I'm not Catholic, but any church deserves that courtesy. Do you have a moment, Sister Agatha? I'd like to speak with you."

Sister Agatha nodded, but as she started to lead the way back outside, he stopped her.

"Not out front, Sister. Those reporters won't give us a moment's peace."

Sister Agatha nodded, then led him out the small side entrance of the chapel. That door, mostly hidden by evergreens, was seldom used. It had been part of the old framework—when the monastery had been nothing more than a big farmhouse with outbuildings.

Once outside, she moved into the shadows and faced him. Behind him she could see the corner of the chapel, and beyond, the parking lot. If any reporters came close enough to listen, she'd spot them. "What can I do for you, Deputy Bennett?"

"Sheriff Green is working this case personally, but I'll be following it closely, too. I know that my mother-in-law came here every Sunday for Mass. Did she ever speak to you about any enemies she may have made?"

Sister Agatha hesitated. "I'm not sure if I should answer your questions, Deputy. As you said yourself, this is Sheriff Green's case."

Just for a second she saw anger flash in his eyes; then his expression became one of polite neutrality. "Sister Agatha, my mother-in-law could be a very difficult woman, but she deserves justice. I owe it to my family to help the sheriff any way I can, though, obviously, I can't officially work the case."

He started to say more, then, hearing voices, turned and saw Louis and Evelyn coming down the steps of the chapel's main entrance. "I better go," he said and hurried over to meet them.

As Sister Agatha walked to the front of the chapel, Sheriff Green approached. Some of the reporters were now hovering around the victim's family, but Sister Agatha's friend Chuck Moody had already left.

"Louis has an iron-clad alibi," Tom said quietly. "We checked with the casino, and the people there remember him. Of course, he could have hired a professional to kill her. The silencer isn't a tool used by amateurs."

"What's the motive?"

"Jealousy or infidelity? Maybe Jane was having an affair. I've found nothing to indicate that yet, but you never know."

"Judging from Louis's reaction and Jane's devoutness, I really doubt that, Tom. Tell me, what was stolen from the cars on the lot? I never heard."

"Two women are missing their garage door openers. That's it," Tom said.

"Considering everything, that's not too bad."

"I'm going to catch whoever did this," Tom said with quiet confidence.

"I know you will. We have faith in you and your deputies, and God's on your side. Don't doubt that for a minute."

"Is your faith really that strong?" he asked, his eyes probing hers.

She nodded. "It's why I became a nun. I may fail God, but He'll never fail me."

Sister Agatha spent most of the night awake in her cell, one of the monastery's small, simple bedrooms. She'd wanted to stay somewhat alert to Pax, who was outside, guarding the grounds.

Sister Agatha occupied her time thinking, reconstructing the events, particularly her last, brief conversation with Jane. Her failure to help a person who'd reached out to her was like a heavy yoke around her heart. She'd prayed for forgiveness, but she needed to do more—like help the sheriff find the killer before he struck again. If someone else died, the weight of her own guilt would consume her.

It was almost four thirty in the morning, time for the Maria bell to ring telling the sisters to rise, when she decided to go speak to the deputy on duty outside. By now, he was probably tired, undoubtedly less guarded, and more likely to talk freely, particularly to a nun. The Great Silence couldn't be broken except in grave emergencies until after Morning Prayers, but she wouldn't be inside the monastery. She'd go outside to speak to the deputy and catch him before he went off duty.

It was still dark when Sister Agatha slipped outside and greeted Pax with a hug. Together, they went around to the parking area, just inside the closed gate. The floodlight, which was connected to a motion sensor, came on, illuminating the area. She could see the sheriff's department vehicle about fifty feet farther up the road. Hearing steps in the gravel to her right, she turned to look.

A tall, slender deputy came out from behind the solid wall that anchored the right half of their metal gate.

"Deputy Bennett?" she asked, wondering what he was doing here.

"No, Sister," he said. "I'm Sergeant McKay. I saw the light come on, so I thought I'd come around and make sure everything was okay."

Pax sat on Sister Agatha's left side, his gaze on the uniformed officer.

"It's about time for our wake-up bells. I was already up, so I thought I'd come out and say hello to Pax. It's been such a trying time for all of us," she said, her voice strained. "To have one of our regulars at Mass killed right here . . . that was quite a shock."

"Nothing surprises me anymore," he said in a somber voice. "After nearly fifteen years as a police officer, I've seen too much of the dark side of human nature."

Sister Agatha studied Deputy McKay. She recalled having seen him at the sheriff's office a few times, but they'd never spoken. The man was in his late forties and had a wariness in and around his eyes that attested to what he'd just said. Police work always seemed to take a toll.

"Did you know Jane Sanchez?" she asked him.

"I knew *of* her, that's all. Supposedly she was a very opinionated woman." He shrugged. "Some people can only hear their own voices."

"Seem like there's a lot of that going around," she answered with a smile.

He laughed, and she was relieved to hear it. She wanted to keep him talking, and lightening the mood would help. "What else have you heard?"

"I understand Mrs. Sanchez had her husband pretty much under her thumb. Though I heard that when she tried that on her son-in-law and daughter, it backfired major league."

"How do you know so much about Jane?" she said, curiosity, not recrimination, alive in her tone.

"Her son-in-law, Gerry Bennett, and I went through the police academy together, and we're friends. Gerry had to live with his in-laws while he and his wife were having their house built, and that was a real nightmare. By the time the house was finished, Gerry and Evelyn were on the brink of divorce. Gerry blamed it on Jane's meddling."

"Mother-in-law problems are fairly common," Sister Agatha said with a rueful smile.

"Yeah, but Gerry's too much like Jane, always has to have the last word. Evelyn was probably stuck in the middle—mother versus husband. Thing is, Jane could be hard to deal with. I saw her a week ago parked outside the station during the noon hour. When I mentioned it to Gerry, he told me that his mother-in-law thought he was cheating on Evelyn and was probably hanging around hoping to catch him with another woman."

"So Gerry and Jane had serious problems?"

His gaze narrowed, and he paused, choosing his words more carefully this time. "If you're asking me whether I think Gerry killed her, the answer's no." He took a breath, then continued. "Gerry can be difficult, but he's a good officer."

"That says something," Sister Agatha said. What he'd already told her about Gerry didn't exactly remove him from the suspect list, though. If he'd really believed that Jane was trying to destroy his marriage, he could have seen her as a threat. And even if she was killed by a professional—well, no one had more contacts in the underworld than a cop.

After a few more minutes of chatting, she returned inside, ready for Matins, which was chanted before daybreak as a counter to the evils that plagued the night.

Two hours later, once Morning Prayers ended, Sister Agatha was called to Reverend Mother's office. After the customary greeting, Reverend Mother invited Sister Agatha to sit down. "I received a call from the Archbishop a few minutes ago. He's very concerned about all the attention the monastery is already getting from the newspapers and media. First because of our involvement with the Good News Meal Program and now with the murder. The fact that cars were broken into didn't escape his notice either."

"There's nothing we can do about the press, Mother, but we'll weather this storm as we have others in the past. At least no vehicles were vandalized, except for ours."

"The Archbishop is worried people will be hesitant to attend Mass, not just here but in town, too, until the criminal is caught. That's why he specifically requested that you help the sheriff gather the information he needs."

"I'll do all I can, but Sheriff Green warned me that the mayor is upset about my involvement in past investigations. He was worried about potential lawsuits, I guess."

"I know how skilled you are, and I'm sure you'll find a way to help out. Your curiosity is as much a part of you as the habit you wear, and you have one important advantage over most people on the outside—your willingness to rely totally on God. He'll always guide those who are faithful to Him."

Grateful that she'd been sanctioned to do the work she'd wanted to see through, Sister Agatha left Mother's office and went to the parlor. Sister Bernarda was at the desk.

"Where's Sister Jo this morning?" Sister Agatha asked. "I just walked past the scriptorium, but only Sister de Lourdes was there."

"Sister Jo's outside with Pax."

"Will she be substitute teaching today?"

"Yes, but she won't be needed at St. Charles until this afternoon, so she'll be taking care of the Good News deliveries once Sister Clothilde gets things ready."

Sister Agatha joined Sister Bernarda, who was standing at the window, and laughed, seeing the young nun playing tug-of-war with Pax and winning by giving him a kiss on the nose. Sister Jo was impetuous and likely to lead with her heart in most matters, and there was an innocence about the child-at-heart that endeared her to everyone.

7

MINUTES LATER, SISTER AGATHA WAS ON HER WAY TO town with Pax riding in the Harley's sidecar. The dog held his nose high into the wind, enjoying all the scents around him. Pax instinctively made the most out of each moment, never worrying about either the future or the past. She envied him that.

Soon she arrived in Jane and Louis's neighborhood. This morning she intended to find out as much as she could about Jane's life. Jane had discovered something disturbing, and Sister Agatha strongly suspected that learning what that was would lead her to a possible motive for Jane's death.

Next door to the Sanchez house, on the left side, stood an old stucco home. A lush carpet of weeds choked what had once been a lawn. Chipped yellow paint covered the wooden trim and front door, but the ground was clear all the way to the mailbox.

This was the best place to start. As Sister Agatha pulled up on the Harley, a woman in her late fifties or early sixties stepped out to the front porch, wiping her hands on a dish cloth.

"I've heard all about you and your dog, Sister," she said after Sister Agatha introduced herself. "I'm Christy White. I guess you're here to help find out why poor Jane Sanchez was killed. It had to be something more than just a robbery gone sour."

"What makes you say that?" Sister Agatha asked instantly.

"The deputies who came by earlier kept asking me who Jane's enemies were. That sure sounded like a murder investigation to me."

"There are a lot of questions that still need answering," Sister Agatha said, purposely remaining vague. "If you can spare a few minutes, I'd like to talk to you."

"Sure, come on in. Bring the dog, too. I'm doing some baking, so we'll talk in the kitchen."

Unlike the exterior, the interior of the house was well maintained, with a comfortable, lived-in look. An afghan crocheted in pastel colors was draped across the back of the dark blue couch, and a macramé hanging covered one wall.

"Those are lovely pieces," Sister Agatha said, gesturing.

"I like working with my hands. It helps me relax."

As they stepped into the kitchen, Sister Agatha saw bowls and floured pans covering all the countertops.

"I'm trying two different recipes at the same time today," Christy explained. "I'll be entering the best one in a magazine contest. Last year I won ten thousand dollars for my blue corn and piñon muffins."

Sister Agatha blinked. "*That* much for a muffin recipe?"

"There's a lot of money to be made in these contests—but you have to win, of course."

Knowing that Sister Clothilde's recipes were second to

none, she considered asking Christy more about it, but before she could, Christy continued.

"But you didn't come here to talk about my cooking, so let's get down to it," she said, stirring a bowl filled with batter. "I've been Jane and Louis's neighbor for many years, and I can tell you that Louis is a good man. I never could stand Jane. Half of the time I wanted to throttle her. But I didn't kill her."

"How come you two didn't get along?" Sister Agatha asked.

"I hated the way she tried to run people's lives—especially Louis's—and it was even worse than usual lately." She lapsed into a long, thoughtful silence, but Sister Agatha didn't interrupt, wanting her to continue at her own pace.

Finally, Christy spoke again. "She meant well, Jane did, but in an attempt to give him a few more tomorrows she was making his todays completely miserable. Do you get me?" Seeing Sister Agatha nod, she went on. "Poor Louis was having a real tough time with all the rules Jane had laid down, too. That's why I'd let him sneak over from time to time for a cup of regular coffee and a doughnut, or take him over to the casino on Sundays so he could enjoy their buffet."

"So you and Jane didn't see eye to eye on much . . ." Sister Agatha let the sentence hang, hoping Christy would fill in more gaps.

"That's absolutely true," Christy answered, meeting Sister Agatha's gaze boldly, "but if I killed everyone I didn't approve of, we'd have a real small neighborhood."

Sister Agatha chuckled softly.

Christy poured the batter into cake pans, then glanced back at Sister Agatha. "Right now, I've got to tell you, I'm more worried about Louis than what happened to Jane."

"Do you think there's any way we at the monastery can help him?"

Christy thought it over before answering. "Louis is mad at God. I don't think he's ready to listen to anyone or anything."

"Thanks so much for taking time to talk to me," Sister Agatha said, standing. "You've been a big help, and I enjoyed visiting with you."

"It was mutual. I work part-time at Rio Casino, in the bakery, naturally, so I'm not always home, but feel free to drop by anytime I'm here."

"Thanks, and please keep an eye on Louis for us. Sometimes it's hard for people going through a crisis to reach out and ask for help. Yet that's the time they need it most."

"It's a good thing he's got friends like you," Christy said. "His only close relatives are his daughter, Evelyn, and her child, but since he doesn't get along with his son-in-law . . ." She shrugged.

"What's the problem between them?" Sister Agatha asked.

"I'm not sure," Christy said. "Louis told me once that Gerry was an irritating jerk. That was back when they were all living next door, but things didn't improve much between Louis and Gerry even after Gerry left."

Sister Agatha walked to the door. "Thanks again."

As she walked with Pax back to the Harley, Sister Agatha mulled over everything she'd learned. Christy had seemed very open, but there was more to her involvement with the Sanchez family. She could feel it in her bones.

8

ER VISIT WITH THE OTHER NEIGHBORS YIELDED NOTHING
new. Frustrated, she returned to the monastery.

As a nun, she'd vowed to let God lead her, to relin-
quish all her own plans and place herself entirely in His hands.
Yet truly letting go of her own opinions and ideas about the way
things *should* be done was the hardest challenge of all.

Knowing that reliable intuitions only came during times of
inner silence, she decided to walk in the monastery's grounds
with Pax instead of going inside. Surrounded by stillness and
peace, she stopped to gaze at a beautiful white butterfly.

Suddenly a brightly colored box came flying over the block
wall that separated their monastery from the vineyard next
door. Startled, she froze, but Pax shot forward and began nosing
the object on the ground.

Sister Agatha listened for whoever had thrown the box but
heard nothing outside the wall, not even footsteps. Whoever

was responsible was either extremely light on his feet or still there.

She drew closer to the foil gift container—about the size of a shoe box—and saw Pax turn it over with his snout. A dead crow tumbled out, a tiny circular piece of white cloth wrapped around its neck like a nun's scapular.

Sister Agatha called Pax to her side immediately and placed him at stay. Crouching, she studied the dead bird. Pinned to its chest was one of their monastery's prayer cards, the small thank-you tokens given to their benefactors. Each contained a promise that the sisters would pray for the donor's intentions. This particular one had the letters AMDG written in her own hand at the bottom. It meant *Ad majorem Dei gloriam*, "to the greater glory of God"—a personal touch she added to each card she handed out.

Hearing a door slam, she turned and saw Sister Bernarda jogging toward her. "Don't touch it!" Sister Bernarda called out. "It could be dangerous."

"I think it's only intended as a warning," Sister Agatha said, stepping aside to give her a clearer look. "I just wish there was some way to tell who originally received that card."

Sister Agatha went over to the wall, pulled herself up, and looked around. No one was within sight. The long-established grape vines were thick with leaves and afforded many hiding places. She waited for a moment, but nothing changed.

"Maybe we should start making the prayer cards more specific," Sister Bernarda said.

"It probably wouldn't have helped, at least not in this instance. There's no way to prove that this card wasn't stolen," Sister Agatha said, studying the crow again without touching it. "Our prayer cards are often left on desks or counters where everyone can see them. I've even spotted a few on office bulletin boards."

"Should I call the sheriff?" Sister Bernarda asked. "I hate to bother him about a dead bird—even one that's meant to symbolically represent us."

"I don't want to legitimize this in any way either, but we have no other choice. We're not supposed to divert the deputy parked outside unless it's an emergency, and this doesn't qualify, but since it's the second threat we've received, Tom has to be told," Sister Agatha said. "I'll stay here and make sure no creature comes along and carries the carcass off." She glanced at Pax, who'd never taken his eyes off the bird. "That means you too, boy."

The bells rang signaling Sext, the midday canonical hour said after the Angelus at Our Lady of Hope.

"If you're still out here after prayers, I'll send you a plate," Sister Bernarda said.

Sister Agatha thanked her and watched as she went back inside. The largest meal of the day was lunch. She was usually hungry by then, as she was now, since breakfast and collation—dinner—were extremely light.

Alone with what their enemy had left, Sister Agatha prayed for all the sisters. What if Sister Gertrude, with her weak heart, had found this? Grateful that things had worked out the way they had, she gave thanks to the Lord.

Sister Jo came out to meet her a short time later with a plate of food. "This is what the people in our Good News Meal Program received today. Sister Bernarda and I made the deliveries. The butternut squash soup is especially good. Why don't you sit over there in the shade while you eat, Sister Agatha? I'll stay and keep an eye on things for you."

Sister Agatha thanked her, then went to sit in the shade of a tall cottonwood while she ate. Just as Sister Jo had said, the soup in particular was very tasty. As she finished her lunch, she heard a vehicle and saw the sheriff pull up.

Tom hurried over to meet them, studied the box and the bird, then gauged the trajectory by raising himself to the top of the wall for a quick look. Finally he came back to join Sister Agatha. "What bothers me most is that I've got a deputy keeping an eye on this place, yet the perp still managed to deliver this package."

Sister Agatha knew that tone of voice. The deputy would have a lot of explaining to do. "To be fair, the officer was ordered to watch the monastery, not the vineyard next door. Even walking the perimeter, with the high wall, he can't see more than two sides at a time, and that's only at the corners."

"I know the wall is too high to see over, but did you notice anyone in the parking area or around the gates?"

Sister Agatha shook her head, as did Sister Jo.

Tom began taking photos of the box, the dead crow, and the general area with a small digital camera.

"Who's on duty this morning?" Sister Agatha asked him.

"Officer Bennett. Originally, I'd planned to keep him on desk duty for a while longer, but with the murder investigation, I'm low on deputies."

"Why didn't you want him out in the field? I know his family's in mourning, but he wasn't close to Jane."

"I'm worried about the pressure he's under and how he'll deal with it."

"Pressure? What do you mean?"

"When a crime's committed that involves a member of a police officer's family, relatives always turn to that officer for answers. Gerry, who's a pain in the butt on a good day, has been pushing everyone in the department for details of the investigation."

"I should have told you that when I spoke to him yesterday, he asked me to pass along any information I managed to get," she said.

"Sounds like Gerry. What did you tell him?"

"Nothing at all, actually."

"Well, watching the monastery is as close as he's going to get to investigating his mother-in-law's murder."

As they approached Bennett's patrol car, Sister Agatha glanced at Tom. "Before you come down too heavy on Gerry, keep in mind that it's likely he was being watched today, too. The person who served up the dead crow undoubtedly made sure Gerry was going to be somewhere else when he made his move."

"You're defending him?" Tom asked, eyebrows raised in surprise.

"No, just pointing out the facts—he was played like the rest of us."

When Deputy Bennett came over to meet them, Tom told him what had happened, fire in his eyes.

Bennett was quick to defend himself. "Sheriff, I've been here *all* morning. No one went past me unnoticed. I also made the quarter-hour foot patrols. But I can't be everywhere at once. It takes me five minutes, give or take, just to walk the perimeter."

"Who came to visit the monastery this morning?" Sheriff Green asked him.

"After Sister Agatha left on the Harley with the dog, a woman visitor drove through the gates and went to the parlor. She stayed for fifteen minutes, then left. Around then, two nuns drove out in the station wagon with a load of food containers, then returned about an hour and a half later. Sister Agatha arrived shortly afterward. Nothing else happened within my view."

"Someone was able to get close enough to throw that box over the wall," Tom argued.

"When did that go down?" Bennett asked, sounding even more defensive now.

"Right before noon," Sister Agatha said.

He considered it briefly, then answered. "They had a crew of laborers at the vineyard most of the morning. I saw them tending the irrigation lines when I went around that side of the property. Any one of them could have tossed the box over the wall."

"Give us a moment, Sister Agatha," Tom said, then stepped away with Gerry.

Although she couldn't hear them, she saw Tom use his radio, and within a few minutes another sheriff's department vehicle drove up. Shortly afterward, Gerry drove away.

Tom exchanged a few words with the new arrival, then came back to join her. "Officer Bennett's got court this afternoon, so I decided to get his replacement over here now. You may have met her already. Deputy Laura Sims used to serve with the Baton Rouge Police Department before she relocated to New Mexico."

"Let me go say hello," Sister Agatha said. She had come across Deputy Sims during an investigation last year.

Laura was a tall, athletic-looking woman with short-cropped red hair. Her bright blue eyes sparkled with life. "Nothing much gets past me, Sister Agatha," she said, shaking Sister Agatha's hand. "It's a skill I developed as the mom of an active five-year-old."

"I'm glad you're here. If you have any problems or questions we can help you with, just let us know," Sister Agatha said.

"Don't worry about anything, Sister. I'm Catholic, and I'll be especially careful not to enter cloistered areas. The nuns taught me too well for that," she answered with a smile.

Sister Agatha found herself liking Deputy Sims more every time she saw her. "That's good to hear."

After saying good-bye to Tom and asking once again to be kept up on any new developments, Sister Agatha walked back toward the parlor.

Before she reached the steps, Sister Jo came out the door. "Reverend Mother wants to speak to you."

"Has something happened?" Sister Agatha asked, quickening her pace.

"I don't know. That's all I was told."

Sister Agatha hurried inside, wishing that she had something encouraging to report.

9

REVEREND MOTHER LISTENED TO SISTER AGATHA'S REPORT, absently rubbing the simple wedding band that identified her as a Bride of Christ. "To what extent has our safety been compromised?"

"I don't think we're in any greater danger than before, Mother," she answered carefully. "We were already threatened once. This is a repeat of the same."

Reverend Mother nodded, lost in thought. "I have new orders for all our externs. Whenever possible I'd like you to travel in pairs when you leave our grounds. And, Sister Agatha, I'd prefer you stop using the motorcycle altogether. It makes you too vulnerable. From now on, use the station wagon unless, of course, you have no other choice."

"Mother, the problem is that the wagon costs a lot more to run and maintain. The gasoline alone . . . well, that car burns up fuel like a jumbo jet."

"God will provide for us, whatever our needs," she said firmly.

Realizing that Reverend Mother's mind was made up, Sister Agatha nodded. "All right, Mother."

Sister Agatha left Mother's office and headed directly to the parlor. Sister Jo was there behind the desk, hanging up the phone. "I'm glad you're here, Sister Agatha. That was the principal at St. Charles. He found someone more qualified to cover the class I was supposed to teach earlier today, but he needs me now to supervise their girls' after-school soccer match. Their coach has had to leave on an emergency. Could you give me a ride? I have to be there in about thirty minutes. Oh, and I guess I'll also need someone to take over parlor duty for me," she added as an afterthought.

"Let me go find Sister Bernarda," Sister Agatha said.

Sister Bernarda was in the chapel. Sister Agatha signaled her silently, and they stepped out into the hall. Sister Agatha then told her about Reverend Mother's new orders and Sister Jo's assignment.

"I was scheduled to pick up a shipment of sacramental wine from the winery this afternoon," Sister Bernarda said. "I need the station wagon for that, so why don't you both ride with me?"

Sister Agatha nodded. As part owners of the winery next door, the monastery nuns had accepted the job of delivering sacramental wine to the area parishes.

Not long afterward, they set out, Sister Bernarda behind the wheel of the Antichrysler. Sister de Lourdes had remained behind to take Sister Jo's place as portress.

"We'll pick up the cases of sacramental wine from Luz del Cielo first, then head over to St. Charles," Sister Agatha told Sister Jo.

"That's fine."

Luz del Cielo Vineyard and Winery was a large estate with a long, winding driveway. As they drove up to the main structure, an old Spanish-style villa with a red tile roof, Sister Agatha saw crews working the vineyard.

The Antichrysler backfired loudly, and Eric Barclay looked up from the vine he'd been grooming. Waving, he hurried over to meet them.

"Just four cases today, Sisters," he said, then signaled one of his men to help load the back of the wagon.

Sister Bernarda and Sister Jo stayed with the Antichrysler, supervising, while Sister Agatha stood a few feet away with Eric.

"How are things going at the monastery?" he asked her in a low voice. "I've been worried about all of you. I see you haven't had time to even get rid of the threat that's scratched on your car door." He pointed to the message, which they hadn't thought to cover. "It was all over last night's TV news."

"We're all being extra careful, and the sheriff's keeping an eye on us, too."

"Aren't you afraid to be out and about?"

She shook her head. "We'll face this just as we have all the other challenges that have come our way—by relying on God," Sister Agatha told him firmly. It was the best answer she could give. "But there's something I'd like to ask. A little after noon today, someone here on the vineyard side threw a box over the wall. There was a very disturbing message inside it. Any idea who might have done that?"

"A deputy has already asked me about it. The problem is that I've had to hire extra laborers recently to get the vines ready for the growing season. There are several new workers here. I've asked around, but I haven't got anything to report."

"If any of your men show a particular interest in our monastery, I'd like to know right away, and so would the sheriff."

"No problem, but you've got me curious now. What was inside the box? The deputy didn't say."

"Keep it to yourself?"

"Of course."

Sister Agatha told him, and he whistled low. Pax's ears suddenly pricked forward and he looked at Eric strangely.

Eric smiled. "Sorry, Pax." He glanced back at Sister Agatha, then added, "I'll keep my eyes and ears open. I won't forget the debt my daughter and I owe you. You're the reason this vineyard is still doing business."

"You don't owe us anything. You made us your business partners, and that's more than we ever expected. We're very grateful, but we would appreciate any help you can give us with this other matter."

"You've got it, Sister."

Once the cases of wine were loaded and the paperwork signed, the sisters were on their way. The drive to St. Charles School took less than fifteen minutes. As they neared the grounds, they saw kids in uniform warming up on the soccer field.

"We'll drop you off, deliver the wine, then come back and pick you up, Sister Jo. If the match isn't over, we'll wait," Sister Bernarda said.

"Thanks," Sister Jo responded. After giving Pax a quick hug, she climbed out of the station wagon and jogged toward the grass field.

As they headed out of town, Sister Agatha studied her aching hands. Her joints were swollen today and hurt like crazy. "I won't be of much use to you unloading the wine, so when we get to San Rafael, do you mind if I go talk to the workers? They've got a crew plastering the wall."

"Go right ahead. I'll concentrate on the delivery," Sister Bernarda answered.

"Thank you, Your Charity."

San Rafael Church was an old New Mexican–style church with two small white bell towers, only one of them finished. The church, formerly in a rural area, had been absorbed into the urban sprawl on the northern outskirts of Albuquerque.

It was only a bit past four, but the crew was already calling it a day, cleaning their tools and policing the work area. Sister Agatha wandered over casually, and before long she spotted Juanita. The young woman was an *enjarradora*—a specialist in the art of *enjarrando*, the craft of plastering with adobe. Juanita had been one of the experts who'd worked on the wall that encircled the monastery.

"Sister Agatha," she greeted. "I heard the news about the murder. I hope the sisters are getting through that okay. It's got to be hard on them."

"Do folks think that visiting our monastery is too dangerous now?" Sister Agatha asked.

She nodded. "A lady got robbed and killed there. It doesn't get worse than that. I keep saying that there's no proof the monastery is dangerous. For all we know, Mrs. Sanchez cut off the wrong guy in traffic on the way to church, so he followed and shot her. But most people don't care about the reason. All they know is that someone was killed there, and the killer's still at large."

Sister Agatha waited while Juanita took a long drink of water from a small bottle she'd attached to her tool belt.

"Have you heard any other theories about Jane Sanchez's murder?" Sister Agatha asked.

"Not me, no. But Dolly Wheeler could probably give you an earful of them. Do you know her?"

Sister Agatha thought about it and then finally shook her head. "The name doesn't sound familiar."

"She and Evelyn, Jane's daughter, were tight at one time—maybe still are. If anyone knows some serious behind-the-scenes type of stuff, like who might have had it in for Jane, it'll be Dolly."

Sister Agatha and Pax rejoined Sister Bernarda moments later. "Do you know Dolly Wheeler?"

"Sure." Sister Bernarda said as they climbed back into the Antichrysler. "She works at St. Charles. She's Mrs. Harper's, the new principal's, administrative assistant."

Sister Agatha pictured the office staff one by one, but Dolly Wheeler's face remained a mystery. "When we get to school, I'm going to the office. I'd like to meet Dolly and ask her a few questions."

"Good luck with that. Dolly's an irritating woman."

"You've dealt with her before?"

"Yes, during last year's Fall Festival I helped her run the school's booth at the fair," Sister Bernarda said. "She's the kind who complains about everything."

Sister Agatha said a prayer, asking to find a way to approach Dolly, one that would enable her to get her cooperation.

They arrived at the school about a half hour later, slowed by commuter traffic heading out of the metropolitan area, and parked in a space beside the big trash bins across from the soccer field. From there, they could see Sister Jo striding back and forth down the sideline, coaching the girls and shouting encouragement.

"She's a natural leader," Sister Agatha said, climbing out of the passenger's side. She then opened the back door to let Pax out and quickly attached his leash.

"The kids are crazy about her," Sister Bernarda said, smiling as they walked along the sidewalk toward the main entrance. A few feet from the door, she stopped. "I think you'll have a better chance with Dolly if I stay out here and watch the game."

"Sister Jo can use some help," Sister Agatha said, remembering that they'd agreed to keep an extra pair of eyes on the new addition to Our Lady of Hope.

Sister Agatha went on to the office, Pax at heel beside her. Someone she knew was in the workroom across from the office, running off copies.

"Hi, Mary. Do you know if Dolly Wheeler is still on campus?"

The young woman made a face. "Please, Sister," she whispered. "Don't say her name. I'm not wearing my crucifix, and that woman's half vampire. She's *always* out for blood."

Before Sister Agatha could answer, a tall, muscular woman with short black hair appeared at the door. The name tag on her crisp white shirt identified her as Dolly Wheeler. "You must be Pax," she said, ignoring Sister Agatha completely and crouching down to pet the dog.

Pax leaned into her without hesitation, letting himself be hugged. Dolly reached into her purse and brought out a small cookie wrapped in clear plastic, then glanced at Sister Agatha. "It's not dog food, Sister, but do you mind? One tiny vanilla wafer won't hurt him."

"Actually, that's one of his favorites. His trainer would often use them as a reward," Sister Agatha said with a smile.

Sister Agatha stared at the woman everyone had warned her would be difficult. She was now happily scratching the dog between the ears. Sister Agatha smiled. Pax had been the answer to her prayer. He'd helped her do what no one else could have—get them off to a good start.

"He's a wonderful monastery pet," Sister Agatha said.

"Animals can be a great comfort during times of stress," Dolly said.

"Things have been rough," Sister Agatha admitted. "Jane Sanchez's murder hit us very hard."

Dolly continued to pet Pax. "It's a nasty business."

"Did you know Jane?" Sister Agatha asked.

Dolly nodded and looked up, meeting her gaze. "I know one shouldn't speak ill of the dead, but I don't believe in mincing words. Jane was an unbelievable pain in the neck."

Sister Agatha wasn't sure how to respond, so she decided not to say anything at all.

Dolly's gaze remained on Sister Agatha, and she suddenly laughed. "I see you probably heard the same thing said about me. At least I mind my own business. Jane wanted to tell everyone exactly how to run their lives—down to the smallest detail."

"I can imagine that would be difficult to deal with," Sister Agatha said, watching as Dolly continued to pet Pax.

"In my opinion, Jane's lucky to have lived this long. Evelyn herself should have throttled her mother years ago. Jane was always finding ways to remind Evelyn that she was adopted, telling her how grateful she should have been that she and Louis sacrificed to give her a home. I think half the reason Evelyn married Gerald Bennett was she knew Jane couldn't stand him."

Sister Agatha nodded but remained silent. Sometimes it was far better not to speak, particularly when someone was on a roll.

Dolly lowered her voice. "The reason I'm telling you this, Sister, is because I figure you're looking into the murder, and I bet you never saw that side of Jane."

"I've heard that she pretty much ran things at home."

Dolly snorted. "You're being way too generous. Jane was a dictator, even to her husband. That's why I think Christy White got into the picture. You know about her and Louis, right?"

Sister Agatha nodded. "They're friends."

"Friends? Hah!" Dolly answered. "But back to Jane. I don't think this murder had anything to do with robbery. That's just what we're meant to believe. Jane made enemies every time she opened her mouth. I think someone had a bellyful, followed Jane, then killed her." As the phone rang, she excused herself.

Sister Agatha looked around the office and realized that it was now five o'clock and most of the staff had left. Taking Pax, she went down the hall and saw Sister Bernarda and Sister Jo waiting for her by the side door. The janitor, Mike Cuevas, was there with them, keys in hand.

He gave Sister Agatha an impatient smile. "There you are, Sister Agatha. I have to lock these side doors once after-school activities are over."

"Sorry to keep you waiting, Mike," she said and hurried out along with Pax.

Sister Jo was smiling broadly. "Sisters, I had so much fun today!"

"So you like coaching?" Sister Agatha asked, though the answer was obvious.

Sister Jo nodded, her eyes sparkling. "Most of all I enjoy the kids." She waved at some students who were walking by on the sidewalk.

Sister Jo was one of the most contented people Sister Agatha had ever met. Sister Jo, in fact, considered being happy part of her duty to God. He didn't like long faces, she'd said once.

"I had to move the car and park across the street because the trash people were coming by," Sister Bernarda said. "We'll have to cross the highway, so stay sharp. People are always in a rush to get home."

Sister Agatha followed her, though Sister Bernarda's pace was brisk and it was difficult to keep up. As they stepped around the corner of the building, Sister Bernarda stopped abruptly and pointed ahead.

"Hey, you! Get away from our car!" she yelled out.

The tall figure in a hooded sweatshirt across the road was waving something in his hand. A heartbeat later Sister Agatha saw new, large, crudely painted letters on the Antichrysler. "He spray-painted our car!"

By then the man had broken into a run.

10

TRAFFIC WAS HEAVY, AND THEY HAD TO WAIT FOR THREE vehicles before making it across the highway. Although the man had disappeared into the trees beyond the parking area, Pax kept straining at the leash. It was nearly impossible for Sister Agatha to keep him from tearing off after the fleeing suspect. His training as a police dog was taking over now.

"I'll catch the guy. Give me Pax, and we'll track him," Sister Jo said.

Every joint in Sister Agatha's body was screaming with pain. Some people's bodies, like Sister Jo's and Sister Bernarda's, were made for running. Hers, afflicted by arthritis, clearly was not. Sister Agatha turned the leash over to Sister Jo, who sprinted off with the eager dog.

Sister Bernarda, aware that Sister Agatha was having trouble, hung back a second. "Are you okay, Sister?"

"I'm fine. Go help Sister Jo."

Sister Agatha approached the Antichrysler from the front, instantly picking up the distinct scent of aerosol paint. As she came around to the driver's side, she saw the new spray-painted message on the already scratched door. It read JESUS SLAVES.

Having seen more than one crude local sign reading PRIVIT DRIVE, she wondered whether this tagger had a spelling problem or had been trying to send some kind of antireligious message.

Three minutes later Sister Bernarda and Sister Jo returned, breathing hard. Sister Bernarda now had Pax on a tight leash, and she was trying to curb the dog's excitement. There was nothing Pax enjoyed more than a chase.

"We tried, but the guy had a head start, and not even Sister Jo and Pax could catch up," Sister Bernarda said. "He had a vehicle one street over, and all we saw was a glimpse of white through the trees as he tore off."

Sister Jo stared at the Antichrysler. "You think he meant 'Jesus saves,' or was this some kind of political comment by a Catholic hater?"

"From what's been happening lately, I'm not at all sure," Sister Agatha answered.

"At least he covered up part of that other threat," Sister Bernarda added with a sigh.

As she finished speaking, Mike came rushing up. "You got tagged," he said, looking at the Antichrysler. "I have to deal with this all the time at school. The important thing is to get rid of the message *immediately*. Once they see they're wasting paint and very few will ever see their message, they move on. I have just the product to take off that spray paint, too. But I better warn you—it may take some of the finish along with it."

"What finish?" Sister Bernarda said wryly. "This car's paint has been finished for years."

"You're right about that." Mike gave her a grim smile. "Let

me help you, and we'll get things back to the way they were. Park next to the building while I go get the cleaner and a roll of paper towels."

Sister Agatha smiled. "Thanks, Mike. We'll take all the help we can get."

Mike looked at the paint, then glanced at Sister Agatha. "What's that supposed to mean?"

"We were just trying to figure that out ourselves," Sister Agatha said.

It took them almost an hour to remove the painted threat. By the time they returned home, it was past collation. All three of them went directly to the kitchen, knowing Sister Clothilde would have set something aside for them.

They weren't disappointed. Sister Clothilde was waiting as they walked into the refectory, their dining room. Pax shot past them, heading to his full dog dish in the next room. Seconds later they could hear him crunching his kibble.

Meanwhile, Sister Clothilde silently brought out a tray with three bowls filled to the brim with hot corn chowder. Two slices of thick homemade bread were beside each.

Sister Clothilde, in her eighties, had taken a vow of silence a lifetime ago and had never broken it. Yet despite it—or maybe because of it—she always seemed attuned to the others' needs. When she'd learned of the Good News Meal Program, she'd stepped in, planning all their menus and preparing the food herself.

Sister Agatha helped her place the food on the refectory table and, after saying grace, began to eat. She hadn't realized how hungry she was until now.

She'd barely had a few teaspoons of Sister Clothilde's special soup when Sister Eugenia suddenly came through the refectory door, a stern look on her face.

"You left this morning without stopping by the infirmary to pick up your pills. I won't have it, Sister Agatha. Just *look* at your hands."

Sister Agatha didn't have to look to know her joints were badly swollen. "It's just the spring weather, Your Charity," Sister Agatha said, taking the pills from her. "It's nothing to worry about."

"You can't ignore the doctor's orders. Once things progress past a certain point, it all becomes harder to manage."

She nodded and quickly swallowed the pills.

"After you've eaten, please go see Reverend Mother. She'd like to speak to you." Then, in a much softer tone, she added, "Your Charity, while you're with her, try to convince her to take something to help her sleep. She hasn't had much rest since, well, you know."

Sister Agatha nodded, noting Sister Eugenia's reluctance to speak of the crime that had been committed practically at their front door. They were all having a difficult time handling what had happened. Yet she alone bore the extra burden of knowing it was partially her fault. This might not have happened if she'd taken time to listen to Jane.

Guilt drove her to find answers now. The only way she had to balance out her failure was to find justice. God would help her. Although she'd failed Him, He wouldn't fail her. Love redeemed all who offered Him a contrite heart.

Once they'd finished eating, Sister Bernarda and Sister Jo offered to clean up. "We'll handle things here while you go talk to Reverend Mother," Sister Bernarda said.

"Thank you, Sisters," Sister Agatha said and hurried out.

Sister Agatha found Reverend Mother outside on one of the benches. After an unusually harsh, wet winter, they all looked forward to recreation, when they could spend time outside in the fresh air.

Despite the fading light of day, Sister Agatha could see that Reverend Mother was exhausted, and her heart went out to her. "Mother, I just spoke with Sister Eugenia. She's very worried about you."

Reverend Mother held up a hand. "I know. She's been wanting me to take those sleeping pills the doctor prescribed. But I tried them before, and they make me too groggy to pay attention to our prayers at Matins. My job is to serve the Lord, and I can't do that if I'm all doped up."

"Lack of sleep isn't good either, Mother," Sister Agatha countered quietly. "You need sleep in order to serve."

"The problem is that I've had too many things on my mind. The Archbishop called again. The reporters have played up the threat to the nuns and are speculating that the death of Mrs. Sanchez is only the beginning and more violence will follow. The Archbishop is worried about the reputations of the monastery and St. Augustine Church. Apparently, he's been getting calls from some of the parishioners who want the diocese to hire parking lot security for local churches."

"Mother, people are just scared," Sister Agatha said softly. "With gang violence on the rise and big-city crime just to the south, all it takes is one dramatic incident to give fear a foothold. Once this killer's caught, we'll have peace again."

"At least we still have the Good News meal deliveries to serve the community and bring the comfort of God's word to them. For that, we can thank Sister Jo and her spirit of giving," Reverend Mother said, then stood.

Together, they walked across the grounds and back to the recreation room. "Providence brought her here to us, I'm sure of it." Reverend Mother added.

"From the looks of it, Providence definitely has a sense of humor," Sister Agatha added, coming to a stop in the doorway.

Sister Jo shuffled past them, two mop heads tied to her shoes. Smiling, she moved quickly to the end of the room, stepped to her left, then pushed off the wall with one hand and spun around on the polished wooden floor.

"What on earth is she doing?" Reverend Mother asked.

"Skating?" Sister Agatha offered.

Sister Bernarda, standing against the wall just inside the room, laughed. "She's buffing up our floor."

"But why?" Reverend Mother asked.

"Sister Jo got sandwiched today between the meal deliveries and the soccer match and wasn't able to take care of the floors. When she tried to sneak in a little work tonight, Sister Eugenia reminded her that, at this monastery, work is prohibited during recreation. That's when Sister Jo decided to get creative," Sister Bernarda answered.

Sister Jo slid to a stop by the table, picked up a can of wax, and sprayed the bottom of the mops. Then she strode off again, a grin on her face. "Wheee. Just like the old duck pond in December."

Reverend Mother laughed. "And here I thought nothing could make me laugh out loud today."

As the bell for Compline sounded, they abruptly stopped speaking. Sister Jo slid to a stop, grabbing the doorjamb to keep from falling. As she reached down to untie the mop heads, the others began to file out of the room, heading for chapel.

Joining her fellow sisters, Sister Agatha knelt and gazed at the altar. "Lord, help me find answers. I failed you once. Please don't let me do that again," she prayed silently from the bottom of her heart.

Soon she began chanting the Divine Office, her voice indistinguishable from those of her sisters.

The next morning, after Terce, Sister Agatha went to the parlor. Sister de Lourdes was already there at the desk.

"I'm glad you're here, Sister Agatha," she said. "A few minutes ago I received a call from Louis Sanchez. He asked that you stop by as soon as you can. He said he needed to talk."

"Thanks, Sister de Lourdes," she said. "Sister Bernarda, Pax, and I will head into town shortly in the station wagon. I'll see him then. We'll make sure to be back before you need to set out to deliver the meals."

"It's not necessary," Sister de Lourdes said. "A few ladies from St. Augustine's will be making our meal deliveries today. Sister Jo will also be free to spell me here once she gets the Good News meals packed and ready for pickup."

"You've got the hardest job, Sister de Lourdes," Sister Agatha said, sympathizing with her. "You have to keep running back and forth between the parlor and the scriptorium, and you also have to make sure the meal pickups go as planned."

"I've devised a system that helps me spend more time greeting visitors and answering the phone. Sister Clothilde does most of the cooking for Good News. Sister Jo packs up the meals. Sister Maria Victoria, Sister Eugenia, Sister Ignatius, and Sister Gertrude get the computer hardware orders for NexCen filled and boxed for pickup. By the time the package express man comes, which is usually late in the afternoon, everything's done."

"How has Sister Maria Victoria been working out?"

"She's great answering the monastery's mail. Words just flow for her," Sister de Lourdes said.

"I'm glad. She really had a tough time as seamstress *and* cellarer. Keeping the books for the monastery was definitely *not* what she was meant to do."

"From disaster to success," Sister de Lourdes said with a smile.

Just then Sister Bernarda and Pax came into the parlor. "I hope I haven't kept you waiting for long, Sister Agatha. I was helping Sister Eugenia go through the infirmary's provisions. She's made a list of medications we need to pick up for her at the pharmacy."

"We'll make that pharmacy stop after we visit Louis Sanchez," Sister Agatha said as they walked out to the Antichrysler, Pax following closely. "He's asked to speak to me."

"Would you like me to go inside with you, or would you prefer to handle this alone?"

Sister Agatha considered it. "I'd like to talk to him one-on-one," she said at last, "but come inside with me. If there's anyone else there, lead them away so Louis and I can speak freely. If no one else is about, excuse yourself and say you've got to take Pax for a walk."

She nodded, understanding. "You want me there to divide their forces, if necessary."

Sister Agatha smiled. You could take the woman out of the marines, but you could never get the marines out of the woman.

They arrived a short time later and found Louis outside, talking to Christy White.

"I'll distract the woman," Sister Bernarda said.

"Wait a sec. I have a better idea," Sister Agatha said quickly. "While I keep them busy, you walk around with Pax and keep an eye out for any eavesdropping neighbor. The day she called me, Jane was worried that someone was listening in on her conversation. She was at home at the time, so maybe it was somebody she knew. There are no fences around, so it would have been easy enough to sneak up and eavesdrop if her window was open."

"Got it. Anything else?" Sister Bernarda asked.

"Yes. Keep watch for a bike with knobby tires. We know the killer had one."

"You've got it," Sister Bernarda answered with a nod.

They walked over to meet Louis moments later. While Sister Agatha remained with them, Sister Bernarda excused herself and walked off with Pax.

"We're very glad you're here, Sister Agatha," Louis said. "Christy's grandson delivers newspapers in our neighborhood, and he's got some information we think you should hear directly from him."

The tone of his voice alerted her. "If he has information, the sheriff needs—"

"That's just it, Sister. Billy won't talk to the sheriff," Christy said. "He's a good boy, but he's got a record. Nothing major, mind you. It's just that he's spent time in juvenile hall and he doesn't trust the deputies."

"But Christy pressured him and he's agreed to talk to you, Sister Agatha," Louis said.

"All right, but be aware that the sheriff will need to be told about anything that's connected to the case," she said. It was possible that Billy's information was tied to whatever Jane had wanted to talk to her about. Maybe everything would fall into place at last. "Where's he now?" she added.

"In my house," Louis said. "Christy's been cooking for both of us."

Sister Agatha followed them into the kitchen. The scent of

freshly fried dough made her mouth water. On the metal table directly in front of her was a teenaged boy wolfing down a huge Navajo taco: a big piece of puffy fry bread topped with pinto beans, lettuce, salsa, tomatoes, and lots of shredded cheese.

"Hi," Sister Agatha said, introducing herself.

He wiped his mouth. "I'm only talking to you, Sister, because Grandma bribed me. *Nobody* cooks like she does," he added with a grin.

"I'm glad that you agreed to talk to me, but if you have information that the sheriff should have—"

"I've got nothing the law can use," he said, interrupting her. "I barely saw the guy who stole Mr. Sanchez's bike. You know I throw papers—deliver newspapers—right?"

She nodded. "Go on, Billy."

"Well, I was in my pickup, throwing the afternoon edition, when I noticed someone walking around the side of Louis's garage. My first thought was that it was the PNM guy, reading the meter, but when I turned the corner, I saw the PNM guy in his truck. The man I'd seen before was heading in the opposite direction on a red bike. Thing is, I didn't really think much about it until Grandma told me that someone had stolen Mr. Sanchez's bike."

"Did you get a good look at the man?"

"No, I barely glanced at him," Billy said, then took another huge mouthful. "I was busy trying to fold the next paper and slip on a rubber band without wrecking my truck. I was running behind that day."

"You're sure it was a man, not a woman?" she pressed, knowing that people often saw far more than they realized.

"It was a guy," he said without hesitation. "Guys walk differently than women."

"What color was his hair?" Sister Agatha asked him.

"Brown—I think. He was wearing a dark blue baseball cap, so I don't know for sure."

"Was he tall?"

"Kinda. He was a lot taller than Mr. Sanchez, and not so . . . stubby."

So that made him over five foot eight, Sister Agatha concluded silently. "You didn't actually see him steal the bike?"

"No, and for all I know it was his own and he'd parked it around the corner. All I can tell you for sure is that he rode away on a red bike. That's why I told Grandma."

Sister Agatha nodded. "Would you recognize the man if you saw him again?"

"I never saw his face because the baseball cap shaded his eyes. And, oh, he was wearing sunglasses. Forgot about that until now."

"What kind of clothes was he wearing?"

"Jeans and a long-sleeved shirt with the sleeves rolled up."

"What color was the shirt?" Sister Agatha pressed. "Was it a service uniform?"

"I remember tan, or maybe cream colored, but that's all I can tell you. I really wasn't paying much attention. I just wanted to finish my route so I could go play Street Cred."

"Come again?" Sister Agatha asked.

"Street Cred, on my computer. It's a hot new game."

Billy finished his meal, sopping up the chile sauce by using a piece of fry bread like a scoop. Jamming it into his mouth, he stood. "I've gotta go. I didn't make it to school this morning because I'm on two-day suspension. I'm grounded, too, so I can't go cruising in my truck unless it's to throw papers. I just came over to Grandma's 'cause I knew she wouldn't rat me out, but I've got to get back before my dad calls to check up on me."

"Have you noticed any other strangers hanging around the area besides the one who may have stolen the bike?" she asked.

He shook his head. "Nope, but you can pass along the information I gave you if it makes any difference."

"The sheriff will have to know, Billy. He's trying to catch a killer. Go tell him yourself. It'll give you some credibility, too, especially with Sheriff Green."

He stood there a moment, looking at her, then glanced at his grandmother. Christy nodded.

"Okay," Billy said. "I'll make the call when I get home. If he sends a deputy by, the whole neighborhood will wonder what trouble I've gotten into now, right?" He grinned, then walked to the door and let himself out.

The phone rang, and Louis went to answer it in the living room. Alone with Christy, Sister Agatha smiled at her. "Thanks for convincing him to talk to me."

"I figured it would help you—and me. You're probably wondering if maybe I had something to do with Jane's murder. People like to gossip, and I know I'm a hot topic right now."

Louis returned to the room before Sister Agatha could answer. "I hope Billy was able to help you, Sister," he said. "People are spreading a lot of nonsense about Christy and me."

"Neither one of us has ever done anything to deserve that kind of trash talk," Christy added.

Sister Agatha looked at Louis, then at Christy. Her instincts told her that they weren't holding out on her, but there were still too many unanswered questions. "Gossip won't convict anyone," Sister Agatha said. "Evidence will. If you want to help, give me a list of Jane's enemies."

"She bugged people sometimes, but not so badly they would kill—" Louis stopped in midsentence as the phone began to ring again, then excused himself.

"Do you agree with that?" Sister Agatha asked Christy.

Christy considered it for a long moment. "This street has no shortage of personality conflicts, particularly when the neighborhood association meets. Tempers always run short, and sniping's rampant. Jane wasn't particularly singled out, though—no more than anyone else with an opinion."

"Who argued with Jane the most?"

"Me," she answered without skipping a beat. "That doesn't mean I killed her. I also argue with my daughter and my grandkid, and they're both still walking around."

Sister Agatha smiled, but questions were racing through her head. "Besides you, then."

She thought it over. "At the meetings, no one in particular."

"Outside those times, then," Sister Agatha pressed.

Christy considered it for a few seconds. "Louis never argued with Jane—which just made it worse for him. The only other people besides me who come to mind right away are her daughter and son-in-law. Jane and Evelyn had huge fights."

"Over what?"

"Near as I can tell, they got into shouting matches over everything. I'd hear them from my kitchen window. Then again, to stop Jane from walking all over you, you had to get ugly from time to time."

Louis returned and glanced at Christy, then at Sister Agatha. "Sister, you're going to have to excuse us. One of the families in our parish lost everything in a house fire, and Father Mahoney asked me if I'd be willing to donate some of Jane's clothing. I said yes, but then . . . well, it was harder than I'd thought. That was the main reason Christy came over. We aren't even close to finished yet, but some volunteers are coming by in a half hour to pick up whatever we have ready."

Sister Agatha stood, then noticed a familiar purse on the

kitchen counter. "Did Jane have two purses exactly alike?" she asked Louis.

"No. A deputy brought that to me a couple of hours ago. The sheriff doesn't need it anymore and thought I might because of the keys and ID stuff inside."

"That was thoughtful," she answered, then continued, after a pause, "I just had an idea. Would you do something for me? Look inside the purse and see if you can tell if anything's missing."

"The sheriff already asked me how much money I thought was stolen, and I told him. It was around a hundred dollars. Besides that, she had one credit card, but it was still there."

"How about missing items that aren't money related?"

Louis picked up the purse and began to set the contents out on the counter.

Seeing the prayer book, Sister Agatha suddenly knew what she wanted to ask next. "Didn't Jane always carry a memo pad in her purse?"

"Yeah, she did," Louis said, checking every pocket and pouch. "It was one of those brightly colored ones. She was always making notes to herself or leaving them for me. Just look at the fridge," he said, waving. "I haven't had the courage to take them down yet."

"So that's missing. Did she keep any other pads around the house?"

Louis scratched his head. "Excuse me for a moment." He left the kitchen and went into the living room.

Sister Agatha heard a drawer open, then another. A moment later, she heard Louis walk into the hall, then the sound of another drawer opening. At long last, he returned to the kitchen. "That's odd. She always left memo pads on her desk and on the bedroom dresser. There were several of them around in that same pink color. Now they're all gone."

"Maybe the deputies took them," Christy offered. "Or the sheriff."

"They would have given Louis a receipt," Sister Agatha said. "I know that from my journalist days."

"Are those pads important for some reason?" Louis asked her.

"You remember that Jane called last Friday and wanted to talk to me about something?"

"Yes, but I still have no idea what that was about," Louis said.

"There's something I didn't mention before. When Jane called, she hung up almost immediately after telling me that she thought someone was listening in," Sister Agatha answered, watching back and forth between the two for a reaction.

"Like me?" Louis asked in confusion. "I might have been in the next room, but I never eavesdrop on purpose."

"Jane did," Christy blurted out.

"Christy!" Louis exclaimed.

"Sorry to be so blunt, but you know she did, Louis. Jane was a snoop."

"Well, I wasn't," he said, his voice soft and strained.

Sister Agatha wasn't surprised about Jane. "She may have meant someone listening in through an open window, or maybe on the phone," Sister Agatha reasoned. Looking over, she noticed that the phone was an older cordless model. Phones like that had a reputation for being vulnerable to bugs, or even neighbors on the same frequency.

"Do you think that's the reason Jane was killed, and it wasn't just a robbery?" Christy asked. "The sheriff should be told about this if he doesn't know already."

"He knows some of it, but I'll speak to him and tell him the rest," Sister Agatha said.

"You're thinking that maybe Jane wrote something down on a memo pad and the killer took them all to make sure nobody else could find out . . . why she was killed?" Louis's voice faded at the end.

"If that's really what happened, Louis, you can trust Sheriff Green to get to the bottom of it," Sister Agatha said. "In the meantime, if either of you thinks of anything, call him right away."

Both nodded.

They were just leaving the kitchen when Sister Agatha heard the sound of metal clanking. That was instantly followed by Pax's frantic barking.

Christy went to the window. "Somebody's broken into my garage!"

Christy rushed out the back door, Louis and Sister Agatha at her heels. When they reached the garage, the right-hand door was half open. Sister Agatha saw Sister Bernarda inside, grasping Pax's leash hard and trying to pull him back. The dog was totally focused on something in the far corner and refused to back away.

Sister Agatha hurried over to help and, as she drew near, heard a dry rattle—a sound she instantly recognized. A rattlesnake was curled in the corner, poised to strike.

D ON'T EVER STRUGGLE WITH PAX, SISTER BERNARDA. You'll lose," Sister Agatha said as she took the leash. "Pax, back," she said in a calm voice.

Pax continued barking but took a step back, then another, used to his handler. Sister Agatha continued until she'd pulled Pax well away from the striking range of the snake.

"He spotted the snake outside and chased it into that corner beside that bike. The garage door was open," Sister Bernarda explained to no one in particular, not taking her eyes off the coiled reptile, which was watching back, its tongue flicking the air.

"If there was a rattler in my yard, I'm glad it was the *dog* who found it," Christy said, standing well behind everyone. "I hang clothes out on the line all the time, and sometimes I come out barefooted."

"We need to call the county. That snake's gotta go," Louis

said. "We have too many kids in this neighborhood. Keep an eye on it while I make a call to animal control," he added, then ran back to his house.

Christy's gaze shifted to the tools scattered all over the floor. "What happened here?"

"That's my fault, too," Sister Bernarda said. "I lost control of the dog, and in his eagerness to get at the snake, he knocked the chair over and the tools."

Christy nodded, but Sister Agatha saw the flicker of uncertainty in her eyes.

"But what were you doing back there, Sister?" Christy pressed.

"I was walking the dog down the easement. You can't tell where the property lines are, but I figured we were okay, not bothering anyone. Then Pax saw the snake . . ."

Christy sighed long and loud. "I've been saving up to get myself a fence, but every time I think I've got the cash, I get hit by a bill I wasn't expecting."

Sister Agatha nodded sympathetically. "We understand, believe me."

"Where did the snake come from?" Christy asked Sister Bernarda after a beat.

"Maybe through the culvert from the drainage ditch. I'm not sure. It crossed right in front of us. I saw movement in the grass, and then the dog took off. I never saw what he was after until it slithered into the garage."

Christy shuddered.

"Who's doing animal control duty these days?" Sister Bernarda asked, still watching the snake. Although it had stopped rattling, it remained coiled, its tongue testing the air.

"Al Marrow," Sister Agatha answered. "He's the one who handled that problem with the coyote a few weeks back."

Al, wearing his khaki uniform shirt and blue jeans, arrived within ten minutes of the call in the county's animal control truck. He was a thin, wiry man with a grim expression, a rough complexion, and numerous tattoos on his arms. Although he looked like a long-term inmate of a state prison, Sister Agatha knew that beneath the gruff exterior beat a very gentle heart.

He nodded to the ladies, then took a look. "Hmm. Western rattlesnake, about average size, maybe four feet. Notice the dark splotches? A western diamondback has those splotches outlined in a pale color."

"Thanks for the Animal Planet moment, Al. Can you just get it out of my garage?" Christy asked.

Al chuckled. "I charge ten dollars a foot, Christy. That comes to forty-five dollars."

Christy looked at him with narrowed eyes.

Al laughed. "Okay, just a joke. It'll take a few minutes, though. I don't want it to get behind something big and heavy like your washing machine."

"What's going to happen to it?" Sister Agatha.

"After I capture it with a loop, I'll release it in the bosque away from any homes. Even a rattler has its place in God's plan, Sister."

Before long, the snake was secure in a burlap sack and Al was on his way.

Once they were back in the Antichrysler and on their way, Sister Agatha was finally free to speak. "That rattler was a godsend. It gave you a perfect way to cover your tracks."

"You're right," Sister Bernarda agreed. "What you don't know is that we were already inside the garage checking out the bike when we found the rattler. As it turns out, the bike was an old model with flat tires, *not* the one stolen from Louis. Anyway, Pax went berserk."

Sister Agatha nodded. "He does that. And he knocked down the tools?"

Sister Bernarda gave her a sheepish smile. "Actually, no. My habit got caught on the bench when Pax tugged at the leash, and when I pulled free it all came tumbling down."

"You certainly had an exciting time. Did you find anything besides the serpent and the wrong bike?"

She nodded. "Something interesting, though it wasn't inside the garage. I spotted something dangling from the outside phone connection on the Sanchez house, so we went up to take a closer look. There was a wire attached there, with one of those double phone jacks at one end. I think that may have been where an outside phone or bug was attached, but only an expert would know for sure."

"When Jane was on the phone talking to me, she was afraid she'd be overheard," Sister Agatha said. "We'll have to tell the sheriff what we've learned, including the part about those missing memo pads." She filled Sister Bernarda in on what she didn't already know.

They'd brought the cell phone, so while Sister Bernarda drove, Sister Agatha told Sheriff Green what she'd learned.

"The information about the memo pads is definitely interesting," he said, "but it's the kind of negative evidence that doesn't really prove anything. What I'm going to do now is send an officer over there to check out their phone and pick up that extra connection."

Sister Agatha's and Sister Bernarda's next stop was the pharmacy. While Sister Bernarda waited for their order to be filled, Sister Agatha went to talk to the clerk stocking the shelves. Silvia Pike had attended St. Charles, and Sister Agatha remembered her well. She'd been devout but had also been a relentless gossip. These days Silvia had become a good source, since her information always proved reliable.

When Sister Agatha greeted her, Silvia's eyes grew bright and she smiled. "Sister Agatha, it's so good to see you again! I loved reading that newspaper article in the *Chronicle* last year about how you helped the sheriff catch a killer. I bet you've got your hands full now, too, with everyone wondering if it's safe to go to Mass with a robber and killer hanging around. Have you received any more threats?"

"We have police protection at the monastery now," Sister Agatha said, not answering her directly. "Tell me, did you know the victim?"

"Jane? Sure, she used to come in here all the time," she said, barely taking a breath. "Louis, too. I don't recall ever seeing them apart."

Except on Sunday, Sister Agatha added silently. "She didn't trust him, or vice versa?" she probed gently.

"Ah, you must have heard the rumor about his neighbor. Well, don't believe it. Jane would have known if something had been going on. Anyway, Louis isn't the kind to stray. He allowed himself to be led around because he really did love Jane. That's my take on it."

"How do you think the rumor got started, then?" Sister Agatha asked.

"I'm not really sure, but you could ask Betty Malone. She's one of Louis's neighbors, and that woman doesn't miss much. She's the president of their neighborhood watch association for a reason."

Sister Agatha made a mental note to pay Betty a visit. "How well do you know Louis, Silvia?"

"Just enough to say hello whenever he came in with Jane.

But I've been friends with their daughter, Evelyn, for years. Evelyn hated Jane. She wasn't even on speaking terms with her half the time. I've got to tell you," she said, lowering her voice and leaning closer to Sister Agatha, "if Evelyn had discovered that her dad *was* having an affair, she would have jumped for joy."

That was certainly an interesting perspective. "Why did Evelyn hate Jane so much? Do you know?" Sister Agatha asked, already knowing that the adoption had been an issue of contention.

"All I can tell you is that I saw firsthand how controlling Jane was back when Ev and I were still in high school. I particularly remember one shouting match out in their front yard. The whole neighborhood must have heard that one. Ev had come home an hour later than her curfew, and Jane went through the roof. She told Ev that she was behaving like a slut and she regretted the day she'd adopted her. What made it even worse is that we were there—me and Allison Williams."

"Do you know if Jane really felt that way?"

"I always thought the real issue was that Evelyn was growing up and trying to become a little more independent. But that kind of argument was nothing in comparison to what came later, after Evelyn married Gerry."

"What happened then?"

"Jane did *everything* she could to try to break them up. Gerry doesn't take lip from anyone, so from day one he argued right back. Things never got any better. Jane would start with the bad-mouthing the second she saw them, telling Evelyn that she'd married a total loser."

"But surely Jane accepted him once the couple had their daughter, right?"

"Didn't seem like it to me, Sister. Just last week, maybe Tuesday, Jane and Louis came here to the drugstore, and she was dissing Gerry to him. Louis looked really embarrassed because he knew I could hear, but Jane just kept running Gerry down. She insisted that Gerry was cheating on Evelyn."

Seeing Sister Bernarda was through at the counter, Sister Agatha knew it was time to go. "It was good talking to you, Silvia," she said, meaning every word.

Sister Agatha and Sister Bernarda hurried back out to the Antichrysler. It was a beautiful, cool, spring day, so Pax had waited for them with all the windows rolled down, under the shade of the store awning. Once they were on their way, he stuck his head out, loving the blast of air that hit his face as they traveled back to the monastery.

"If Jane thought Gerry was messing around, that could have been what she wanted to talk to me about," Sister Agatha told Sister Bernarda on their way home. "The problem with gossip is that I don't have any evidence to back it up, and the sheriff is going to need more than hearsay."

"You should probably still tell the sheriff so he can follow it up if he feels it necessary, don't you think?"

Sister Agatha nodded, then brought out the cell phone and made the call.

Twenty minutes later, they were back home with the medications. Pax had gone into the inner courtyard to play alone with his favorite rope toy, tossing it into the air or shaking it.

While Sister Bernarda met with Sister Eugenia, Sister Agatha stopped by the chapel to pray for guidance. Turning to the Lord, she placed the matter in His hands, then, with all the love in her heart, focused solely on Him.

Sister Agatha came back out of the chapel some time later, her spirit renewed, and headed to the parlor. She was halfway down the hall when she saw Sister Bernarda hurrying to meet her.

"Have you seen Pax?" Sister Bernarda asked quickly.

"Not since we returned. He went outside to play with his rope, remember?"

"Sister Clothilde had a treat for him, but she couldn't find the old guy anywhere."

Alarmed, Sister Agatha and Sister Bernarda went to the parlor, where they found Sister de Lourdes.

"Have you seen Pax?" Sister Agatha asked her quickly.

"Yes, he went with Sister Jo in the Harley. She got a call from a Mr. Stevens, who asked why he hadn't received his lunch today. So she got the address, made up another meal, then took off with it immediately."

"Mr. Stevens? We've never delivered to someone with that name, have we?" Sister Bernarda asked.

"Maybe he's new," Sister Agatha suggested.

"That's what Sister Jo concluded, too," Sister de Lourdes said. "She was upset about anyone missing a meal, so she left in a hurry. Since she couldn't find the car keys, she took the bike."

Sister Bernarda reached into her pocket and brought out the keys. "Oops. My fault."

"I'm curious about this delivery. Would you call St. Augustine's and have them verify the name, Sister de Lourdes?" Sister Agatha asked.

After a minute on the line, it became obvious that there was no Mr. Stevens on the list.

"She's been set up," Sister Agatha said, her voice rising in fear. "Any idea where she was going?"

"She repeated it aloud as she wrote it down. It's 800 something Calle de Elena," Sister de Lourdes replied.

"That's less than five miles from here. Let's take the

Antichrysler and see if we can catch up to her," Sister Agatha said to Sister Bernarda. She turned back to Sister de Lourdes. "Call the sheriff and tell him what's happening." Sister de Lourdes nodded and picked up the telephone.

"Let's go," Sister Bernarda said, leading the way to the door. "I'm the one who forgot to put the keys back, so I'm driving."

Sister Agatha's heart was hammering against her rib cage as they passed through the monastery gates. Sister Bernarda at the wheel, they traveled as quickly as they could down the dirt road, heading for the highway. The car backfired in protest, a common event that they'd learned to ignore.

When the cell phone rang, Sister Agatha grabbed it instantly. It was the sheriff. "I ran the address on our database. There's no 800 block of Calle de Elena. It only goes up to 700. I don't have a deputy in that area, but I'm sending one to check out the entire neighborhood."

"It could have been just a crank call, but then again, it might be more serious than that. What should we do?" she asked Tom. "She doesn't have the cell phone, so I can't call to let her know she's been tricked."

"Limit your search to the roads leading away from your own neighborhood," he said. "I'll work the area from Calle de Elena toward the monastery. Call if you spot the Harley."

"Thanks, Tom, and you do the same. At least she has Pax with her."

"That's very good news."

Sister Agatha kept praying and searching while Sister Bernarda drove slowly down the gravel road, checking at each side road for tracks or a dust trail. Suddenly, catching a faint roar in the distance, Sister Agatha sat up.

"Slow down to a crawl," she said. "I could have sworn I heard that 'potato potato' rumble of the Harley."

"There!" Sister Bernarda said, pointing. Through gaps in the trees and the undergrowth they could see flashes of the red and white Harley. It was on the other side of the irrigation ditch, closer to the river, going in the same direction they were, but on a parallel road.

"It looks like she's heading back to the monastery," Sister Bernarda said, "but she sure took the long way."

"She might have taken the left turn after the winery instead of the right," Sister Agatha said. "We should be able to catch up to her at the bridge."

Although Sister Bernarda sped up, causing another backfire, the Harley got there first and drove on through the intersection. Recognizing the Antichrysler, Sister Jo came to a stop and waved at them. Pax barked happily.

"She's safe." Sister Agatha said, sighing.

The Harley accelerated on ahead. "Race you to the monastery!" Sister Jo called out.

Hearing the wail of a siren, Sister Bernarda pulled to the side to let the deputy go past them. Sister Agatha's eyes widened a second later as Sister Jo was pulled over. "Rats! I forgot to tell the sheriff that we'd found Sister Jo."

She picked up the cell phone and called in quickly. "No, it was our mistake. I'm *very* sorry," Sister Agatha said, then explained. After apologizing to Tom again, she placed the phone down.

"He's angry, and I can't blame him. He pulled the deputy off monastery duty to help us search."

"So the monastery was left unguarded because of us?"

"That's the way it shapes up," she said. As they pulled out into the road, she could see the deputy walking back from the cycle to his vehicle. "At least he's going to be able to go back now."

Sister Jo followed the deputy's vehicle, and the Antichrysler brought up the rear. A short time later, as they drew close to the monastery, Sister Agatha saw the deputy's department vehicle once again parked across the street from their entrance. They waved as they went by, and then continued up the monastery's driveway.

Inside the open gates, Sister Bernarda parked next to the Harley. A second later, Sister Jo came out of the parlor, Pax at her side.

"Thanks for coming to check on me," Sister Jo said. "I was stupid, falling for that fake Mr. Stevens's call. Then I took the wrong turn after leaving the highway and had to come back the long way. At least I got the chance to try out the Harley. That's sure one cool ride, Sisters!"

"Why didn't you even attempt to find one of us? Sister Bernarda had the car keys. And are you licensed to operate a motorcycle?" Sister Agatha asked.

Sister Jo's mouth fell open. "Well, no, but I knew how to drive it, and Mr. Stevens sounded so . . . disappointed. I figured there wouldn't be any harm in taking the motorcycle on a quick delivery."

"If you'd called St. Augustine's and checked, you would have known it was a crank call," Sister Agatha replied. "We were worried sick that you might have been lured into a trap by . . . you know."

Sister Jo paled under Sister Agatha's steady gaze. "A killer, like with Jane Sanchez? I didn't think of that. I was just worried that some poor elderly man would go without his only hot meal of the day. But Our Lord must have been protecting me. On Calle de Elena I passed another deputy."

"A deputy?" Her words sparked Sister Agatha's curiosity—the sheriff had said there was no officer in the area. "What exactly did you see?"

"He was meeting some guy in a baseball cap. The man was holding a big envelope in his hand, too," she said. "I didn't get a close look at the deputy, so I can't tell you who he was."

"What happened then?" Sister Agatha asked, leading the way back into the parlor.

"Once I found out that the address I was looking for didn't exist, I turned around and came right back to the monastery."

Sister Agatha shook her head in frustration. "No, regarding the deputy's meeting. What can you tell me about that?"

"Not much. As I said, I didn't get a good look. All I noticed was that the deputy was tall and wearing his tan uniform and cap. Sunglasses, too." She paused, then added, "Come to think of it, he had something in *his* hand, too . . ." She squinted, and a pensive look came over her face. "I think it may have been a camera."

"Anything else?" Sister Agatha pressed, keeping her voice low since the portress was on the phone.

Sister Jo thought about it a moment, then finally shook her head. "I don't think so. And I really am sorry if I worried you. It never occurred to me that I was being punked."

"Punked?" Sister Bernarda asked.

"Scammed. Set up," Sister Jo added in explanation.

"Welcome to the twenty-first century, Sister Bernarda," Sister Agatha said, finally finding a reason to smile. Looking back at Sister Jo, she grew serious once again. "Okay, it's over, but let's all learn from this and not be fooled again. Keep in mind that we still don't know the extent of the threat against us, but one woman has already died. One of us—maybe you—could be the next target." Sister Agatha met Sister Jo's gaze and held it.

"I'll be more careful next time. I'll make it up to both of you, too. What if I take a double shift as portress? How's that?" she asked brightly.

Sister de Lourdes beamed Sister Agatha a hopeful smile.

"All right. Sister de Lourdes will be grateful for the help. One more thing—did you ever think to inform Reverend Mother that you'd left the monastery grounds?" Seeing Sister Jo shake her head, a mortified expression on her face, Sister Agatha continued. "An extern needs to get permission before leaving the grounds. That's our rule, except in a grave emergency, of course."

"I'll tell Reverend Mother what happened right away," Sister Jo said, then excused herself and left the parlor.

Sister Agatha stood by the window, looking back down the road, lost in thought. After a few minutes, Sister Bernarda cleared her throat. "Okay, what's bothering you? Is it something to do with the meeting Sister Jo witnessed—the deputy and that civilian?"

"You read my mind," she said, turning around. "Maybe it's just my imagination working overtime, but I can come up with some interesting explanations for what she saw."

"Like what?" Sister Bernarda pressed.

"What if it was Gerry Bennett paying off the person who murdered his mother-in-law, or maybe someone he enlisted to help with the logistics, like stealing Louis's bike?"

"Then again, it could have been just another deputy receiving information from an informant," Sister Bernarda countered. "Maybe the man in the baseball cap gave the deputy the envelope after Sister Jo went by. It could all have been perfectly legitimate."

As the bells for the Angelus rang, Sister Agatha glanced at Sister Bernarda. "Let's join the sisters at prayer. Then, after Sext and our meal at one, we'll head back into town and see what we can dig up."

Closing up the parlor, they returned to the peacefulness of their cloister.

12

A FTER THEIR MEAL, REVEREND MOTHER APPROACHED Sister Agatha. "Follow me to my office, child."

Moments later Sister Agatha sat down across from the abbess. She could see Reverend Mother was deeply troubled about something.

"This morning we received four crank calls and six disturbing e-mails," Reverend Mother said at last. "Though they came from different locations and e-mail addresses, collectively they're threatening to harm us—for no stated reasons. I reported these to the sheriff, and Sister de Lourdes sent copies of the e-mails to his computer. Sheriff Green said that it could all be the work of one person. The calls in particular seem to be so. Sister de Lourdes said that although the caller was trying to disguise his voice, he sounded pretty much the same each time."

"E-mails from the same person can come in from multiple addresses, too," Sister Agatha answered.

"Although the deputies will continue to watch our monastery, I'd like us to take all the precautions we can as well. That's why I called you here. How much danger do you think we're facing? We won't close the monastery, of course, but we could send some of our sisters elsewhere until the crisis is past."

Sister Agatha took a slow, deep breath, then let it out again. "Mother, I think we're being manipulated. Sister Jo reported what happened to her over at St. Charles, and we've been the victims of vandalism and dirty tricks. But I think the real issue is Jane Sanchez's murder. Whoever killed her is trying to confuse us and the sheriff."

"So you believe that we're in no danger?"

Sister Agatha paused for several seconds. "We can't afford to assume we're safe or that someone is just out to scare us. On the other hand, I just can't figure out a motive for whatever's going on, unless it has to do with Jane Sanchez."

"Our monastery has always been a place of safety, and our older sisters in particular are having a very difficult time coping. We need to put an end to this situation, child." She stared at the statue of the Blessed Mother, then, at long last, added, "As of right now, you'll have no other duties except helping the sheriff find out who killed Jane Sanchez."

"Mother, if I may make one small request?"

"What is it, child?"

"I'd like to be able to travel to town alone during daytime hours whenever I need to do so. Seeing two of us together in the station wagon isn't going to dissuade anyone who really wants to come after us. The Harley is much more practical, and, oddly enough, seeing me on the cycle makes people smile and puts them in a good mood. I've also noticed that I get more cooperation when I'm alone with Pax."

Reverend Mother considered it, then nodded. "All right,

but if any extern has to go into town after dusk, I still want you to travel in pairs. The rest of the time you may use the Harley—as long as you continue to take Pax along."

"Thank you, Mother."

"I also wanted to thank you for going to check on Sister Jo. Some of what happened wasn't her fault, but I'm glad you reminded her of our rules. Now that I've spoken to her, I'm sure we'll never have another incident like that again."

Sister Agatha left Reverend Mother's office and went directly to the parlor. Sister Bernarda was behind the desk just hanging up the phone as she came in.

"I'll be taking the Harley and running the errands in town with Pax this afternoon. Mother's okay with that," Sister Agatha said.

Sister Bernarda nodded in approval. "Pax is the best second you could have. Between his running speed and those huge teeth, he can do far more to protect you than I could."

Sister Agatha laughed and realized she hadn't done that in several days. It felt good. "Give me the list of afternoon errands that need to be done. I'll take care of those while I'm in town and be back as soon as possible."

Sister Bernarda handed her a sheet of paper, and Sister Agatha studied it for a moment. "Onion sets, drippers, hose, connectors, and other irrigation supplies. I should have room in the sidecar for this. These are for the drip system Sister Jo has drawn up for us?"

"She claims it'll save us a lot of water, even if we just use it for the roses and other perennials. We can do the work ourselves, and the materials are cheap," Sister Bernarda said. "The nursery you suggested, Southwest Gardens, carries everything we need."

"I was hoping it would. That's the place where Jane

Sanchez worked. We've done business there before, and I know the owner."

"You were hoping for a chance to go there on business so you could ask them about Jane?" Sister Bernarda asked.

"Yes," Sister Agatha admitted.

"Go with courage and leave the rest to Him," Sister Bernarda said resolutely.

"Amen to that."

Sister Agatha was in the Harley with Pax a short time later. With his huge panting grin, Pax was enjoying the feel of the wind whipping past his face to the utmost. She, too, loved the sense of freedom that came from being on the Harley and always took time to thank the Lord for this blessing.

By the time Sister Agatha arrived at the nursery, the onion sets and other supplies were in a small cardboard box waiting for her. She paid for the order, then went to speak to the owner, Josh Douglas, about Jane.

After seeing to Pax, who would remain in the sidecar in the shade of a cottonwood tree, she went to find Josh. She found him out back beneath a shaded work area, transplanting seedlings into hand-painted clay pots. In his midsixties, Josh still led a very active life. He wasn't the kind who'd ever even consider retirement, even though his years as a policeman were past.

"Hey, Sister Agatha. I'm sure glad you sisters have decided to go with a drip system. Saves a ton of water."

"We have a new nun at Our Lady, and she's helping bring our garden into the twenty-first century. So how's business, Josh?"

"Fine, but maybe I should be asking *you* that question. Any news? I heard that the monastery also got some threats outta that."

"It's true, and I'm trying to help out," she said with a nod. "The situation affects us directly."

"I see your point," he answered with a nod. "I've given some thought to what happened, and I'm satisfied that nothing about her work here was connected to the crime. Jane was our book-keeper, which kept her away from the rest of the staff—a good thing, because she could be very controlling. But she was a great worker and always made us look good at the end of the year."

"Did she ever talk to you about family or personal problems?"

"Of course she did. Jane was a gossip and had lots of issues with her daughter and son-in-law. Jane was sure he was cheating on Evelyn and was doing her best to catch him in the act. She'd even started bringing the car to work instead of having Louis drop her off so she could go find Gerry during her lunch hour and check on him. Those are hard facts, and exactly what I told the sheriff."

"She sounds obsessed," Sister Agatha said. "How'd that all work out for her?"

"I don't know, but I do know that Jane came back from lunch one day last week acting really strange. I didn't ask her about it because I really didn't want to know."

"Do you think she saw something that upset her?"

"Maybe, but if she'd seen Gerry messing around, I'm almost sure she would have said so. It was the kind of thing she'd want *everyone* to know. Jane really wanted to get Evelyn away from Gerry. She hated that guy."

Sister Agatha shook her head, now realizing that her brief conversations with Jane after Mass had only shown her the tip of the iceberg. How could anyone so pious on Sunday become so bitter and hostile the rest of the week? "Obsession of any kind can take over your life."

"I hated having to tell the sheriff any of this. I think it was Jane, not Gerry, who had the problem. Still, it gives Gerry a motive for wanting his mother-in-law out of his hair permanently. That's not the kind of information I could withhold with a clear conscience." He met her gaze. "Anyway, I know Tom Green won't let this ruin his objectivity when it comes to Gerry Bennett."

"It's too soon to do much except gather information," Sister Agatha assured him. "There are way too many possibilities and confusing clues to sift through."

"Gerry's argumentative and controlling, just like Jane was," he said. "I know that from experience. In my book, that's probably why they never got along. Gerry's a tough guy, and he only shows his softer side around his daughter, Mary. I've seen him here with her, picking out flowers he was going to plant by her playhouse—one he built on his own. Anyone who sees that side of him would never forget it."

"What you're telling me is that Gerry's hard to know and it works against him?"

Josh nodded. "My judgment as a retired cop—and a father to six children."

Thanking him, Sister Agatha went back to the Harley. It was a beautiful afternoon and the perfect time to pay Betty Malone a visit. Ever since she'd spoken to Dolly, she'd been meaning to drop by Betty's home.

Sister Agatha took a side road and arrived at Betty's a short time later. Apparently having heard the motorcycle coming up the street, Betty had come out to meet her.

"You've got perfect timing, Sister. I just made some cheesecake, my favorite comfort food," she added with a laugh.

Sitting in the kitchen moments later, Sister Agatha tasted Betty's cheesecake and smiled. "This *is* wonderful!"

"Over the years, I've added a few things here and there. I'm glad you like it."

Sister Agatha ate slowly, relishing every bite. Drenched in a semisweet sauce with cherries, it was truly decadent.

"So what brings you here?" Betty asked casually, taking small bites from a slice of plain cheesecake she'd cut for herself.

"I wanted to ask you a few questions about the Sanchezes, but first I would ask that our conversation stay between us. Is that okay with you?"

"Sure. I'm an old hand at keeping things to myself. Never cared much for gossip, you know."

"Neither do I, but right now I really need information, and you're the best person I could think to ask."

"Is this about Louis and Christy?" she asked with a long, heavy sigh.

"That, and other things. From your kitchen window you have quite a view of both Christy's and Louis's yards. What can you tell me about their relationship? Was there really more going on between them, as people keep hinting?"

Betty hesitated. "I understand why you're asking, and I'll help you, but from what I know about those two, the gossip is way off the mark. Mind you, I've seen plenty of signs that Christy might have a thing for Louis, but Louis would have never stepped out on Jane. Louis's primary interest is *food*, not women. What got people talking is that Christy's a lonely woman."

"So you haven't seen anything that might suggest there was something going on between her and Louis?" Sister Agatha asked quietly. "Or that it's possible that Christy killed Jane—her competition?"

"No way," she answered firmly. "That wouldn't have gotten her anywhere, and she knew it. Jane and Louis loved each other, despite their differences."

Sister Agatha nodded, understanding far more than Betty's words had revealed. This was a quiet neighborhood, one where neighbors often stood together on issues. Despite the occasional disagreements, violence didn't play a part in their lives.

"What do you know about Jane and her son-in-law? Did those two really hate each other that much?"

Betty nodded. "That part of the gossip is true. Jane would have done anything to break them up. The entire neighborhood knew that. It was one of the reasons Evelyn finally stopped coming by to see her parents. She hadn't been by for at least a couple of months. Evelyn adores her father and really wanted him to get to know his granddaughter. With Jane gone, maybe what's left of Louis's family will get back together. It's just very sad that this had to happen first."

"We've been praying for all of them, and will continue to do so," Sister Agatha said. "Thanks very much for your help, Betty. This *will* stay between us, don't worry about that." With a sheepish smile, Sister Agatha used her fingers to pick up a few crumbs of cheesecake still on her plate. "And thanks so much for sharing this wonderful dessert," she said, licking what was left off her fingertips.

Betty smiled. "Would you like another slice for the road?"

Sister Agatha shook her head and smiled. "Thanks, but no. I'm full, so another slice would definitely come under the header 'gluttony.'"

"I'm sure God will look the other way just this once," Betty said with a twinkle in her eye. "You could also look at it as an act of charity. This old woman would love to know that her cheesecake's all but irresistible."

"In that case, who am I to disappoint?"

Betty placed a slice in a small plastic container, poured a

generous portion of cherry sauce over it, then sealed the lid tightly. "There you go."

Sister Agatha placed the container on the floor of the sidecar, anchoring it inside the coils of the irrigation hose. Pax looked at it longingly, then at her.

"Nothing doing, guy. That piece is for Reverend Mother. If there's anyone who deserves a treat, it's her. She's had it rough these past few days."

Sister Agatha and Pax were on the way back to the monastery minutes later. As she drove, she mentally reviewed everything she'd learned, trying to sort out the relevant and factual from the rest.

Glancing into the side mirror as she changed lanes, she noticed an old white van coming up quickly behind her. She pulled slightly to the right and cut back on the throttle, motioning with her left hand for the vehicle to pass her. Instead of passing, however, the van inched even closer.

Sister Agatha speeded up, trying to keep a safe distance between them, and took a good, hard look in the rearview mirror. The road vibration made it hard to see the driver's face, who was sitting well back in his seat and wearing a hat and sunglasses.

Again she motioned the driver to pass, slowing and pulling way over to the right, nearly on the shoulder. This time he got the message and accelerated quickly, rocketing past her.

Then, without any warning, the van swerved into her lane. "Look out!" she yelled.

Sister Agatha touched the brakes and pulled to the right as hard as she could without risking going head over heels. As they hit the soft ground near the ditch, the wheel of the sidecar holding Pax dug in and the bike pulled hard to the right. For a second she thought they were going to roll, but the rear end stayed put.

"Down!" she yelled to Pax, hoping he'd hear her and duck into the cockpit of the sidecar.

Fighting to remain in control of the Harley, Sister Agatha forced the handlebars back to the left, holding on with a death grip, more worried about hitting something than being able to stop. The soft ground slowed the bike quickly, but it was shaking and vibrating like a leaf in a windstorm.

Gritting her teeth, she held on, tapping the rear brake as much as she dared. The big Harley trembled and bounced as they barreled through knee-high grass and weeds.

Finally, in a thick cloud of dust, they slid to a stop just a few feet from the wire fence that lined the roadway. Looking toward the highway, she could see the rear end of the van that had forced them off the road racing away, picking up speed. It had a sign on the rear doors, but at this distance she couldn't make out the lettering.

Whispering a prayer of heartfelt thanks that neither she nor Pax had been injured, she sat back on the saddle, taking deep breaths and trying to stop shaking. Pax was still flat on his stomach, but his head was turned toward her, and he was panting from excitement.

"I've got to report this driver to the sheriff right now, boy," she said to Pax, turning off the engine.

As she reached up with trembling hands to remove her helmet—a cell phone call was impossible when the helmet covered her ears—she looked down the road and saw that the van had turned around and was racing back once again in their direction.

"He's coming back. Lord, help us!"

She switched on the ignition and turned toward the road, her thoughts racing. If he was planning to sideswipe them, her best counter was to throw off his timing. Heart hammering, she waited, planning on sitting still, then accelerating forward, back toward the fence, at the last possible second.

As the van reached the center line, she revved up the engine, the bike now in gear.

Sister Agatha concentrated on watching the van's front tires. The second they turned, she'd cut loose. But the van held its position.

She glanced back up at the driver's face, hoping to get a good look at him, and suddenly realized that he was holding something big in his hand. A head . . . she could make out a face . . . and hair . . . Before she could complete the thought that was forming in her mind, he hurled it in her direction.

Sister Agatha ducked and prayed that the helmet would do its job and protect her from—whatever it was. A heartbeat later, something splattered against her visor, and she felt something warm and wet strike the back of her hand. The noxious smell nearly made her gag. She prayed that it hadn't been brains escaping from a decaying, severed human head.

13

ER BREATH CAUGHT IN HER THROAT AS SHE SAW THE
goo that was running down her visor, but at least it wasn't
blood or brains.

Forcing herself to swallow the panic that was making it
hard for her to think straight, she looked around. That scent . . .
she recognized it. It was overripe fruit. Then she saw the mess
on the road ahead. The impact point held an overripe melon
and what appeared to be a wig and a Halloween mask of a man's
face. Seeds, rind, and rotten pulp had splattered everywhere,
including on the Harley and herself.

The idiot in the van had set her up, placed a face mask over
a rotten melon, then attached a wig to the top. With just a split
second for her to see what was coming, he'd obviously hoped to
scare her to death—and he'd almost succeeded.

The smell was getting worse. Pieces of overripe fruit had
splattered her from head to foot, much of it sticking to her

habit. Turning off the engine, she dismounted and brushed away the larger bits and pieces. In the process, some of the gooey slime smeared into the fabric, leaving a gleaming film. "Oh, yuck!"

Watching for traffic, she stepped out onto the road and picked up the wig. It was black and stringy—not counting the sliver of melon rind still attached by glue—and looked to her like the ones sold everywhere at Halloween. There wasn't much hope of getting anything useful from it, but she still brought it back to the sidecar and dropped it inside. It was evidence. She also picked up the mask, the latex image of an ugly man, holding it by the elastic strap.

Pax, who'd escaped being slimed, was still lying down. He sniffed at the wig and mask, snorted, then looked up at her.

"Yeah, I know, they stink major league," she said. "You can sit now, boy," she added. "Just don't mess with these goodies. They're for the sheriff."

After cleaning herself off as much as she could, finishing with her hands, she reached for the cell phone and got the sheriff on his private line seconds later. "I was just run off the road, Tom," she said. She gave him the highlights of the incident.

"I have a deputy heading north out of town. If the van's still in the area, he may be able to find it using the description you just gave me. In the meantime, drive back to Bernalillo, but go slow enough so you can get off the road if you have to. I want you here at the station so you can file an official report."

By the time she reached the sheriff's office, Tom was waiting. He was at the front talking to one of his deputies and, seeing her, came over immediately.

124

As they headed down the hall, Pax tugged at the leash, wanting to visit his friends in the bullpen. He knew he'd be able to mooch a doughnut or two there. Sister Agatha pulled him closer to her, but Tom just smiled.

"Let him go. The officers always enjoy seeing him."

As she did, she saw Fritz Albrecht watching from one of the desks. She nodded to him, then followed Tom to his office. "I called you as soon as I could," she said.

Tom closed the door, looking at the stains on her habit, then sniffed the air. "Interesting smell. Just so I'm sure I got it right—the van nearly struck the Harley on the first pass?"

"I think he wanted to force me off the road, maybe cause me to have an accident without risking injury to himself. When it didn't work, he followed up with the melon, which he'd obviously intended to use eventually. He wasn't aiming to hit me with it, I don't think. He wanted my fear to do the job for him and cause me to wreck," she said, then added, "I recovered the wig and mask for you, handling both as carefully as I could. They're the cheap Halloween costume kind."

"Where are they?"

"In the sidecar. Just follow your nose."

"I'll have a deputy go get them," he said, then stepped out into the hall.

After he came back, Tom said nothing, lost in thought for several moments. At long last, he spoke. "This has gone beyond scratched messages, threatening e-mails, and phone calls. You've made a very dangerous enemy who has obviously decided to up the stakes."

She told him about her visit to the nursery and the Sanchez neighborhood, and what she'd learned. "The question that needs to be answered is whether I was the target—you know, me personally—or was it the monastery?"

"Does it matter? *You're* the face of the monastery in the community."

"Yes, but so are Sister de Lourdes and Sister Bernarda. Are they in danger, too? And what about Sister Jo?"

"I wish I could tell you," he said with a shrug. "Let's go back to what we know. You've given me a description of the van. Now tell me about the driver. Was it Gerry Bennett? He seems to be the focus of most of what you and I have been hearing lately."

"I don't know. It all happened too fast, and he was shaded by the vehicle's interior. I thought about it on the way here, too, but the only things I remember clearly are his sunglasses and hat . . . baseball cap, I think. I was just too busy trying to keep Pax and me alive to see anything else."

He nodded. "I hear you."

"But the white van, it was an older model, I think, and had a sign on its side and across the rear doors. The lettering was blue. I wish I could tell you what it said, but I couldn't make it out."

"The colors will help. At least we can rule out plain white vans or other white vans with different color lettering."

"Unfortunately, that still leaves a lot of possibilities," she said. "White vans with signs are everywhere."

"I'll check Gerry Bennett's location during the time of the incident. Until I have something other than vague gossip, I can't bring him in."

"I understand." Sister Agatha signed the statement he'd had typed up, then left with Pax minutes later. Anxious to wash the smell of rotten melon off the cycle before returning home, she pulled into Paul Gonzales's gas station. Some of the greenish pulp had splattered on the sidecar and stuck there, as well as on the engine itself, and the heat from the air cooled V-twin was enhancing the smell. Seeing Paul busy with a customer, she drove the Harley around the back of the building, where she knew he kept a hose hooked up.

Placing Pax at stay safely out of the way, she washed off the sidecar. She then sprayed the engine with a fine mist, afraid a cold stream might crack something. Worried about what she'd tell Reverend Mother once she got back, she took her time. If only she could give Mother some real answers instead of having to report yet another threat.

Paul came up moments after his customer had driven off. "So what's new with you, Sister Agatha?"

She put the hose down and, borrowing a rag, began wiping down the Harley. "Paul, did you happen to see a white van with a blue sign on the side go by, say, in the last hour or so?"

"Lots of white vans around, but yeah, as a matter of fact I remember one. He didn't pull in, but he stopped at the light. It caught my eye because the van was from a plumbing company and I've been meaning to talk to a plumber. I'm thinking of buying a power washer for customer cars."

"What plumbing company was it?" she asked, putting him back on track.

"Royal Flush Plumbing. The lettering looked like pipes, complete with joints and connectors."

She nodded, now remembering what had just been at the edge of her focus before. "Did you get a look at the driver?"

"No, it was the name of the company that caught my attention. It struck me as funny, that's all."

"Thanks, Paul." Sister Agatha handed the rag back, then called the sheriff and gave him the information.

Tom listened, and she heard him typing on his computer. "Bad news," he said. "That van was stolen about an hour ago. I've got the report right here in front of me."

"If you find it abandoned somewhere, you might be able to get prints."

"I wouldn't count on that if I were you," he cautioned. "So far, nothing's been straightforward and simple on this case."

Sister Agatha drove back to the monastery slowly. She'd have to update Reverend Mother, but she had nothing to report that came even close to good news.

She arrived just in time for Vespers and joined the sisters in prayer. "O Lord, make haste to help me," she prayed from the depths of her heart.

After collation, recreation started. Sister Agatha looked for Reverend Mother but was unable to find her, so she went to join Sister Bernarda. She was on one of their outside benches reading a letter.

"Excuse me, Your Charity. Have you seen Mother?" Sister Agatha asked her.

"Sister Eugenia pulled rank, and Reverend Mother is lying down in the infirmary finally getting some sleep. Sister Eugenia managed to find something, a nonnarcotic, that Reverend Mother was willing to take to help her rest."

"What was it? Do you know?"

"A New Mexican folk remedy, an herbal tea, that apparently works wonders."

"I'm so glad to hear this," Sister Agatha said. For more than one reason, too. She hadn't been looking forward to updating Reverend Mother tonight.

"Something's troubling you. I can always tell," Sister Bernarda said, folding up the letter and placing it back into the envelope. "Would it help you to talk about it?"

"Maybe," Sister Agatha said. She sat down on the *banco* outside their vegetable garden and watched Sister Jo and Sister Ignatius uncoil the black irrigation hose, straightening it out and placing rocks on the ends to hold it in place until the coils relaxed.

Sister Agatha filled her in on the afternoon's events. "I'm not sure if the driver was striking out at me specifically. Heaven knows I've made plenty of enemies over the years. But that phony head he threw at me . . . that was a taunt as well as an implied threat. It's not the kind of thing one does to a generalized target. The whole incident has a more personal feel to it." She paused, then added, "Or am I saying that because it happened to me?"

"He was playing with you, Sister Agatha. If it really was the same man who killed Jane Sanchez, he probably wasn't intending to do the same to you, at least not today. He wanted you to fear him first. He might have done the same thing to Jane in the days or hours leading up to the murder. You mentioned she'd seen something and wanted to tell you about it, right?"

Sister Agatha nodded. "But if it had been an attack like today, she'd have called the police, don't you think?"

"Maybe not if the attacker had *been* the police, like Gerry Bennett?" Sister Bernarda suggested.

"I see your point. But if she'd known for sure, she would have used that knowledge. That would have given her the perfect ammunition to get rid of her son-in-law, if she could have proven that Gerry was harassing her."

"We're reaching," Sister Bernarda said firmly. "Judging on the facts and the nature of the attack, I believe *you* were his target. Think. You're the only one who rides with Pax on the Harley."

Sister Agatha stared at her fellow extern, her thoughts suddenly racing. "Maybe I've been looking at this from the wrong angle. What if he was after a specific person . . . but got the target wrong?"

Sister Bernarda gave her a puzzled look. Then comprehension dawned over her features. "You're thinking about Sister Jo and what she saw while on that crank delivery call, aren't you? She's about your size and weight, and on the motorcycle, one nun looks pretty much like another. She was also wearing a helmet that day and riding with Pax. Someone could have easily assumed that was you. You're the one who drives the Harley—everyone knows that."

"Exactly. Although she took off her helmet briefly, from a distance, people tend to only see our habit."

"But Sister Jo barely saw anything at all, if I remember her story correctly."

"Maybe the little she did see was threat enough," Sister Agatha answered. "What if one or both of the men involved in that exchange are now worried that she may be able to identify them? What she saw may have been connected to a crime—like bribery, for example. Remember the big envelope?"

"Have you spoken to Tom about this?" Sister Bernarda asked.

"He's already checking up on Gerry Bennett. But maybe I should call—"

Before she could say anything more, the bells for Compline rang. Sister Bernarda stood and, bowing her head, hurried inside. Sister Agatha followed her.

It was the next day, well after Morning Prayers—which at one time had been called Prime—when she met Sister Bernarda in the parlor.

"You'll be going to see Sheriff Green this morning, won't you?" Sister Bernarda asked.

Sister Agatha nodded. Sister Bernarda's reminder was simply

her way of covering the bases. The marine in her didn't like leaving things to chance.

"I'll tell him what Sister Jo witnessed that day on Calle de Elena and see what he has to say," Sister Agatha said.

"On your way there, you might also make a mental list of anyone you think might have a grievance against you. That's just in case we're way off base on this."

"I'll do that," she answered gently, knowing Sister Bernarda was worried about her.

"Have you spoken to Reverend Mother yet?"

Sister Agatha shook her head. "Sister Eugenia said that Mother's sleeping late and *nobody* has permission to wake her up this morning. Mother apparently got up in the middle of the night and couldn't get back to sleep. Sister Eugenia brewed some more of her special tea, and after that, Mother was out like a light."

"I wonder what was in that tea," Sister Bernarda mused.

Sister Agatha smiled. "Sister Eugenia said that it was star-shaped anise and another herb. Together they can knock you for a loop, particularly if the tea is made strong and you're already tired. And Mother was. She's been working much too hard."

"Then you better work even harder to find answers so Mother doesn't have to worry so much," Sister Bernarda said, then added, "I'll let Mother know you've gone as soon as she's available again."

After saying good-bye, Sister Agatha went outside. It was a beautiful morning. The almost cloudless sky was a brilliant blue, and the temperature was still pleasantly cool. She knew it wouldn't last. By this afternoon the wind was supposed to reach forty miles per hour. Curtains of sand and blowing dust would rise like waves, blanketing everything and limiting visibility. *That* was typical of New Mexican spring afternoons.

Enjoying the weather while she could, and thanking the Lord for the morning, she whistled for Pax. The giant dog came shooting from around the corner with one of his favorite toys, an old stuffed sock, still in his mouth.

"Pax, road trip!"

Without hesitation the dog gracefully jumped into the sidecar, the toy still firmly clamped in his jaws.

On the way to town Sister Agatha kept a sharp eye on other vehicles. Refusing to let fear master her, she focused on the business at hand and tried to think of anyone who might have had a grievance against her. Most of the names that came to her were people who were still in prison . . . as far as she knew. Their relatives could be a problem, but they hadn't been before, so there was no reason to think they would be now.

She'd already reached Bernalillo before she remembered the problem Tom was having with the mayor regarding her cooperative work with the sheriff's department. Pulling over in front of a coffee shop, she decided to give him a call first, then let him decide when and where to meet.

After finding out where she was, he decided he'd come and meet her for coffee. While Pax remained at stay in the cycle, out of the sun, she went inside. Sister Agatha ordered a cup of coffee, then found a booth where she could see outside clearly and watch the dog.

Tom arrived about five minutes later and joined her at the booth. "Next time just come to the station. I needed the break this morning, and getting away was too tempting to pass up, but if we meet like this again it'll look like we're sneaking around. That'll just make things more interesting to Fritz and his boss— not to mention my wife."

"I never thought of that," she admitted.

"No problem. Had you called ten minutes earlier, I would

have insisted you come to my office immediately. I was dying for an excuse to get rid of the defense attorney across my desk. He wanted me to drop all charges against his client—a real lowlife."

"With all the pressure of a murder investigation on top of a political football game, I was trying to make things easier for you," she said, then smiled as the waitress brought coffee for Tom and refilled her cup.

"So what's been going on?" Tom asked after the waitress walked away.

She quickly repeated the stories she'd heard about Jane's obsessive behavior concerning her daughter's marriage and ended by describing her conversation with Jane's boss at the nursery.

"I've already spoken to Gerry about this," Tom said. "I also got the details about Jane's snooping. He told me that he and Evelyn separated briefly and he began seeing Laura Sims. His mother-in-law found out about it and threatened to do all in her power to get his marriage to Evelyn annulled on grounds of adultery. He knew she didn't have the power to make that happen, and he told her so right to her face."

"Annulments in the Catholic Church are harder than blitz to get," she said slowly.

"According to Gerry, Jane knew she was just shooting blanks, hoping the threat would scare him into giving up trying to save his marriage. When she found out that he and Evelyn were in counseling and that their marriage was back on track, she really lost it. She started checking up on him and tailing him, thinking she could catch him with Laura. She'd even have her cell phone handy, ready to take pictures."

"Has anyone used the missing phone since it disappeared?"

"There's been no activity whatsoever. Usually when a cell phone's stolen, the thief uses it extensively for a short period of time, then throws it away, but we've got nothing."

"Then we go back to the big issue. Does Gerry have an alibi for the time of Jane's death?" Sister Agatha asked.

"He was home alone, which is where you'd expect him to be at six thirty in the morning on Sunday," Tom said. "So if you're asking me whether he's a suspect, the answer's yes, but he's not high on my list, despite what was going on between him and his mother-in-law. That's not just because he's one of ours either. I know the guy, and I trust what my gut tells me about him. He's irritating at times, but he's not a cold-blooded killer."

"Remember that Jane wasn't an easy woman to get along with—at least according to virtually everyone I've spoken to who knew her. She presented herself differently to me, but I'm a nun. Most of those who knew her outside church saw a different side of Jane. Gerry had a good reason for disliking her intensely. He's also supposed to be a passionate person, and his marriage was being threatened."

"All good points."

"What about Deputy Sims? She would have some of the skills the killer demonstrated, and she has, or had, a relationship with Gerry. Have you looked into her whereabouts?"

"She was on patrol no more than a few miles away from the monastery. She's our newest officer, so she gets the unpopular shifts, like weekends."

"So it's possible she might have stopped by the monastery during Mass. Jane wouldn't have been alarmed by a woman deputy. She might have even welcomed the opportunity to get into the face of the woman who'd dated her married son-in-law. Also, if Laura waited until the last second to pull out her pistol, that would certainly explain why Jane never called out for help."

"But what would Sims's motive be? Killing Jane would have eliminated the one person who was working hard to pull Evelyn and Gerry apart. If she'd wanted Gerry bad enough to kill someone, her target would have been Evelyn, his wife."

"That's a valid point, but Sims still had the means and opportunity to carry out the crime. I know you hate even the possibility that one of your people might be implicated, but don't rule her out—not yet, anyway." Sister Agatha lapsed into uneasy silence.

"Something else is bothering you, isn't it?" he asked after a moment. "And that would be the second reason you wanted to talk to me this morning?"

She nodded, then recounted what Sister Jo had seen the day she'd tried to make the phony Good News lunch delivery on Calle de Elena. "We don't know what the meeting between the deputy and that man was about, but I'm wondering if maybe Sister Jo saw something that was meant to stay secret. That would explain why that man tried to run me off the road with a stolen plumber's van. Maybe one of those two decided to permanently silence the nun on the cycle and make it look accidental."

"The two men on that side street—it was the deputy who took the envelope from the guy in the cap?" he repeated, verifying it.

"That's what Sister Jo said. Was there a special operation going down at the time, a snitch providing information, maybe?"

"Not that I know about—and I would have known if we'd had something major going down. But give me a chance to look into it some more. Any contact an officer makes with a source has to be logged into a report, though the identities of the informants are usually disguised using pseudonyms or code names."

"There's another possibility we need to take into account, too, though it's not directly related to what we've been talking about. Have any of the people I've testified against in the past been released from jail recently?"

"Give me a sec," he said, bringing out his cell phone. He called the station, asked the duty officer to access a database, then waited. A minute later, Tom heard and repeated an address, thanked the officer, then ended the call. "She got one hit—Del Martinez. Remember him?"

She nodded. Del had owned a roofing company in town and had been as crooked as they came. Worst of all, he'd clearly blamed her for his arrest and subsequent imprisonment.

"He swore he'd get even someday," she said slowly.

"I remember. He dove right across the table at you, and one of the bailiffs had to subdue him."

She nodded. "He managed to grab my arm, and when they Tasered him, I got some of that jolt myself. But, Tom, that incident happened three years ago. He has a family and a life to salvage. Wouldn't he have more important things to worry about now that he's out of prison?"

Before he could answer, Tom's cell phone started to buzz. He spoke for a moment, then ended the call and stood, placing a few bills on the table for the coffee and a tip. "I've got a situation— an armed robbery. I'll give you a call when I'm free, and we'll go pay Del Martinez a visit together."

"You could be busy for hours. I've got his address now, so let me try a different approach—something more low-key," she said.

He gave her an incredulous look. "Low-key, you?"

"Have a little faith," she called to him as he hurried toward the door.

14

WITH DEL MARTINEZ'S ADDRESS IN HAND, SISTER Agatha drove away in the Harley with Pax and headed to the man's home. It was located in a residential area west of the station and close to the river. As in so many older neighborhoods here, one house could be a McMansion of brick and stone while the one next door was a crumbling adobe house built during the Great Depression.

Sister Agatha drove down the narrow, winding street, searching for house numbers on the mailboxes. Finally she found Del's address, a small stucco home badly in need of paint. An old Chevy Impala was in the driveway and an early seventies Dodge pickup with a missing hood was parked in the front yard astride a crumbling sidewalk.

From the fresh tire tracks, Sister Agatha knew the Chevy was still running, though half of the body was now gray primer paint, and the rear bumper was missing. The pickup was ready for the salvage yard. The rear tires were flat and the engine was missing.

She parked the Harley and removed her helmet, looking around. She could hear music coming from farther down the driveway, which ended at a detached garage, but nobody was in sight.

Placing her helmet on the saddle, Sister Agatha, with Pax at her side, made her way toward the music, which seemed to be coming from the garage. A radio blaring Spanish music was drowned out in bursts by the machine-gun rattle of an impact wrench. Pax's ears stood erect, alert to the noise, but he remained calm, having heard it all before during his police training.

As Sister Agatha approached the open garage, she heard the clang of a tool hitting the concrete floor. A man was at the front of the garage, bending over the engine compartment of a white Toyota sedan. About that time, he turned his head and noticed her and Pax.

It wasn't Del, but there was a family resemblance. The man was tall and thin and had long black hair that brushed his shoulders. She was about to introduce herself when he suddenly turned, picked up a large wrench, and came toward her.

Pax bared his teeth and immediately stepped in front of her. Although she had Pax on a leash—she always did when they were away from familiar territory—the dog was straining and pulling at his collar, his low growl making it clear he meant business.

"If you put that wrench down, the dog will relax. We're no threat to you," she said in a quiet, calm voice.

"Tell that to Del, Sister Agnes, or whatever you call yourself. *You're* the one who put him in prison."

She heard another oath, and a man rolled out from under the car and stood. She recognized Del Martinez right away, though his head was shaved and the scar along his cheek was new. "Sister Agatha—as if I wasn't having a bad enough day already."

Del placed his hand on the other man's shoulder. "Ease up, bro. Can't afford bail this time."

"But—"

Del took the wrench from the other man's hand and slid it into the pocket of his gray overalls. Pax quit snarling immediately, but his hackles were still raised.

Sister Agatha pulled him closer to her. "Del, how are you?" she asked softly.

"As free as they'll let me be, Sister," he said coldly. "What are you doing coming around here? Haven't you messed up my life enough already?"

"I'll show them the street," the other man spat out, pushing up the sleeves of his gray sweatshirt.

Del put his arm out, blocking his brother's path as the dog growled again. "Excuse my brother Martin, Sister Agatha. He's been working three jobs to pay the bills since our company went belly up."

"Yeah, thanks to your lies," Martin muttered.

"Del," Sister Agatha said, focusing exclusively on him, "I know you want to live a normal life again—to be with your family, to be free, as you said a moment ago. You've served your time, so if there's any way I can help you now, all you have to do is let me know. If you need a job, I'd be happy to talk to any of the business owners in town on your behalf."

"Save it. You've done enough already," Del said, glaring at her. "No insurance, no money for gas, no nothing, but me and my family get by. Before, we were doing okay. Now, thanks to you, we're busting our butts fixing up junkers for a few dollars here and there."

"That's good, honest work. You should be proud of your skills and ingenuity. If I hear of anyone who's in the market for inexpensive transportation, I'll tell them about you."

"*Vete*," Del answered in a taut voice. "Get out," he repeated in English. "Now! I want nothing from you, and neither does my family."

"Tell her, bro," Martin said.

Sister Agatha heard a door slam, turned her head, and saw two women striding purposefully toward them from the rear of the house, their fists clenched. One of them she recognized as Del's wife, Gloria. Pax began to growl at them, his tone low and menacing.

The sudden realization that she was trapped between the two groups sent a chill up Sister Agatha's spine. She tightened up on the leash, determined to curb Pax's reaction as much as possible. She didn't want to turn this into a full-blown confrontation.

"Hey, old crow. You've got a lot of nerve coming here."

The words came from the short, stocky, dark-haired woman on the left. She stopped about ten feet away and crossed her arms over her chest.

"My Martin's a roofer, and he was working for Del. We would have been just fine if you hadn't stuck your nose into our business. I miscarried, Sister, and I blame *you* for that. If our lives hadn't been turned upside down that wouldn't have happened."

"I'm so very sorry that you lost your baby," Sister Agatha said gently, feeling her pain. The loss of an unborn child was enough to cast a permanent cloud over any woman's heart. "But you can try again, can't you?"

"And bring a baby into this—barrio?" she said, waving her arm around the garage. She looked over at Del's wife, who nodded. Both took a step forward.

In an instant, Pax's hackles rose and he snarled, lowering himself and cocking his body in preparation for a lunge. His body language made his intentions crystal clear.

The two women froze in their tracks.

Sister Agatha looked back at Del. "If you have a change of heart and decide that I can be of help, just call me," Sister Agatha said, pulling Pax in closer to her. "The dog and I will leave now."

Never taking her eyes off them, she walked around the women, keeping Pax between her and potential danger, and headed down the driveway toward the Harley. After she could no longer see the others, Sister Agatha kept an eye on Pax, who continued to look back even as they walked.

It seemed to take a heart-pounding eternity to reach the motorcycle. She'd never felt such hatred in her life. Unnerved, Sister Agatha got under way as soon as possible, thankfully without incident.

Sister Agatha arrived at the monastery well after one, which meant that she'd missed the main meal of the day.

As she walked into the parlor, Sister de Lourdes stood up and smiled. "Sister Clothilde saved you a sandwich and some vegetables from lunch," she said and pointed to the edge of the desk. A small tray and a thermos had been set there.

"That's welcome news! I'm very hungry."

Sister de Lourdes invited her to sit and eat at the parlor's desk. "Enjoy your lunch, Your Charity," she said. As Sister Bernarda, her replacement, came in, she added, "It's time for me to get back to the scriptorium."

"How's Sister Jo working out in there?" Sister Agatha asked before Sister de Lourdes could leave.

"She's already replaced our Good News meals list with a

spreadsheet that includes names, addresses, and a delivery schedule. There's also a separate file for the people St. Augustine serves. She doesn't want to get tricked again by a crank caller like the one we had the other day."

After finishing her lunch, Sister Agatha went to talk to Reverend Mother. Sister Eugenia's herbal tea remedy had worked wonders, and the abbess looked alert and much refreshed.

As Sister Agatha told her about the incident with Del Martinez and his relatives, she saw the abbess frown. "We'll have to go back to the way things were," Reverend Mother said. "You'll travel only in the station wagon, accompanied by another extern as well as Pax."

"Mother, we just don't have enough externs to go around, not with Sister de Lourdes working in the scriptorium most of the day and the Good News Meals Progam well under way," Sister Agatha said gently.

"My mind's made up, child."

Sister Agatha bowed her head. "I'll tell the others, Mother."

Sister Agatha left Mother's office and went down the hall. They would no longer be able to divide monastery duties like delivering the noontime meals, dropping Sister Jo off at school, or picking up prescriptions and groceries. Yet a part of her was undeniably relieved.

When Sister Agatha walked back into the parlor, Sister Bernarda, taking her turn as portress, handed her an envelope. "This came for you," she said.

Sister Agatha opened the small envelope, and as she caught her first glimpse of what was inside, her heart froze.

"What is it?" Sister Bernarda asked immediately.

Not trusting her voice, Sister Agatha pulled out the two photos and held them out to her. One showed her and Pax riding the Harley down a residential street. The other showed her inside Smitty's grocery, where the extern nuns were frequent shoppers. In each photo, a large X had been drawn over her head with a black marker.

"Both those photos came from a computer printer," Sister de Lourdes said, looking over as she stepped into the parlor. "That first photo of you at Smitty's was taken up close, but it's blurry and low quality, like you'd get from a cell phone camera. The one of you riding the Harley came from a higher-quality camera, one with a high shutter speed. Notice that it's a lot sharper than the other one, though you're moving," Sister de Lourdes added. "The sheriff might be able to figure out what brand of toner was used and, from there, the brand of printer."

Sister Agatha took a deep breath and pushed back her fears. "The problem is that the crime lab will take weeks and weeks to give him an answer—and that's assuming they have the budget for the tests. Maybe he can go low-tech and lift some finger-prints from the photos or the envelope itself." She prayed that she hadn't inadvertently smudged whatever might have been there. "Two of us need to go see the sheriff right away. Which one of you would like to go with me?"

"I'll take over as portress and keep the parlor open," Sister de Lourdes said.

Moments later, Sister Bernarda and Sister Agatha were in the Antichrysler, on the way to town. Pax had stayed behind this time. He'd proven that he had an incredible gift for helping Sister Gertrude relax, and the elderly nun was having blood pressure problems again. Pax was not only a great watchdog, but he also doubled as an excellent therapy dog whenever the need arose.

"I know the photos frightened you, but you need to push that fear aside now," Sister Bernarda said softly.

"After all that's happened, that's easier said than done. Whoever sent these photos has some serious business in mind.

For a while there, I was convinced that the killer just wanted to distract us because he didn't want us focusing on the murder. But these photos took planning and show clear intent."

"It also means someone has been watching you closely when you're in town—close enough to take the pictures, anyway," Sister Bernarda said. "Taking that a step further, you must have seen him at one point or another, too. The big difference is that you never realized who, or what, he was."

15

THEY ARRIVED AT THE SHERIFF'S DEPARTMENT WITHIN twenty minutes. Tom had seen them both come in and, as if sensing trouble, led them to his office immediately. As they passed by the bullpen, Sister Agatha noticed Fritz Albrecht watching. This time she didn't even bother to nod.

"What's happened?" Tom asked as he closed the door.

Sister Agatha handed him the envelope containing the photographs. "Chances are the sender didn't leave any fingerprints, but I thought you'd want to check anyway."

"Good thinking."

"Do you think the person threatening us is also Jane's killer?" she asked, struggling to keep her voice from wavering.

"Yes. Otherwise it's all too coincidental."

"What about the stolen plumber's van, Tom, the one that forced me off the road? Has it been located?" Sister Agatha asked.

He nodded. "It was abandoned east of I-25, up near Placitas. One interesting thing, too. The plumber swears that he locked the van, but although the van was definitely hot-wired, there was no sign of a break-in."

"Prints?"

"A million of them, most of them belonging to the owner and his partner, as well as dozens of smudged ones. Nothing that'll lead us to the suspect, though. Before you ask, we didn't get any prints from the mask or wig."

Sister Agatha nodded somberly. "I'm finding it hard not to take his threats personally, particularly after seeing those photos."

"I don't blame you. He may have had a passing interest in Sister Jo, but you're the one he's focusing on now. Of course, you're the one with the investigative background—the nun who has been linked in the past to the solution of several crimes. I think this is like a game to the killer, and you're the one being played."

"Sister Bernarda and I are going to pay Smitty a visit next," Sister Agatha said, glancing at her fellow extern. "I have a feeling that photo of me at his store was taken recently."

"Smitty has surveillance cameras at his store these days. See if you can get his permission to check out the video," Tom said. "If there's anyone paying particular attention to you, give me a call."

"Can you give me a copy of those photos? If I look at them long enough, I might be able to come up with something myself," Sister Agatha said.

After they left the sheriff's office, Sister Bernarda glanced at Sister Agatha. "Smitty's video cameras don't work half the time. He keeps them up there mostly as a deterrent."

"Let's ask anyway. We've got nothing to lose." She paused,

then in a sad voice added, "I wish I could go back in time. I'd give anything to undo the past. If only I'd taken time to listen to Jane when she called! If I'd at least tried to talk to her long enough to get more information, I wouldn't feel so bad."

"Don't let guilt master you. We're all human, and we make mistakes. Our Lord always forgives us because He knows that, too. Focus on what you have to do now," Sister Bernarda said. "That's the best way to serve Him."

At Smitty's, after saying hello to the two cashiers, Sister Agatha and Sister Bernarda went to the rear of the store and found Smitty at his desk.

"Hi, Sisters! What brings you here?"

"We came to ask you a favor," Sister Agatha said. "We'd like to view some footage from your surveillance cameras. We need to check the times when I was last here."

He grimaced. "I wish I could help you, but although the cameras are still working, the video recorder quit recording. I'm upgrading to a new digital system that's scheduled to be installed later today." He looked at one and then the other. "What's going on?"

Sister Agatha told him about the threatening photos.

He looked distressed by the news. "I overheard an odd conversation between some kids recently," he said slowly. "Now I'm wondering if that's somehow connected to this. Word is that Sister Jo saw Jane's killer—a man riding a bicycle and packing a pistol. Since you're the crime solver . . ."

"Sister Jo couldn't have seen anything. That's just flat-out impossible. Nobody inside the chapel can see the parking area through the stained glass windows, and the doors were closed when the crime was committed," Sister Bernarda replied flatly.

"Sister Bernarda's right. Any idea where they would get such a crazy story?" Sister Agatha asked.

"Beats me, but that's what the kids were saying."

After thanking Smitty, they left the store in silence. Sister Bernarda glanced over at Sister Agatha. "So where to now? Should we go talk to Sister Jo? My guess is that she said something during the soccer match that her students managed to twist all out of proportion."

"I'll catch up to her this evening and find out what she said," Sister Agatha replied.

During recreation that evening, Sister Agatha sat alone on the bench near the statue of St. Joseph. She needed time to think before speaking to Sister Jo about the stories her students were spreading. Right now the young nun was playing with Pax, like children enjoying what was left of the day. Just watching them vastly improved Sister Agatha's spirits, and helped to ease the burden of responsibility she still felt over Jane's death.

Sister Bernarda was right—she wasn't to blame. Intellectually, she understood that. Emotionally . . . that was another matter. All she knew was that she'd have an easier time sleeping once justice was served.

With that goal in mind, she glanced down at the photo of her on the motorcycle with Pax. The neighborhood didn't look familiar. Trying to retrace her steps mentally, she silently reviewed all the errands she'd run last week.

She heard a sudden loud squeal and quickly looked back up to see Pax jumping, trying to get the tennis ball away from Sister Jo. She tumbled backward laughing and then threw it for him.

"She's certainly a breath of fresh air," Sister Bernarda said, joining Sister Agatha.

"She's been a blessing to us, and we have something to offer her, too, so it has worked out perfectly," she answered.

"Just look at her. Her spirit's so free," Sister Bernarda said. "You and I wear watches, always conscious of the time—or lack of it—but she doesn't even bother with one. She told me once that the bells here and at school are all she needs."

Sister Agatha inhaled sharply. "That's it! I *knew* I was missing something. Look at these photos. Now notice the arm of the nun on the motorcycle. The wind blows back the sleeves."

"No watch . . . but you *always* wear yours—" Her eyes widened. "That was Sister Jo!"

"Put that together with what the kids are saying. I'm more convinced than ever that at least some of our problems are linked to what she *saw*." Sister Agatha waved. "Sister Jo," she called out.

The young nun came over immediately, Pax trailing happily after her.

"I need to talk to you. Will you sit down here on the bench for a moment?" Sister Agatha asked.

Sister Jo did as she asked and gave her a worried look. "Did I do something wrong?"

"No," Sister Agatha said, then sighed and managed a thin smile. "I'd like you to think back to your trip on the Harley—when you got that fake meal delivery call. This is very important, so I'd like you to close your eyes and visualize everything you saw that day. I want details, so think hard, Sister."

Sister Jo obeyed her request. "I found that street, Calle de Elena, on the street map for Bernalillo we keep in the parlor drawer. Then I loaded up Pax and the lunch and went directly to town, taking the main road all the way. When I reached the street, I started at the 100 block and drove south, checking the house numbers. At the end of the street, there was another side road that ran half a block and dead-ended at the ditch bank. I had no idea where to go next, so I looked around for anyone who could give me directions."

"What happened next?" Sister Agatha pressed.

"I spotted a sheriff's department car parked in the shade of a big tree. A deputy in uniform was standing beside the driver's door. I slowed down, wondering where the 800 block was from there, and noticed the deputy was holding something . . . a camera, I think . . . but I'm not sure about that. A man handed the deputy an envelope, then got into a black SUV across the street and drove off. Then the deputy saw me, so I stopped across the street and waved. I called out, asking where the 800 block of Calle de Elena was. The deputy told me there wasn't an 800 block, so I thanked him and drove away. I realized that either I'd written down the wrong address or someone had punked me."

"Then you came back, and met us on the way?" Sister Agatha concluded.

"Exactly."

Sister Agatha nodded. "Now think back. Try to envision the deputy's face."

"I can't. I was across the road, and he was in the shade, wearing sunglasses and his uniform cap," she answered.

"Okay, so tell me about the other man, then. Was he taller than the deputy?"

She closed her eyes again, her eyebrows knitting together. "The deputy was kind of tall, but maybe they were close to the same height. The other guy had a blue baseball cap on." She thought for a moment. "I remember that, as I was driving away, the deputy raised whatever he had in his right hand. Come to think of it, he might have been taking a picture of the Harley. It's a classic."

"That was very good. Thank you, Sister Jo," Sister Agatha said.

Sister Jo's expression brightened. "I'm glad I could help."

"There's something else I need to discuss with you," Sister Agatha said, her tone serious once more. "Did you know that some of the kids in Bernalillo are saying that you *saw* the killer?"

"*What?* I never said anything of the sort! Some of the kids at school came up to ask me about that particular Sunday, so I told them how sad we all were, and how we were praying for the family daily. Naturally, they were also curious about the crime itself. I didn't want to talk about it, but I did answer one question. I told them that the murder weapon had probably been a pistol." In a hesitant voice, she added, "I may have also mentioned that the police thought the killer rode away on a bicycle."

"Kids talk, and somewhere along the way the details got embellished," Sister Agatha said. "Be *extremely* careful what you say to the students. If I'm right, their interpretation has placed you in the killer's spotlight."

Sister Jo drew in a sharp breath. "I heard about the photos you received. Are you telling me that the threats were aimed at me?" Her eyes widened, and she continued before Sister Agatha could answer. "Then I can't stay here with all of you anymore. I'm a danger to everyone."

Sister Agatha held up one hand. "Stop. First we'll tell Reverend Mother. Then we'll figure out what needs to be done next. We have police protection, so there's no reason to panic, but I need you to *focus*. Is there *anything* else about your trip into Bernalillo that sticks in your mind? Something that may have led the bad guy to see you as a greater threat to him than, say, the rest of us?"

She shook her head. "I've told you all I know!"

"Let's pray for help right now," Sister Agatha said. Bowing her head, she led them in the Our Father, then the Memorae, a prayer to the Virgin Mary, asking for her help.

"I've always loved that prayer to Our Lady," Sister Jo said in a much calmer voice after Sister Agatha finished.

"So do I," Sister Agatha said. "Now let's try again. Close your eyes, think back, and describe what you saw on that dead-end street."

Sister Jo did as she asked. After several long seconds, she smiled slowly. "The deputy's car was a regular department vehicle, white with those brown markings and the image of the gold badge on the driver's door—but I just remembered something else. There was a brown number 73 between the front bumper and wheel. The front corner of the car was in the sun instead of the shade, so it stood out clearly. One more thing," she added in an excited voice. "The envelope that was handed from one to the other—it was small and thick, like the ones we use to package computer video cards for NexCen."

"Well done!" Sister Agatha said. "Now why don't you go play with Pax some more? He loves this time of day."

As she moved away, Sister Agatha looked at Sister Bernarda. "We should have started with a prayer. That never fails to center a person's thoughts."

Before Sister Bernarda could answer, the bells rang for Compline, and it was time to go inside.

16

L ONG AFTER COMPLINE, THE NUNS REMAINED IN CHAPEL, deep in prayer. The monastery was defined by silence. Yet that outward peace was only a manifestation of what they strived to maintain within. It was in that stillness of the soul that God's gentle whispers touched awaiting hearts.

Sister Agatha reached out to Him wordlessly, asking for His help and His protection. No answers came. Refusing to give up, she remained where she was.

Then, in the soft glow of the flickering candles, she became aware of a gently shimmering light on the left wall. As a flash of lightning suddenly illuminated the chapel, it became a brilliant figure as tall as the ceiling, its bright outline filled with colors.

Tzuriel, the monastery's angel. She knew it in her heart. Before the words had even formed in her mind, the figure vanished.

Sister Agatha looked around the chapel at her fellow sisters.

Sister Ignatius remained kneeling, her head bowed, a peaceful smile on her face. The rest were staring at the wall in stunned silence.

Sister Agatha knew what they'd seen. Though she'd never be able to prove that it hadn't been a trick of the light filtering through their stained glass window, her heart whispered a different truth.

Another hour of prayer elapsed before they all left the chapel. After Reverend Mother's final blessing, the Asperges, the sprinkling with holy water, each of the sisters retreated to the solitude of their cells. Until the bells rang again, they'd remain alone with Him who was faithful.

The next morning, Sister Agatha went to serve as portress while Sister Bernarda and Sister Jo worked to get the Good News lunches ready. She sat down at the desk and, knowing it was imperative that she tell Tom what Sister Jo had remembered, dialed his office.

Tom listened closely as she told him about the squad car's number. "Hang on a minute," he said when she finished.

Sister Agatha listened to the sound of typing; then Tom picked up the phone again.

"I know who Sister Jo saw—at least which deputy is assigned to that vehicle," he said. "I'll be asking him about this myself, but I can't tell you who it is and risk compromising an undercover op."

"Is that what she saw—an ongoing undercover operation?" Sister Agatha pressed, following her instincts.

He paused. "I'll have to check the records, but from the description, I'm fairly sure that's what was going on that morning."

Sister Agatha noted his momentary hesitation. The identity of the deputy had obviously disturbed him.

"Who was the officer?" She was afraid she already knew the answer. "You *know* I can keep whatever you tell me in strict confidence. I can also read the numbers myself on department vehicles, so it's something I'm bound to discover sooner or later."

There was a long pause, then Tom finally responded. "Vehicle number 73 is assigned to Deputy Gerald Bennett."

Sister Agatha continued as portress for the rest of the day, giving Sister Bernarda and Sister Jo the opportunity to deliver the Good News meals and then catch up on their work as sacristans. Sister de Lourdes, who'd been working double time trying to keep up with her scriptorium work as well as take over as portress whenever needed, also deserved a break.

Sister Agatha welcomed her own return to familiar routines because, through them, she always found the peace that allowed her to think clearly. Though none of the sisters would have ever put any undue pressure on her by careless comments, they had a right to expect results. The case had to be solved soon.

In an effort to get a new perspective on the events of the case, she twisted the facts around in her head as the day passed. She was deep in thought at the parlor desk when a possibility she hadn't considered before suddenly came to her. Tom had been disturbed by the possibility that there'd been an undercover op going on he hadn't known about—but what if Sister Jo had seen exactly what she'd been set up to witness?

Maybe the deputy had engineered things so a nun would inadvertently witness the meeting. That theory was intriguing—but it had one major loophole. How could the deputy who'd photographed Sister Jo on the Harley have known for sure that a nun, any nun, would be there at that particular time?

The answer to that question came to her later that night during the Great Silence. As Sister Agatha once again went over the sequence of events, she suddenly realized that the crank call must have come from the deputy. It was the only thing that made sense. The entire community knew about the Good News deliveries, and the fact that Our Lady of Hope provided a portion of the service. A call to the monastery at the right time, and a plea for help, would have been enough to set things in motion. The only things the deputy couldn't have known were which nun would come and what form of transportation she'd be using. The Antichysler and the Harley were both well known, though, so all the deputy would have had to do was get into position and wait.

The photo's implied threat was clear—but maybe she'd misread the intent. It could have been the killer's way of taunting them, of showing them that they were at his mercy.

As plausible as that was, it was still just one more theory. There were many variables left to explore. What she needed to do was talk to Sister Jo again.

The Great Silence pulsed with a life of its own within the walls of the monastery. As it happened, newcomer Sister Jo lived inside St. Francis's Pantry, where one of the rooms had been converted to a bedroom for overnight visitors. Willing to stretch the rules just a bit considering the seriousness of the matter, Sister Agatha hurried outside to talk to her, Pax at her side.

The small building—the original residence on the property— was dark as she approached, but Sister Agatha was fully prepared to wake Sister Jo if need be. She had to check a few facts and find out if, at long last, she was on the right track.

Sister Agatha knocked loudly on the door to St. Francis's

Pantry, but no one answered. Her initial annoyance soon turned to worry. Only the completely stone-deaf could have slept through the din she'd created. Even Pax had flinched every time she'd banged her fist against the door.

Taking her flashlight, she shined it through the open window of the guest room in the back. The small bed was still made, and Sister Jo was nowhere to be seen.

Sister Agatha swallowed the bitter taste of fear that touched the back of her throat. There was no need to panic yet. Sister Jo had been with them at Compline. She couldn't have gone far without a vehicle, and none had been heard leaving the grounds. Maybe she'd returned to the chapel, or perhaps opted for a walk in the garden before going to bed.

Sister Agatha searched the grounds carefully for footprints. The earlier rain had softened the earth, and thanks to the beam of her flashlight, she could see the imprint of Sister Jo's shoes clearly. With a relieved smile, she followed the trail.

Sister Agatha didn't worry again until she saw that the tracks led directly to the tall, heavy garden gate. Beyond that high wall was the winery's vineyard.

As Sister Agatha drew closer, she could see that the combination lock was open and hanging on the hasp. Sister Jo had left the grounds, and the gate was still unlocked, probably so she could get back inside later. Determined to find answers, she followed.

Sister Agatha slipped out the gate silently, Pax leading the way. Suddenly the big dog's ears pricked up and he shot forward, alerted by a sound only he'd heard.

Trusting the dog's instincts for trouble, she ran after him, toward the river. As they reached the end of the vineyard, which bordered a shallow irrigation ditch, she heard a woman scream.

Directly ahead, in the glow of the moon, she could see a

man in a dark hooded sweatshirt struggling to push Sister Jo's head down into the water. Pax snarled and shot forward. Seeing the blur of motion, the man turned and threw up his arm just as the dog struck. Sister Jo's assailant was knocked back and almost fell as Pax sank his teeth into his forearm.

Sister Agatha had expected a yowl of pain, but the man only grunted, shook his arm, and tried to pull free. Unable to manage it, he reached into his jacket and pulled out an object about the size of a cell phone.

Suddenly there was a bright flash, and Pax yelped, falling to the ground. Free, Sister Jo's assailant leaped across the ditch and raced into the bosque, the wooded area beyond.

Sister Agatha reached Sister Jo's side a heartbeat later and pulled the sputtering nun to her knees.

"Are you okay?" Sister Agatha asked her.

Sister Jo wiped the water from her eyes and, still coughing, nodded. Just then Deputy Sims came rushing up.

"She's okay," Sister Agatha said, then pointed. "Her assailant went toward the river!"

The officer nodded once, aimed her flashlight in that direction, then took off.

Seconds later Sister Agatha saw Eric Barclay running toward them, carrying a big flashlight.

"What's going on? I heard a woman scream!" He aimed the flashlight beam at Sister Jo, saw she was soaked and muddy, and helped her to her feet.

"I'm okay," Sister Jo managed. "Help Pax. He got shocked."

Sister Agatha reached down and stroked the dog, who had his head up now, though he still looked dazed. She then ran her hand across his side where he'd been shocked. There was no burn, only a few singed hairs. "He was just stunned. He'll be okay."

Even as she spoke the dog rose to his feet, ears up. Sister

Agatha continued to pet him as Deputy Sims returned. "I heard a vehicle and followed the sound, but he got away clean. All I saw was dust rising off the road. Did any of you get a good look at him?"

Sister Agatha shook her head. "He had on a hooded sweatshirt—it was either blue or black—and he had a Taser, which he used on Pax. He obviously came prepared. He wasn't even fazed by the dog."

"Let's check the ground for blood," Sims said.

Sims and Eric both used their flashlights but found nothing except water and mud from the ditch.

"The way Pax bit down on his forearm, there should have been plenty of blood," Sister Agatha said. "He crunched down hard and shook his head."

Sister Jo nodded. "Pax's teeth should have torn right into the guy's muscles."

"If he brought something to take out the dog, maybe he also knew enough to pad his arm," Sims concluded.

"Either that or it was a prosthetic," Sister Agatha answered.

"I called this in, and Sheriff Green's on his way over. He wants to check out the incident firsthand," Deputy Sims said.

Sister Agatha glanced at Eric. "Did you see or hear a vehicle?"

"No. I was outside checking the irrigation systems when I heard the scream."

Sister Agatha studied the ground and saw a half-smoked cigarette, the burned end crushed. Before she could give it more thought, Sister Bernarda came rushing up holding a flashlight and a cell phone.

"I thought there was something going on out here! I heard a scream, then saw Deputy Sims go racing past the front gate." Sister Bernarda looked at the young nun and exclaimed, "Sister Jo! Did you go for a swim?"

"No, I was bobbing for crawdads," Sister Jo mumbled, then managed a weak grin.

Sister Agatha quickly filled Sister Bernarda in on what she knew, then looked back at Sister Jo. "You have some explaining to do, Your Charity. You can start by telling us what you were doing out here at this time of night."

Sister Jo cringed, then sneezed.

Seeing Sister Jo shivering, Sister Agatha relented. "Let's go back to your room first. We can talk there after you dry off. Is that okay, Deputy?"

"That's fine," Sims replied, still searching the ground with her flashlight.

"Better give me something to tell Reverend Mother," Sister Bernarda added. "She saw the lights, too."

Sister Agatha looked back at Sister Jo. "In one sentence or less, what were you doing off monastery grounds at this hour?"

"I . . . needed a cigarette. That's mine, Deputy," she said, pointing to the ground. "He smashed it when he grabbed me from behind."

"I didn't even know you smoked." Sister Agatha closed her eyes and opened them in a gesture of impatience. "I hope that cigarette was worth it."

"I'd just lit it," she answered in a thin voice. "The man came from nowhere, and the next thing I knew he was pushing my face into the water."

"If you'll let this be a lesson you'll *never* forget, then maybe some good can come from this terrible incident," Sister Bernarda said.

Sister Jo nodded miserably, then hugged Pax. "You're a brave boy, Pax. Thanks!"

Sister Agatha took Sister Bernarda aside and softly added,

"Let Reverend Mother know what happened, but emphasize the bottom line—a major tragedy was averted tonight."

Almost thirty minutes later, Sheriff Green, Sister Agatha, and a now warm and dry Sister Jo sat together on metal folding chairs in St. Francis's Pantry. Sister Agatha had brewed them all a cup of hot tea. Nights in the desert, even in spring, could be cold, especially when the sky was clear.

"Start from the beginning, Sister Jo," Tom said, "and don't leave any details out, even if you think they're unimportant."

Sister Jo nodded, now humbly contrite. "I used to be a smoker and still get cravings from time to time. When I found out that Deputy Sims smoked, I decided to beg a cigarette off her. Well, more than one. I shouldn't have . . . but it was never more than one at a time," she added in a thin whisper. "When we become nuns we give up a lot, but there are two things I don't think I'll ever stop missing. Cigarettes are one," she said with a sheepish smile.

Sister Agatha nearly choked on her tea, but Tom smiled.

"He said not to leave anything out," Sister Jo added quickly, seeing the annoyed expression on Sister Agatha's face.

"Stick to the events," Sister Agatha said.

Sister Jo nodded. "I've been walking off the grounds each night after Compline. We all know the combination to the lock at the gate, so I'd open it up, go out for my smoke, then come back and lock it back up again. I wasn't smoking on our grounds, and with a deputy keeping watch around the outside, I figured I wasn't hurting anyone."

"Your actions endangered me, Pax, and you," Sister Agatha said firmly.

Tom shot her a hard look, and Sister Agatha swallowed her anger and fell silent.

"I know, Sister Agatha. I messed up big-time," Sister Jo said. "The thing is, I'd always wait until *after* the deputy had circled the wall. That way, since the area had just been checked out, I figured I'd be perfectly safe."

"My guess is that he was waiting for you. He knew your routine—and the deputy's," Tom said. "Deputy Sims should have never made her rounds at predictable times."

"She doesn't," Sister Jo said quickly. "But it's always within a half hour or so," she added in a barely audible voice.

"Did your assailant say anything to you?" Tom pressed.

"All I heard was one word, 'finally.' But I may be wrong about that. By then, my head was below water and I was trying hard to hold my breath."

As a tear rolled down her face, Sister Agatha's heart went out to her. Sister Jo had been through a lot in the past few hours. "From now on, you'll sleep inside the monastery. I'm sure Mother will agree and find a place for you. If nothing else, the laundry room can double as your cell—or maybe even the parlor."

Sister Jo nodded. "And I'll never touch a cigarette again. Not *ever*. But that other craving of mine . . ."

Sister Agatha glared at her.

"Cokes, the ones from Mexico," she added quickly. "They're made with real sugar, not corn syrup. When I was up in Santa Fe, there was a Mexican restaurant within walking distance that had them, so they were easy to get. I haven't had much luck since I moved here. But I'll give those up, too."

Tom started to laugh, then covered quickly, clearing his throat instead.

Leaving Sister Bernarda to help Sister Jo pack up her

belongings, Sister Agatha stepped outside onto the grounds with the sheriff.

"This was carefully planned, Tom. There can be no doubt about that. I think Deputy Bennett may have figured out, either from your questions or from my visit to the station, that Sister Jo was the nun on the Harley that day on Calle de Elena. Or maybe he's heard the stories from St. Charles students. We've recently discovered that some of the soccer team kids think that Sister Jo saw the killer on the bicycle."

"There's still a question about who was assigned unit 73 that day, but I can guarantee you one thing. If I've got a dirty cop hiding behind his badge—a killer—I'll get him," he said in a low, determined voice. "Count on it."

"I'll pray that you're able to find him quickly, Tom, before it leaves a stain on the other officers who serve with honor," Sister Agatha said.

17

THE BELLS RANG AS USUAL AT FOUR THIRTY THE FOLLOW-
ing morning. Sister Agatha got up with a groan, trying to
find it in her heart to bless the bell ringer. She hadn't
managed to get much sleep last night with so many questions
still running through her mind.

As she got to her feet she saw the pills, courtesy of Sister Eugenia, on the chest of drawers by her bed. There were two slices
of bread there, too, since her medication couldn't be taken on an
empty stomach.

Well past Morning Prayers she finally caught up to Sister Jo
in the refectory. She was hard at work, cleaning.

"Can you use some help finishing up here?" Sister Agatha
asked.

Sister Jo looked up from where she was kneeling, wiping the
baseboards, and gave her a hesitant smile. "The baseboards are

done, but I haven't wiped the chairs, the dining table, or the sideboard."

Looking over at their sideboard, Sister Agatha noted the human skull kept in plain view. It was there, in a central location, to remind the sisters of their own mortality. She always avoided looking at it when eating. After all these years, it still gave her the creeps.

"Hand me a cloth. I'll take the table and chairs," Sister Agatha said.

They worked quickly, Sister Jo softly humming stanzas from the Magnificat, her soprano voice, melodious and soft, proclaiming the greatness of God.

Sister Agatha was walking around to the other side of the communal dining table when she heard a thump and Sister Jo's gasp. She turned just in time to see the skull rolling toward the edge of the sideboard.

Like a shortstop spearing a line drive, Sister Jo dove to catch it, but missed. The skull struck her fingertips and bounced onto the brick floor. Sister Jo lunged again, groping for the skull with her outstretched hand, but the skull bounced away, spinning like a top. A second later, it hit the corner, bumping the wall so hard its jaw fell off.

"*Now* what have I done?" Sister Jo scrambled to her feet. The skull was upright in the corner, more toothless than before, but still staring. "I broke his jaw! All I was trying to do was get a spider off his forehead. I went to squish it with my dustcloth, but then both took off on me!"

"Accidents happen," Sister Agatha managed, trying not to burst out laughing. The truth of it was she couldn't remember the last time anything like that had happened.

"I feel terrible about this! What am I going to do?"

"I think it's just an artificial skull—a model intended for anatomy classes. See if you can reattach the jaw."

Sister Jo picked it up and, after a moment, snapped the jaw back on with a click. "There! It's fixed!"

"While you return the skull to its place, I'll put away the cleaning rags," Sister Agatha said. "Then we have to get going. We're scheduled to meet with Sheriff Green. He wanted to talk to both of us in the parlor this morning."

Tom was already there with Sister Bernarda when they walked in. Sister Jo sat down and looked at him with a pained expression.

Sensing her tension, Tom walked to the parlor window, then glanced back at her and Sister Agatha. "It's an almost perfect day outside. Let's talk while we walk."

Sister Jo smiled brightly. "That sounds like a wonderful idea, Sheriff!"

Sister Agatha gave Tom an almost imperceptible nod. He'd played it right. She, too, had a feeling that Sister Jo knew more about her assailant than she realized, but recent events had undermined her self-confidence, as evidenced by her reaction to knocking over the skull.

Leaving Sister Bernarda to act as portress, they walked outside. Tom allowed the silence to stretch for a few minutes, then finally spoke. "So tell me, Sister Jo. The man forced your head under the water, but from Deputy Sims's report, and your own words, I'm assuming he didn't actually try to drown you. You were able to get your head back out of the water in time to take breaths. Is that correct?"

Sister Jo looked up at him and nodded. "Each time I thought I was about to drown, he'd yank my head back up. Then, as soon as I'd caught a breath, he'd push me back down."

She paused, then looked at him with new understanding. "So he was just trying to scare me, right?"

Tom started to answer, but his phone rang. He stepped away from them for a few moments, finished his conversation, then signaled Sister Agatha.

She joined him. If she'd read his expression accurately, something had just taken an unexpected turn.

"Good news," he said. "Or bad news, depending on who you are. I've been following up on unit 73. Gerry *was* on patrol during the time Sister Jo drove down Calle de Elena but, according to Dispatch, gave his location as southern Bernalillo during the critical time interval. That's across town."

"But less than ten minutes away, Tom. Gerry could have lied about his location, too," she concluded.

"It's possible, and our units don't have GPS systems yet, so we can't verify his alibi. The thing is that last night, when Sister Jo was attacked, Bennett was home with his wife. Evelyn vouches for him."

"So what do you think? Is Gerry in the middle of this somehow, or not? It wouldn't be that unusual for a wife to cover for her husband."

"The first alibi isn't solid. That's why I'm following up on this, trying to find a citizen or two who can confirm his location during Sister Jo's ride." He shook his head. "Even if I can't, my gut's telling me that Gerry's not our man."

"What we need to do is figure out how it's possible for unit 73 to show up beside Calle de Elena at the same time the officer was driving it across town. Saints are supposed to be capable of bilocation, but I doubt cars are similarly blessed." Sister Agatha turned around and suddenly realized that Sister Jo had disappeared.

Noting it too, Tom immediately jogged to the squad car across the street from the monastery. Sister Agatha followed him. Once they cleared the open gate, they saw Deputy Sims standing beside the monastery wall, talking to Sister Jo.

As Sister Agatha and the sheriff joined them, Deputy Sims quickly wiped away the white powder that covered her lips.

"Deputy," Tom said coldly. With only that word, he managed to convey extreme displeasure.

"I'm sorry, sir," Laura said, swallowing quickly. "Powdered sugar." She looked down and brushed more white powder from her uniform.

Sheriff Green didn't say a word.

"Please don't be angry with her," Sister Jo said quickly. "I knew she got into trouble because of what happened to me last night, but she *was* doing her job. If it's anyone's fault, it's mine."

Sister Agatha knew Sister Jo couldn't have slipped her a doughnut. They didn't have any at the monastery except on rare occasions. "Cookies?" she asked, seeing the small napkin-covered treat in Deputy Sims's hand.

"Better than ordinary cookies," Sister Jo answered. "It's Sister Clothilde's new recipe. She calls them Miraculous Munchies."

"She has a winner with these," Laura Sims said with a sheepish smile.

Sheriff Green glowered at her. "I'd like to see you in my office after your relief arrives."

"Yes, sir," she said, instantly serious.

Sister Jo looked completely mortified. "Please don't let her get into trouble on my account. I was only trying to thank her for last night."

Sheriff Green gave Sister Jo a puzzled look, then relaxed. "I'll forget the whole thing if you'll talk to me about the day you saw unit 73 on Calle de Elena. Are you up to it?"

Sister Jo took a deep breath, then let it out slowly. "You bet, Sheriff."

"Good. Think back to the sheriff's deputy you saw that day," Tom said. "I need you to visualize the things that caught your eye, like his cap and uniform."

Sister Jo said nothing for several moments as they crossed the parking area, walking around the circular garden in the center. Twice, she glanced back at Deputy Sims as if studying her. At long last she spoke. "Deputy Sims's uniform is different—a bit, anyway."

"Different how?" he asked.

"Not the color. That's the same. The belt he wore, *that* was different," she said firmly.

Sister Agatha and Tom exchanged a quick look as Sister Jo's eyes narrowed and she struggled to remember specifics. "The color was the same, black, and there was that weave pattern, but the officer I saw by car 73 had a lot of extra things attached to his belt."

"What kind of extra things?" Tom asked her.

"Deputy Sims carries a pistol, and so did the deputy I saw, but there were several extra black pouches on that officer's belt. It caught my eye because I was having a problem with the rosary fastened around my cincture. Then I saw how many things were attached to *his* belt, and promptly apologized to Our Lord for complaining."

Sheriff Green led the way back to the main gate where Deputy Sims stood. "Do you have extra clips you can attach to your belt to show her what they look like?"

Deputy Sims walked over to the trunk of her squad car, opened a metal box, then brought out two ammo magazines, each in a black pouch. She attached them to her belt by metal clips.

"Like that?" Tom asked Sister Jo.

She nodded. "A bit, but he had more of them, four, I think. He also had a flashlight in some kind of loop, and something with an antenna . . . a hand radio, maybe? And chrome hand-cuffs. I remember that because they shined, even in the shade where he was standing."

"How many of your officers carry that much equipment?" Sister Agatha asked.

"There are a few I can think of offhand," Tom answered. "Most of them are on the SWAT team, or are ones who've been forced to fire their weapons on duty."

"The *Chronicle*," Sister Agatha said suddenly, thinking out loud. "They'll have photos of crime scenes ranging from family disputes to auto accidents. Anytime an interesting call goes out over the radio, they check it out. Sister Jo can look for similar equipment configurations in photos there. That wouldn't em-barrass any officers, or tip off the one she actually saw."

"Good idea," Tom said. "I'll meet you there."

Sister Agatha looked at Sister Jo. "Looks like you and I will be making a trip to town."

They set out shortly thereafter, leaving Pax behind. Once at the *Chronicle*, unfortunately, the search proved to be more time-consuming than they'd expected. Two hours passed as Chuck Moody systematically pulled up every single photo they had on file, showing each one to Sister Jo. In return for his cooperation, Sheriff Green had agreed to give him an exclusive on the devel-oping story.

By noon, based upon height and equipment, they'd nar-rowed the field to three tall, slender officers: Sergeant Michael McKay, a deputy named Craig Goodwin, and Gerry Bennett. Deputy Sims had been ruled out because Sister Jo had been con-vinced that the officer was male, not female, and Deputy Sims's belt configuration hadn't matched.

They went outside, and Sister Agatha motioned Sheriff Green aside while Sister Jo got into the Antichyrsler.

"Tom, Gerry Bennett's name pops up every time we look into a new aspect of this investigation."

"It seems that way, but he might have been set up. Or maybe Sister Jo's memory isn't as flawless as we think. Let's see what I get when I check out the other two officers. Then I'll decide what the next step should be."

"What about Pax's attack the other night? He mauled that man's forearm. Have you seen signs of that type of injury on the arm of any of your men?"

"No, I haven't. With our uniforms being long-sleeved, I've had to look extra hard at the way the deputies handle themselves, but nobody appears to be injured."

"What I still don't get is why witnessing the exchange of an envelope would be enough to warrant an attempt on Sister Jo's life—that is, unless it was Bennett paying off whoever killed Jane," Sister Agatha said.

"That's a real stretch. Keep in mind that we have no real evidence that Bennett was behind the murder. All we know for sure is that the two didn't get along. There's also the possibility that the attack on Sister Jo is unrelated. Maybe it was a transient who felt threatened, or a voyeur who was afraid he'd been discovered."

"Then why attack her instead of running away? I'm sure the threats all tie in to what she saw, Tom. We're dealing with a suspect who has some serious know-how, too. Look at the evidence— a small-caliber weapon with an effective silencer, someone playing psychological warfare with e-mails, now a night stalker with a stun weapon and knowledge of how to deal with police dogs. The very fact that there was no blood on the scene of Pax's attack proves that the man knew how to keep himself from being torn to shreds. Doesn't all that sound like the same highly trained individual?"

"Those are good points. I'm guessing you've got a theory that pulls all those events together?"

She nodded. "Consider last night. The man who attacked Sister Jo brought along a self-defense weapon meant to immobilize an opponent. If he'd really wanted to drown Sister Jo, instead of just trying to scare her, he would have shot her full of electricity. Then, while she was stunned and unable to defend herself, or scream for help, he could have easily held her head underwater. Or he could have just brought his silenced pistol."

"Makes sense, and I'll give you this much—it's looking more and more like the perp is one of *my* people," Tom said, his voice hard. "But all I can do right now is continue my investigation and try to weed out the innocent."

"Let me help you. We have two very different ways of approaching a case, and by sharing information, we'll get to the answers faster—and maybe save another life."

"What have you got in mind?"

"For starters, I'd like to speak with Officer Bennett alone."

"*Not* going to happen. For legal and a host of other reasons, I insist on handling my own men," Tom answered emphatically.

Before she could argue, Sister Agatha's cell phone rang. She looked at the caller ID and said, "It's Sister Bernarda. Give me a moment."

Sister Jo had been called to St. Charles to substitute teach for the remainder of the day. As Sister Agatha drove her to the school, she noticed that the young nun looked almost relieved to go back to teaching, a world she knew well. She couldn't blame her. When Sister Agatha pulled up in front of St. Charles, Sister Jo almost ran inside.

Twenty minutes later, as she and Tom had agreed, Sister Agatha walked through the doors of the sheriff's department. Fritz was nowhere to be seen. Learning from the duty officer that Tom was in his office with Deputy Bennett and that she'd been asked to join them, she hurried down the hall. Although Tom's door was closed, she could hear loud, angry voices on the other side.

Sister Agatha knocked, and Tom opened the door, inviting her in. As she stepped into the room, Bennett glowered at her.

Sister Agatha took a seat, and Bennett immediately rolled up both his sleeves and bared his arms. "See? No bite marks, bruises, not even a scratch. I'm being framed. Can't you two see that?"

"Jane tried to ruin your marriage," Sister Agatha said. "I heard she was tracking you during her lunch breaks, hoping to catch you cheating on Evelyn."

"Like I didn't know," he spat out. "She'd even snap photos of me with her cell phone whenever she'd see me talking to women deputies. I hated my mother-in-law. I won't deny it. The old bat was determined to destroy my marriage. But understand this—I had absolutely nothing to do with her death, and I have no idea who killed her. I am *not* guilty, and I won't allow anyone to convict me based on a ton of hearsay."

"Your name keeps coming up in this investigation, Deputy," Sheriff Green said, "so, officially, you're a person of interest. That's as far as it goes, for now. If I had any real evidence, you would have been suspended. You know how this department works."

Bennett shook his head, a disgusted look on his face. "What galls me is that you're still not sure I can be trusted, are you, Sheriff?"

"Give me a chance to complete this investigation, Gerry. It's not like you're the only one on our list."

"Who are the others?"

Tom shook his head. "This is *my* case, not yours, Deputy. You know better than to ask that."

"Then I'm out of here. I won't work someplace I'm not trusted, Sheriff." He took off his badge and slapped it down hard onto Tom's desk.

Tom pushed the badge back in front of Gerry. "Put this back on, Deputy. I'm advising you to take bereavement leave with pay. Spend some time with your family, and use this as an opportunity to cool off."

Gerry hesitated for a moment, looked over at Sister Agatha, then took back his badge and pinned it on. "Okay. You make sense, boss. My wife and daughter need me right now anyway."

Once Gerry had left the office, Tom leaned back in his chair. "This is going to get a lot worse before it gets better."

"Tom, I have an idea. Let *me* look into this from the outside. The envelope Sister Jo saw being passed might have been a payoff. If we speculate that money was exchanged, that means there's a deputy out there with spare cash. You won't be able to get a warrant to look into your men's bank records, and it wouldn't do much good even if you could. No officer with half a brain would sock that money away someplace where it could be traced. But I can nose around unofficially. Let's see if Sergeant McKay, Craig Goodwin, or Deputy Bennett has made any large purchases lately."

"I'm under orders to keep you away from my department. I can't agree to that," Tom replied.

"No, but you can't stop me from doing this on my own. Just remember that a nun can talk to a lot of neighbors without raising even the slightest suspicion."

Tom thought about it for a moment. "Be careful not to get yourself into any trouble. If one of my officers has to bail you out, everything's going to hit the fan."

"All I want to do is find out which of the officers is showing signs of a recent windfall."

"Do *not* confront these men, and don't let what you're doing leak to the public—or, worse, the press. That includes Chuck Moody."

"He already knows we're checking into those three officers, Tom, and I need Chuck to provide me with their addresses. He can be trusted to keep his mouth shut for now."

"He's *your* source, Sister Agatha. You control him," Tom said. "Meanwhile, I'm going to update my résumé in case the mayor gets wind of this."

After leaving the station, Sister Agatha called Chuck, who quickly provided her with the officers' addresses. She didn't bother to ask him where he got the information, and he didn't volunteer his source.

Sister Agatha drove to Craig Goodwin's neighborhood first since it was closest. The deputy lived in an older section of town just west of the main highway, with modest housing. Nothing about his home, a rental, set off any alarms. Speaking to some of Craig's neighbors, Sister Agatha learned that the deputy was young and single. He lived a quiet life, and his spending patterns were modest at best. Goodwin drove a ten-year-old pickup. The seventies-era muscle car undergoing restoration beneath a canvas shelter in the backyard looked like it belonged to a man who enjoyed tinkering with cars. If he'd taken any bribes recently, he'd also had the intelligence to keep from spending that cash ostentatiously.

Disappointed but not discouraged, Sister Agatha decided to stop by Bennett's home next since it was between where she was and Michael McKay's. As she drove down the nearly deserted residential street, she saw no car in the driveway or carport, and from the drawn curtains it didn't appear that Evelyn was home.

Sister Agatha parked the Antichrysler and took a leisurely stroll around the block, cutting through the alley so she could see the Bennetts' backyard. There was an inexpensive swing set, a handmade playhouse, and an old brick barbecue that dated from the sixties. They also had an ancient picnic table, one of those redwood ones with the matching benches. Sister Agatha remembered one in her own backyard when she was growing up.

She was on her way back to the Antichrysler when she suddenly spotted an adult man's bright red bicycle in the yard next door. It was a long shot, but since it matched the description of Louis's stolen bike, knobby tires and all, it wasn't something she could afford to ignore.

With a bright smile, she waved at the man wearing ear protectors and safety goggles as he fed a piece of lumber through a table saw.

The first four "Yoo-hoo, sirs" went unheeded. The man, in his early sixties, finally finished the cut he was making and turned off the saw. Taking advantage of the silence, she called out to him again. This time, the man turned around, surprised to see her standing by the fence.

"Can I do something for you, Sister?" he asked, removing his ear protection.

"I was just admiring your bike! It looks almost new."

"Yeah, that's what I was thinking. I was cleaning out my garage, hauling stuff over to the big trash bin the county brought for our neighborhood's cleanup day, and there it was, sitting right on top. Someone had just tossed it in, apparently. I got it out and brought it home. Even the tires are new. People throw out perfectly good things these days. I thought it might have been stolen, but it didn't have a license plate and there was no name on it anywhere. So I figured I'd watch the newspaper for a few days, and if it wasn't listed as missing, I'd sell it."

He opened the side gate and let her into his yard. "The reflector's broken, but otherwise it's in perfect condition. You interested?"

Sister Agatha studied the bike. "I think I know someone who might be."

18

THE MAN SMILED. "SEND HIM OVER. I'M RETIRED, USU-
ally here, so anytime's good. Joe Gomez's the name," he
said, offering her his hand.

Sister Agatha shook it. "I'm Sister Agatha, Mr. Gomez. It's
a pleasure to meet you."

"That's where I found the bicycle," he said, pointing toward
the easement behind his property.

She looked at the big green metal bin again, having passed
by it just a few minutes earlier.

After thanking Mr. Gomez, Sister Agatha made her way
back in the direction of the Dumpster. Suddenly she was very
glad she hadn't brought Pax along with her this morning. Knowing she might have to climb in there herself was bad enough, but
dogs love trash, and if Pax had been around he'd have insisted on
jumping in, with or without her.

As soon as she reached the Dumpster, Sister Agatha realized

it was taller than she'd initially thought. Even standing on a metal support, she could only see the debris and trash at the full end.

There was no other choice. She'd have to climb in, and the full end was the place to do it. Grateful that she was wearing the black sneakers she reserved for motorcycle use instead of her usual convent sandals, Sister Agatha pulled herself up and over. She landed on an old door lying atop some broken cinder blocks. Normally, nothing could have compelled her to crawl inside a giant trash container. Yet pieces of evidence were still missing, and something was urging her to keep looking.

The bin was only half full, and most of the items thrown inside it were worn-out appliances, scrap building materials, and broken furniture too big for normal trash pickup. Except for that one corner, where someone had dumped in branches from pruned rosebushes, the search wasn't as hard as she'd expected. Though the missing piece of reflector was nowhere to be found, what kept her in the bin searching was the hope that the killer had discarded the murder weapon here.

She was using a piece of wood to shift some of the lumber resting on the bottom when she heard a dull metallic clunk. A few feet in front of her, resting between two broken pieces of plywood, she found the frame of a partially disassembled automatic pistol.

She made no attempt to touch it. Instead, she reached for the cell phone and called Sheriff Green.

"I'll be there in less than ten minutes. Don't let *anyone* near that trash bin."

As Sister Agatha crawled back out, a telephone lineman parked beside one of the phone boxes along the easement saw her. He waved and jogged over.

"I knew the monastery was having some tough times, Sister, but I never realized things were this bad." He reached into his pocket and pulled out a twenty. "God bless you."

Stunned, Sister Agatha stared at the twenty in her hand. As the man walked away, she suddenly realized what had happened. He'd thought she'd been scavenging. Seeing the man driving away in his repair truck, she knew she couldn't give the money back now. She placed it in her pocket. With a gentle sigh, she took comfort in the sure knowledge that God would bless him a thousandfold for the gift he'd just given them.

Hours later, Sister Agatha was sitting alone in the sheriff's office. When Tom came back in, he placed a hot dog on a napkin in front of her. "Lots of mustard, chili, and onions, just the way you like it."

"You remembered my weakness for hot dogs! Thanks," she said, taking a large bite.

He filled her in after swallowing a huge bite from his enormous submarine sandwich. "You stumbled across a treasure chest of evidence this morning, Sister. Not even the mayor is going to complain this time. Your find could crack this case wide open. Underneath all the rose cuttings, crime scene officers found the rest of the pistol, including a crude but effective silencer. It was patterned from a design available in a widely circulated early seventies publication called *The Anarchist Cookbook*. They also found the magazine—loaded except for one round—and a spent .22 shell casing. The bad part is that they were unable to lift any prints at all. It's especially frustrating because human blood was found on the outer metal casing of the silencer, and its type matches the victim's."

"Have they test-fired the pistol yet, and did the bullet

match the slug recovered from Jane Sanchez's body?" Sister Agatha asked.

"The bullet that killed Jane was too deformed for us to make a positive match, but the firing pin strike and the ejection marks on the recovered shell casing match the pistol. That's how we were able to determine that it was fired from the same weapon."

"So what now?" she asked.

"The serial number on the pistol was filed down, but we'll be sending the frame to another lab. Maybe experts there can recover some of the numbers using an acid etching technique. If we're lucky, we'll find out who the original owner of the weapon was, and that'll narrow the field some more."

"Anything else?"

Tom nodded. "We also found Jane's cell phone in that Dumpster. It had been stomped to pieces but I sent the SIM card and the rest to a forensic lab to try to restore the memory. I checked, and not all the data is stored on the card, so we might get lucky, who knows?"

"Jane struck me as someone from the written message generation," Sister Agatha said. "What about those missing memo pads? Find any?"

"As a matter of fact, yes. There were three or four pads, all hot pink, right next to the cell phone. Jane's fingerprints were on the bottom of two of the pads. I asked the lab techs to check for impressions of words on the paper—in case Jane had written something incriminating that had slipped past the killer. I mean, why else would the killer want to take them?"

"Has Louis identified the red bicycle at Mr. Gomez's as the one Jane gave him?"

"He didn't have to. Jane had saved the sales receipt from the bike shop, and the serial numbers match."

"The killer obviously saw no need to change those—he

knew that the bike couldn't be used to positively ID him unless he'd left his prints on it—but the way he removed the serial numbers from the gun and dumped the physical evidence screams of someone well acquainted with police procedure. All that points right back to Officer Bennett, who conveniently lives within a stone's throw of that trash bin."

Seeing Tom scowl, she added, "The problem with all this, of course, is that the trail's much too obvious. Any police officer would know better than to go through all those evidence-concealing measures, then turn right around and dump the murder weapon, the bicycle, and all the rest within sight of his own home. The killer must have known that the bicycle would be found by the next person using the bin. Any kid walking by would have pulled it out."

"Agreed. So if we assume Bennett was set up and rule him out, that leaves Goodwin or McKay—and no apparent motive."

"Goodwin leads a very simple life, from what I managed to learn. He doesn't strike me as the kind who'd be money hungry." She described what she'd seen.

Tom nodded. "He likes to tinker with cars. If anyone in our department is having a problem with their personal vehicle, he'll fix it for a six-pack and the cost of parts. Still, he might have a money stash and is just waiting for things to blow over before he starts setting himself up with a first-class auto shop."

"What do you know about Sergeant McKay?" she asked and saw him stiffen. "Tom, I'm sorry," she added softly. "I know this is hard on you, having to decide which one of your deputies has gone bad."

"My people all work hard and give the job everything—including, at times, their lives. Our department has a lot to be proud of, but when one officer is dirty, the rest of us pick up the smell. That's an incredibly frustrating fact of life, particularly because most of my officers live for the department. The trail of divorces is ample proof of their dedication to the job," he answered.

"The sooner you find the deputy who betrayed the department's trust, the quicker you'll be able to get back to normal," she said, standing. "I'm going to check out McKay next. If I find anything you need to know about, I'll be in touch right away." Tossing the empty napkin into his trash can, she added, "Thanks so much for lunch."

"Watch yourself. McKay's off duty right now." Tom glanced down the hall. "Where's Pax? Did you bring him into town? You need him with you these days."

"He's got infirmary duty, but I'll go back for him. Reverend Mother prefers for us not to go out alone when at all possible."

"She's right. Danger could come from anywhere—and probably when you're least expecting it."

Sister Agatha returned to the monastery. After leaving word for Reverend Mother about her progress, she went to find Pax. As she walked in through the garden gate, she saw the dog jumping up into the air, chasing butterflies. She chuckled softly, envying his carefree life.

Sister Agatha whistled for him, and Pax came rushing over. Soon they were on their way to town in the Antichrysler. Sergeant Michael McKay lived in Questa Verde, one of the newer neighborhoods. The homes here all looked pretty much the same except for the exterior paint color.

It didn't take her long to find McKay's home. His squad car was parked in the driveway of the two-car garage. Next to it was a humongous pickup with the type of option package that usually made men salivate—extra lights, trim, toolboxes, mirrors, oversized chrome wheels, big bumpers, and a fancy paint scheme.

Sister Agatha drove past his front window even slower than the twenty miles per hour the speed limit sign called for, trying to sneak a peek inside. As she did, she caught a glimpse of an enormous flat-screen TV. She'd seen plenty of big TVs before, but this one was about the size of the wall. McKay was there, too, a beer bottle in his hand, intent on the basketball game he was watching.

"We need to get a closer look, Pax. Let's park a street away, then walk back. No one will bother us. Most people will assume we're here to ask for donations and do their best not to make eye contact." She remembered the telephone company man who'd given her the twenty. "Of course, there *are* exceptions."

As they approached the deputy's home, she slowed her step. She wouldn't risk walking directly past the front window in case he happened to look out or could see a reflection of the window on his big-screen TV. They'd met before and spoken briefly when he'd been on duty outside the monastery, so if he saw her here he'd know he was under suspicion.

The backyard was encased by cedar fencing, but the gate was unlocked. Alone, she knew she'd make almost no noise, so Sister Agatha signaled Pax to stay and went through silently, closing the gate behind her out of habit.

The first thing Sister Agatha noticed was the huge stainless steel gas grill. This man clearly had a thing for *big*. The outdoor appliance looked incredibly expensive. There was a large work surface, four main burners, a split-fork rotisserie, and two infrared side burners—at least that was what their labels said. McKay could cook for the entire neighborhood with this setup. Compared to this hardware, Deputy Bennett's grill was from the Stone Age.

She was edging around an outdoor dining group with a round inlaid mosaic table when she heard a deep-throated growl. It didn't sound like Pax.

Sister Agatha turned her head and spotted a rottweiler near the far corner of the house. Muttering a "good boy," she started a slow backpedal toward the gate. She'd taken only a few steps when the dog came at her. Acting instinctively, she hopped onto a metal side table and stepped over onto the grill. She stood in the center of the work surface, one foot on either side of the burners.

The fence was three feet away. Sister Agatha wondered if she could make the jump without snagging her long habit on the wooden rails. Inching closer, she put out her foot. Just then the big black dog lunged upward, barely missing her heel with a snap of his jaws.

The dog was obviously trained not to bark, merely to attack. The realization frightened her as much as the possibility that McKay would catch her dancing atop his outdoor kitchen. She glanced toward the window and noted with relief that he was apparently still engrossed in the game.

Grateful for the impulse that had led her to close the gate, she called out, "Pax, speak!"

When Pax began to bark, the rottweiler took off and ran to the gate. The black and tan dog didn't bark back, but his low growl made her skin crawl.

While the two dogs spoke in their own language, Sister Agatha stepped over onto the top rail of the cedar fence. She jumped down onto the ground on the other side, going into an instantaneous crouch to absorb the fall, and called Pax to her.

Soon they were hurrying away, heading toward the ease-ment road behind the homes. Once they were several houses away from McKay's, they walked back along a shallow drainage ditch that directed rainwater away from the cul-de-sac ahead. At the curb, standing between houses, she stood under the shade of a locust tree and caught her breath.

A tall man with a ramrod-straight back came off the porch of his home and approached her. "Can I help you, Sister?"

"Hello," Sister Agatha said brightly, thinking fast. "I came to invite you and your neighbors to daily Mass at Our Lady of Hope Monastery. The sheriff's department is now keeping a careful watch over us, and we wanted people to know that they'd be safe."

"Most of my neighbors work, so I'm not sure they can make weekday Mass, but you're welcome to talk to anyone you find," he said, not responding directly to her invitation. "I'm Hugh Eberly, the head of the Neighborhood Watch Association. I heard a dog barking a few minutes ago and came out to see what was going on. Did you happen to spot anything unusual while you were walking around?"

"A dog barked at us a while ago. The animals around here aren't used to seeing a nun's habit, I suppose," she answered with a smile. Gesturing to McKay's squad car, she continued, "I can't imagine you'd have much of a crime problem with a deputy living in the neighborhood. Having his department vehicle in plain sight is a great deterrent, don't you think?"

"You never know these days," he said sadly.

"Our deputies must have finally gotten that raise they've been wanting," she added offhandedly. "That's some fancy truck!"

"I haven't heard anything about a raise. McKay inherited some money from his father, so that's probably why he was able to buy that truck. His dad passed away last month in Amarillo."

"I'm sorry to hear that. It's hard to lose a parent."

"I don't think they were close," Hugh answered.

Sister Agatha glanced at her watch, then back at him. "I have to be on my way. Please remember that our chapel is always open and ready to welcome everyone."

Once in the Antichrysler, Sister Agatha called Tom and

updated him on McKay's recent spending spree, mentioning what she'd seen in his backyard.

"You had *no* business whatsoever going onto his property, Sister. McKay's a law enforcement officer, and he deserves more respect than that. You were lucky you didn't get caught—or worse."

"Tom, I did what you couldn't so we could get some answers. This new information can be useful. Or have you already investigated McKay's newfound wealth and just not bothered to mention it to me?"

"*Back off McKay*," he said, his voice suddenly very hard. "Am I clear?"

"I've barely gotten started," she protested.

"There's a legal issue in play here that makes it impossible for me to say any more. You *have* to back off."

Sister Agatha knew an order when she heard one. Was it possible that another agency was already investigating McKay and Tom had just found out?

"All right, then," she said. "Have you heard if the lab will be able to reconstruct the serial numbers on the weapon I found?"

"I checked with them a short while ago. They believe they can but have no idea how long that's going to take. The state crime lab is always backed up, and the situation is even worse these days because of all the budget cuts they've had."

After saying good-bye, Sister Agatha sat quietly in the Antichrysler with Pax. Although the key was in the ignition, she didn't start the engine, not wanting to waste precious gasoline until she knew where to go next. While she gave the matter some thought, her cell phone rang.

"Sister Agatha, I'm glad I got you. This is Chuck at the *Chronicle*. I think you better come over."

"What's wrong?"

"I'd rather show you when you get here. And, Sister? Brace yourself."

His words had sparked her curiosity, and she drove there as quickly as the speed limit would allow. She was at the *Chronicle* five minutes later, and Chuck greeted her at the door.

"Come in, Sister. There's something I want to show you," he said, leading the way to his desk. He then reached into a manila folder and presented her with a handwritten letter.

Sister Agatha scanned it quickly. The letter had been written to the editor of the *Chronicle* by Del Martinez's wife. The woman blamed her husband's recent conviction and prison sentence on what she claimed was Sister Agatha's biased and misleading testimony. She told of the suffering her family had endured and accused Sister Agatha of coming by their home and threatening to have Del's parole revoked.

"None of this is true. You know that, right?" Sister Agatha asked Chuck at last.

He nodded. "That's why I wanted you to see it. With your background, I'm sure you can write a killer rebuttal letter, and I can print both side by side."

She considered it for several long moments, then shook her head. "No. I won't dignify these accusations with a response. Folks familiar with the case will already know it wasn't just my testimony that got Del sent away—it was all the physical evidence, the money trail, and the other witnesses who were also ripped off. Del and his family are trying to avoid taking personal responsibility for their own actions, that's all."

"Point all that out in a rebuttal letter, Sister. It can't hurt."

She shook her head. "No, I can't do that. It's just not our way. We follow in the footsteps of Our Lord, and fighting back like this isn't part of the package I signed up for," she said with a smile.

"Are you sure, Sister? I've got to go to press, and if you change your mind a few hours from now, it'll be too late."

"That's all right, but thanks for letting me know in advance." Sister Agatha remained seated, her fingers entwined around the rosary that hung from her rope belt.

Chuck smiled. "What's up, Sister? You've got something else on your mind."

"I could sure use a favor, Chuck, but you'd have to keep this to yourself for now. Is that okay?"

He grinned even wider. "Same deal? I get the story first?"

"If there is one, yes," Sister Agatha answered.

"Then shoot."

"I'd like you to use the *Chronicle*'s Internet connection to access the obit columns of an Amarillo, Texas, newspaper. I need whatever you can find on the death of Sergeant Michael McKay's father."

Chuck did a search for the last name McKay, and two showed up, but they were sisters in their late twenties who'd died in an automobile accident. As Chuck continued working time passed slowly. Sister Agatha had just begun wondering if McKay had made up the whole story about his father's death when Chuck suddenly let out a whoop.

"Got it! I decided to check into the archives for the name Michael McKay, and here's what I found," he said, pointing to the screen. "This account names him as the only surviving member of Henry McKay's immediate family. Deputy McKay's father didn't die last month, though. He passed on six years ago," Chuck said.

"Interesting," Sister Agatha muttered. "With Michael being the only close relative still alive, I doubt any legal issues over a will would have taken *that* long to resolve."

Sister Agatha sat back, considering what she'd learned. She'd have to give Tom the news soon, too, though he'd asked her to back off. Of course, Tom knew that obedience had never come easily to her.

"I better get going," she said, standing. Maybe she'd be graced with divine inspiration between here and the station. She had to find a way to tell Tom what she'd learned without starting World War III.

As she stepped outside, she spotted someone crouched down beside the Antichrysler. At the sound of the exit door, the woman looked up, and Sister Agatha immediately recognized Del Martinez's wife. She'd been letting the air out of the front tire. From what Sister Agatha could see, the rear tire on that side was already flat.

Sister Agatha kept a firm hand on Pax, who was straining at the leash, growling. Then, hearing a click behind her, she turned her head quickly and saw Chuck taking a photo with his cell phone.

Gloria Martinez stood up and glared at Sister Agatha. "Go ahead, let your dog attack. I'll sue, and it'll cost you plenty."

"I have no intention of turning the dog loose," Sister Agatha said, forcing Pax to sit quietly with a snap of the leash. "We forgive our enemies. It's what Our Lord asked us to do and one of the best ways we have to honor Him in our daily lives."

"I'm not so sainted, and I've got the sheriff on speed dial. Get away from Sister's car," Chuck ordered. "And you're on private property. If you don't leave right now, *I'll* press charges."

Sister Agatha placed a hand on Chuck's arm, holding him back, then looked back at Gloria. "*You* know the truth, Gloria. I didn't send your husband to jail—his own actions did. There was more than enough evidence to convict him, even without my testimony."

Sister Agatha saw the raw pain that flashed in Gloria's

eyes and gentled her tone as she continued. "You're hurting inside, and you want to strike out. I understand that. You're human. But you're only going to make things worse for Del and yourself this way. The last thing either of you needs is more bad publicity."

Gloria took a step back, tears running down her face, then ran to a sedan parked just down the street.

As Gloria's car sped away, Sister Agatha breathed a sigh of relief. "Thank God. That could have turned very nasty."

Chuck studied the flat tires. "At least she didn't damage the tires. The valve cores are still here on the ground, and all I have to do is screw them back in with the same kind of valve cap tool she used. I can get you rolling in fifteen minutes. I've got a small compressor in my car's emergency kit."

As he walked over to his car, Sister Agatha kept her hand on Pax's head. It wasn't for the dog's benefit as much as her own. Pax was calm now, but she wasn't. Petting the dog always soothed her and helped get her thinking back on track.

Chuck returned, parked his vehicle next to hers, screwed the cores back in with a special valve cap, then hooked up the compressor to a dashboard outlet. "I'm running the photo of Gloria Martinez letting the air out of your tire right next to her letter," he said, inflating the Antichrysler's tires.

"You don't have to do that."

"Sister, that's balanced news, and that's what I do as a reporter. No way I'm not running it."

She knew from his tone that she wouldn't dissuade him, so she didn't press the issue.

After the tires had been inflated, Sister Agatha slipped behind the wheel. "Thanks for your help, Chuck. Next time I'm in town I'll bring you some of Sister Clothilde's cookies," she promised.

"No way I'm turning that down!" he said with a twinkle in his eye.

Sister Agatha knew exactly what she had to do next. She had to go talk to Tom. Bracing herself, she called ahead to let him know she was coming.

Tom saw her arrive, and after one look at her, his expression changed and turned dour. He knew her visit wouldn't bring him news he'd welcome.

"My office, right?" he asked in a taut voice as she came up to him.

"I think you'll prefer it that way. Will it create any more problems with you-know-who?" She cocked her head toward the area where Fritz Albrecht had his desk.

"He's not around at the moment," Tom answered. "By the way, I spoke to the mayor a while ago. I told him that I was using you as an informant, and unless he wanted me to start paying you like we usually do with snitches, he shouldn't complain."

"Imagine, me, a snitch. How'd he take that?" Sister Agatha tried to suppress a grin.

"I don't know. He hung up on me." Tom led the way down the hall, then invited her in. "Let me guess," he said, taking a seat behind his desk. "You've done something I'm going to regret even more than dissing the mayor?"

"You may not like what I did," she admitted, "but you need to know what I found out." As she'd hoped, her words immediately caught his attention.

Tom sat up a little straighter and leaned forward, resting his elbows on the desk. "Go on."

She told him what she'd learned, then waited, sensing that he was more intrigued than angry now.

"It shouldn't surprise me that you didn't let this go," he said at last, then expelled his breath in a hiss. "McKay has a high-profile alibi for the time of the murder, Sister. He was playing a round of golf that morning, and in addition to the others in the foursome, the clubhouse staff was also able to verify his presence. McKay bought a three-hundred-dollar driver right before tee time."

"Where does the high-profile part come in?"

"One of the golfers in the foursome was State Senator Holman."

She sucked in her breath. Another promising lead had just gone up in smoke.

"If you insist on investigating McKay, make darned sure he doesn't catch you snooping around, Sister Agatha. He's currently seeing an anger management counselor—a requirement after a nasty incident. Michael might come across as overly polite and calm these days, but that's only because he wants the counseling sessions to end. Believe me, you never want to see the other side of him. We're also looking into a departmental issue that concerns him, but that's something I absolutely can't discuss further."

Sister Agatha was about to speak when Tom's phone rang. He listened for a bit, then said, "I'm going to put you on the speakerphone, Chuck."

"I wanted you to know that a private citizen visiting the *Chronicle*'s office had her car vandalized by Mrs. Gloria Martinez. She said it was payback from Del Martinez, her husband. I'm calling because I wondered if Martinez's parole officer should be notified about this."

"Who was the citizen?" Tom's gaze fastened on Sister Agatha; he already suspected the answer.

"Is that necessary?" Chuck asked.

"Yes," Tom said firmly.

"It was Sister Agatha from Our Lady of Hope, and the vehicle involved was the monastery station wagon."

Tom glared at Sister Agatha, and the temperature in the room suddenly seemed to drop fifty degrees. "Okay. I'll handle it from here. Thanks for letting me know, Chuck." He switched off the speaker and took a deep, slow breath. "Want to tell me what that was all about, Sister?"

"It was no big deal," Sister Agatha said. She quickly filled him in. "The woman's in pain, Tom, and going a little crazy, that's all."

"I'll have a deputy go talk to Del. His family situation shouldn't spill over onto the nuns. He's got to stop passing blame and learn to handle his own messes."

As she stood up to go, he placed a hand on her arm. "Do yourself a favor and stay away from Sergeant McKay, Sister. Like I said, there's a lot going on with him right now. Let me handle that myself."

"Okay," she agreed. "Actually, I think that we've been going around this the wrong way. From now on I'm going to focus on finding out who the *other* man was, the guy who handed the deputy the envelope."

"That could be just about anyone. How do you plan to narrow down the suspect list?"

"Judging solely from Sister Jo's description, I think it's the same man who's been targeting me."

"You didn't have much of a description for me right after the incidents occurred, but now that you're calmer, do you want to go through some mug shots?"

She nodded. "It may not help, but it can't hurt, as they say. I have to go pick up Sister Jo at St. Charles. Okay if I bring her back here and we both look? She saw the two men on Calle de Elena."

"Excellent idea."

A half hour later, both nuns were seated at one of the desks in the station, leafing through books filled with photos. They examined every face carefully, but after a while, the sea of men became one giant blur.

Sister Jo gave Sister Agatha a look filled with desperation. "This is hopeless."

Sister Agatha leaned back in her seat, feeling dejected. "I was hoping a face would jump out at us—that a part of our memory had retained something we weren't even aware of. It doesn't look like that's going to happen."

Tom came in and knew at a glance that their efforts had been fruitless. "You've been trying hard to force it. Let it go for now."

"Maybe the man we're looking for doesn't have a record—at least not yet," Sister Jo said.

Sister Agatha glanced up at Tom quickly. "We could be looking in the wrong direction. Maybe we should be concentrating on a regular member of the community—one who has a lot to lose. What Sister Jo saw may have been a blackmail payoff, not a bribe."

"The problem with that theory is that instead of narrowing down the field, it widens it to every white male in the county."

"I know," Sister Agatha answered softly.

They left the station a short time later. As they reached the station wagon, Sister Agatha looked at her watch. "If we go back right now, we'll make Vespers. I need the quiet of the chapel and time to pray, so let's head home."

Sister Jo nodded and smiled. "Do you think Tzuriel will come see us again? Sister Ignatius has told me all about him."

Sister Agatha gave her a surprised look. "Do you really believe in our angel?" she asked, curious to know how the newcomer perceived the story.

"I know what I saw after Compline that night in chapel," she said, nodding. "People these days are taught that it's only real if you can feel it or touch it, but Our Lord taught us differently."

Sister Agatha looked at her and nodded, lost in thought. Pondering Sister Jo's words, they headed home to the monastery.

Though it was the middle of the night, Sister Agatha remained in chapel, deep in prayer. She wasn't sure what to do next and desperately needed guidance.

As she looked up toward the altar, she saw the flicker of a shadow on the wall to her right. Trying, and hoping, to see the form of an angel, she stared at it hard, but nothing happened. It was only the play of light from the candles.

Frustration bit into her. Giving up, at least for tonight, she rose to her feet. She'd tried so hard to make things happen!

Her own words replayed themselves in her mind, and, horrified, she realized what she'd been trying to do. She had no power to *force* anything. What on earth had she been thinking? Servants obeyed, they didn't issue orders or make demands, and she was a servant of God. As the knowledge of what she'd done cut through her weariness, she prayed for forgiveness.

Minutes passed, and slowly she began to see things from a new perspective. All this time she'd been trying to get answers through sheer willpower, just as she'd tried to make the play of light and shadow coalesce into angel form—but mysteries weren't solved by following preconceived notions.

As she let go of her old opinions, a new idea formed at the back of her mind. Everything she'd learned so far indicated that the suspect was hiding in the community. If she was going to find him, that's exactly where she'd have to look.

Thanking the Lord, she walked out of chapel noiselessly and went to her room. It was time to rest.

19

FTER MORNING PRAYERS, SISTER AGATHA SET OUT with Sister Jo and Pax in the Antichrysler. Sister de Lourdes and Sister Bernarda would be helping get the lunch meals ready today. A parishioner from St. Augustine's would come by to help them make the deliveries if the station wagon wasn't back in time.

"You and I are going to do something completely different this morning. We'll start by walking around the town hall and looking at the faces of people there—men, actually. Let's see if we can find anyone of interest," Sister Agatha said. "If we do, be careful to avoid looking surprised."

"I get you. I'll just smile at everyone. You think we're dealing with political corruption of some kind?"

"People of influence usually have many secrets."

Sister Jo nodded thoughtfully. "Like Peter Aragon, the

council member who lost some of his support when the church got the Good News Meal Program. But he's not our man. I remember seeing his photo and the former program director's in the St. Augustine Church bulletin."

A half hour later, they were inside the two-story city hall, walking down corridors and glancing in doorways. Many people said a quick hello. Others offered to help them find whatever office they were looking for. After about twenty minutes, and two passes around the pink adobe territorial-style building, they walked back outside.

"I'm sorry, Sister Agatha, but I didn't see anyone I recognized. All those people were strangers to me, but then again, I'm still new to the area."

"Don't feel bad. Most of them were strangers to me, too," Sister Agatha admitted. "I have very few friends in high places—well, except for the Highest Place," she said, pointing up.

As they sat together in one of the *bancos* on the front patio, Sister Agatha struggled not to let her discouragement show. She'd been so sure that they were on the right track.

Sister Jo reached down to pet Pax, her gaze wandering around aimlessly. "Now, *he* looks familiar, but I've never met him before—not that I remember, anyway," she said.

Sister Agatha, immediately alert, glanced around. "Who are you talking about?"

Sister Jo pointed at a billboard across the street. It showed real estate developer and state senator Dwight Holman. The billboard was preelection, at least five months old, and was starting to peel around the edges, but the man's face was clear.

"It's possible you saw him at our monastery," Sister Agatha said and reminded her of his visit. Then, after a beat, she added, "Let's go to the *Chronicle*."

Sister Jo followed, smiling and nodding to everyone who passed them on the grounds and in the parking lot.

"You're always so happy," Sister Agatha said with a smile of her own.

"What's not to be happy about? I'm doing the work I love, and today I even get to hang out with you and Pax."

"You like hanging out with Pax and me?" Sister Agatha asked, surprised.

"Sure! Exciting things always happen around you two, Sister Agatha."

Sister Agatha had to admit she enjoyed being with Sister Jo, too. It was a blessing to be with someone who made the most out of every moment. She had no doubt that Sister Jo was very close to the Lord's heart.

"Are we going to look at more photos?" Sister Jo asked.

"Yes, but only of Senator Holman. Maybe there's a photo on file that'll show him wearing a cap, like the man you saw with the deputy."

Sister Jo's usual smile turned to a worried frown. "What if I still can't confirm that he was the one with the deputy?"

"No matter what happens, the problem's in God's hands, and we'll trust Him to handle everything in the right way."

"Then let's go for it, Sister Agatha!"

As they drove into a parking slot outside the *Chronicle*'s only building, she remembered that she'd promised Chuck some of Sister Clothilde's cookies. "Rats! I totally forgot," she said, then explained. "Remind me to bring him some next time, Sister Jo."

"I have two cookies inside my pocket. They're still wrapped up in a napkin," Sister Jo confessed, pulling them out.

Sister Agatha looked at her, surprised. "How did you get those? They look a bit like Sister Clothilde's new recipe."

"They are, but this version of Miraculous Munchies has piñons and less powdered sugar," she answered. "I work a lot in the kitchen helping prepare the lunch meals. Since I'm already there, Sister Clothilde has designated me as her official taster."

Sister Agatha smiled, knowing that was just like Sister Clothilde—rewarding any of them who went that extra mile. "Would you mind giving those to Chuck?"

"Not at all," Sister Jo answered. "I'm sure they're wonderful. Sister's cookies always are."

A moment later, Chuck greeted them as they came through the door. "Hey, Sisters. What brings you here so early in the morning?"

"Early?" Sister Agatha checked her watch. "It's a little after nine."

He took a sip of his coffee and gave them a bleary-eyed look. "Sister, I'm usually here well past midnight every day. Anything before 11:00 A.M. is early." He offered them coffee. Then, as he took the cookies from them, his eyes brightened considerably. "Thanks!"

Seeing that he was in a far better mood now, Sister Agatha continued. "Chuck, we need to do a computer search on Dwight Holman. Can you help us?"

"Ah, Holman. I recall our most recent article on the freshman senator," he said. "It was a delicate issue. About a month ago, Holman rear-ended another vehicle, and there was a fatality. We had to be real careful not to print anything that couldn't be verified outright. Holman's a close friend of the mayor and could have brought some serious pressure down on us—more than a small press like ours could take."

"I don't remember hearing about that accident," Sister

Agatha said, "but then again, we don't subscribe to any of the local papers, and we don't have a television."

"We were the only news outlet that carried the story. That's what made it even more interesting to me." They all huddled around Chuck's new computer as he called up the information. "Here's the story," he said, pointing to the screen. "Holman's sedan rear-ended another car that had slowed down because of poor visibility. At the time it had been raining hard. The other driver, Beatriz Griego, a Mexican national and legal resident of the United States, died."

They stared at the photo of the damaged cars, plus one of the victim and another of Holman. "That could be him," Sister Jo said at last, "but I'd need to see him in person wearing a cap to be sure."

Sister Agatha looked over Chuck's shoulder, reading the article. "I see Holman was cited for following too close."

"That's all he got, too. The passenger in Griego's car wasn't injured and gave the police a statement releasing Holman from any culpability. She claimed that Griego had nearly come to a stop in the lane because she'd been distracted talking on her cell phone, and that's why Holman's vehicle had struck them."

"You don't buy it?" Sister Agatha asked, reading him accurately.

"I really dug deep on this story, and there were things that didn't fit. For one, according to other drivers I've spoken to, the rain in the area wasn't that bad. And it was only four in the afternoon, not after dark, so visibility couldn't have been that low. The whole thing has a stink to it, but I've never been able to prove anything."

"Sounds like someone worked hard to hush things up quickly," Sister Agatha said.

"I searched the Web sites of the area newspapers and the local television stations, too, but they barely mentioned the accident," Chuck said.

"Do you have the name of the officer who responded to the call?" Sister Agatha asked.

He opened another screen on his computer, then answered her. "Sergeant Michael McKay."

Sister Agatha considered everything she'd just learned. Holman . . . and McKay? She remembered the sheriff telling her that during the time of Jane Sanchez's murder, McKay had supposedly been playing golf with Holman. Maybe she'd just found the connection.

"He didn't show up for court, so the case was thrown out," Chuck added.

"I'm assuming they did a Breathalyzer test at the accident scene, particularly since it resulted in a death, is that right?" Sister Agatha asked.

"No. A field sobriety test was conducted, but there was no Breathalyzer on record. Sheriff Green was really upset about that, but by the time he found out, it was too late. McKay was suspended for a week without pay for not following protocol, and Holman got ticketed for following too close. That was it."

"There was no lawsuit?" Sister Jo asked. "Everybody sues nowadays, and after all, Holman did get a ticket for a traffic violation."

Chuck shook his head. "Lawsuits are public record, and I haven't seen a thing. The victim didn't have any close relatives in the area, apparently, or maybe they were paid off under the table."

It didn't surprise her that Tom hadn't mentioned any of it.

He prided himself on his department. Things like this rarely happened, but when they did, he usually clamped down on everything and everyone.

What had come as a shock was hearing that McKay had gotten off with only a brief suspension. That just didn't sound like something Tom would do. Maybe he was still following up on it, and that was the reason he'd wanted her to back off.

"I'd like to talk to the passenger in the victim's car. Do you have her name?" Sister Agatha asked.

"Carmen Morales. I tracked her down, but to be honest I didn't have much luck questioning her. Her English is pretty spotty."

"I can help. I was born Angela Montoya and raised in a Las Cruces household that spoke Spanish nearly as much as English," Sister Jo said.

"Tell me where I can find Carmen," Sister Agatha added, glancing at Chuck.

"I don't know where she lives, but I do know she works for Katherine Brown."

"The architect?"

"Yes. Katherine has an office adjacent to her home, so once you look up her office in the phone book, you'll have both addresses."

Thanking Chuck, Sister Agatha got ready to leave, and Sister Jo followed. Soon they arrived at a large pueblo-style home. From what she could see, there was a detached smaller studio at the back of the driveway. The sign over the door announced it as Brown Architectural.

"Do we talk to the owner first," Sister Jo asked, "or go to the house and try to find Carmen?"

"Judging by the three high-end cars parked by the studio,

my guess is that Katherine's with clients. Let's go to the main house and see if Carmen answers the door."

Sister Agatha parked by the side, well away from the studio, and then led the way up to the front door. The doorbell had a pretty tone, like distant church bells.

A moment later, a young Hispanic woman opened the door. Before Sister Agatha could say a word, she gasped, dropped a feather duster, and ran toward the back of the house.

"Go around! Stop her at the back door," Sister Agatha called out to Sister Jo.

As Sister Agatha hurried inside after Carmen, she held on tightly to Pax, who at the moment wasn't sure if this was a game or not. The race was short, and Sister Agatha managed to corner Carmen in the kitchen. Beyond, she could see Sister Jo standing outside the door.

"Why on earth are you running? I mean you no harm," Sister Agatha said gently.

"*Déjame!*" She said, recoiling from her and Pax. "*No sé nada.*"

Sister Agatha's Spanish was rusty, but she caught that much. *Déjame* was "leave me alone," and *no sé nada* meant "I don't know anything." The fact that Carmen had run and felt compelled to say that told her a much different story.

Ordering Pax to sit and stay, she softened her voice even more and continued. "*Estás en este país legalmente?*" Sister Agatha said, asking if Carmen was in the country legally.

Carmen's eyes widened, but she said nothing.

"Relax," Sister Agatha said quietly. "I'm not Immigration. *Soy monja, una hermana. No inmigra,*" she added, telling Carmen that she wasn't part of the border patrol, that she was simply a nun—she hoped. Sadly, her accent and command of the language were so bad, she wasn't one hundred percent sure whether she'd said she was a nun or all wet. She never could remember the difference between *monja* and *mojada*.

The woman's eyes narrowed with distrust. "He say that *inmigra* come dressed like nun," she said, pointing. "Like *you*."

"No, I really *am* a nun," Sister Agatha said calmly. "*No tengas miercoles,*" she said and saw the woman's puzzled face.

"You just told her not to have Wednesdays," Sister Jo said, stepping inside the room. "*No tengas miedo,*" she said, "*that* means don't be afraid."

"He said you would come dressed like nun to fool me—and send me back," Carmen said.

"I'm *not* part of Immigration," Sister Agatha repeated firmly. "Who told you that crazy story?"

"The *policía*. He say if I talk to anyone I go to jail—then back to Mexico."

"Which deputy told you that?" Sister Agatha asked.

Seeing her hesitate, Sister Agatha lowered her voice and met her gaze. "Won't you help me? If you do, I promise to pray for you—that *you* might receive a blessing, too."

"And if I say no?" she asked.

"I can't force you to do anything. If you won't help, then we'll leave."

She nodded slowly, fear slowly melting away from her features. "I help. The deputy was Mac Cai," she said, pronouncing it carefully.

Sister Agatha wasn't surprised. "Tell me what happened the day of the accident."

The woman took a deep, shuddering breath. "Beatriz gave me ride because it rain, but wipers not work so good in her car. Then bam! I use seat belt, but Beatriz . . ." She shook her head, and a silent tear ran down her face. "I no can help. The steering wheel . . . her face. Then policeman come."

"McKay was the officer who arrived first?" Sister Agatha pressed.

"No. First officer *más joven* . . . young, and not tall. He help me to his car and put me in backseat. Then Mac Cai come. He talked to Señor Holman. Very soft. I couldn't hear. Then Mac Cai helped Señor Holman into the front seat of his police car."

"You mean the backseat," Sister Agatha corrected. The rear seat of a police cruiser had no door handles and no way for a suspect to get out.

"No. Front," she insisted.

"Before putting him in the car, did the deputy make him walk a straight line, or touch the tip of his nose?" Sister Agatha asked, demonstrating.

Carmen shook her head. "No. He just put him in car . . . and they shake hands."

Like friends, Sister Agatha mused silently.

"Mr. Holman no walk very good. Had too many *cervezas* that day," Carmen added quietly.

"Beers," Sister Jo translated.

"That one, I got," Sister Agatha said, then looked at Carmen. "And you signed a statement, right?"

"*Sí*, but my English not so good. Mac Cai wrote and said to me just sign. He said keep my mouth shut."

Sister Jo glanced at Sister Agatha. "I don't get any of this. Why would Sergeant McKay tell her that Immigration would come for her masquerading as a nun?"

"McKay must have known that I'd become a threat to him if I found out about this. And he was right. Now that I have, I'm not letting this go." Sister Agatha turned to Carmen once more.

"*When* did McKay tell you to be careful about speaking to nuns?"

"He come to my apartment. Yesterday at night."

Sister Agatha nodded pensively. At long last they were on the right track.

20

BEFORE SISTER AGATHA COULD SAY ANYTHING ELSE, A woman came through the back door. Sister Agatha recognized Katherine Brown from her photo in the yellow pages.

"Hello, Sisters," she said with a smile. "I saw your monastery's famous wheels outside. If you wanted a donation, you should have gone straight to my office."

"You were with clients, and actually I wanted to talk to your housekeeper," Sister Agatha said, shaking her hand.

Katherine glanced over at Carmen, then reached into her pants pocket and brought out several bills. "Here you go, Carmen," she said. "Thanks."

The young woman muttered a quick "*Gracias,*" then hurried out the front door, where a sedan was waiting for her. Within seconds, the car disappeared from view.

"Something must have upset Carmen. She forgot to schedule

a time to come next week. What did you say to her?" she demanded, glaring at Sister Agatha.

"Did you know she's in this country illegally?"

"How would I know something like that?" Katherine countered smoothly.

"Do you always pay your employees in cash?" Sister Agatha countered.

"She prefers it that way." Katherine stood at the window, looking out at her driveway. "I wonder if I've just lost my housekeeper," she added with a sigh.

"Do you know about the accident she had?"

"It couldn't have been her fault. She was just a passenger," Katherine answered flatly.

"Would you give me Carmen's phone number in case I need to talk to her again later?" Sister Agatha asked.

"I don't have it, and no address either. Beatriz, God rest her soul, recommended Carmen to me and handled all the arrangements—until the accident. All I know about Carmen is that she's reliable and incredibly honest. She even returns quarters she finds between the sofa cushions."

Sister Agatha held her gaze. She had a feeling Katherine was telling her the truth. "If you see Carmen again, will you let me know?"

Katherine exhaled softly. "She won't be back. People like Carmen survive by staying under the radar. If somebody shows too much interest in them, they disappear like puffs of smoke and reinvent themselves elsewhere."

"Thanks," Sister Agatha said.

They were back inside the Antichrysler when Sister Jo's stomach suddenly growled loudly. Sister Agatha laughed. "Thanks for the reminder. It's time for us to head home and get something to eat. Afterward, you and Sister Bernarda can use this vehicle to make the lunch deliveries."

A short time later, driving the Harley, Sister Agatha was back on the road, knowing there was still a lot of work to be done. Pax, as usual, was in the sidecar.

Sister Agatha went directly to the sheriff's station and walked inside with Pax at heel beside her. The mayor's aide was seated at a desk in the bullpen, but he was engrossed in a conversation with a deputy and didn't see her come in.

Sister Agatha continued to Tom's office and knocked on his open door.

He glanced up from his computer keyboard, a look of pure relief spreading over his features.

Sister Agatha gave him a bemused smile. "That must be some report you're working on if you're this eager for an interruption."

He laughed. "You have no idea. I've spent the better part of the morning nitpicking details and sorting through bureaucratic jargon. This is, no doubt, the mayor's revenge for my latest act of defiance." Tom leaned back and studied her. "What have you got for me?"

She closed his office door and took a seat. As she told him what she'd uncovered concerning Holman's car accident, his expression grew somber. "So what do you think?" she asked at last.

"Our chances of finding Carmen now are slim to none. My guess is she's already left town. But I've been working on something else that may pay off." He met her gaze and held it. "What I'm about to tell you doesn't leave this office, clear? The mayor is tight with Holman, and I don't want this coming back at me or you."

"No problem."

"I've had an internal investigation under way for several weeks now—long before the murder. I have reason to believe that we have a dirty cop in the department, one with a strong political ally. That's why I've been moving slow. If this department makes enemies among the powers that be, our budget will be one of the first things to go south. So we've been watching our step at the same time we've been gathering evidence. Gerry Bennett was working on this with me, doing a lot of the field interviews."

"Does your investigation involve State Senator Holman?" she asked.

He nodded. "Holman must have heard my footsteps coming up behind him. Word is, he's hired himself an attorney—Mike Langley."

Sister Agatha's eyebrows rose. Langley was a top defense attorney known for skillfully manipulating juries.

"Langley's been around since your journalism days, so I know you've heard of him," he said. "As for Holman, he's built a solid power base by handing out favors whenever he can. When the county tried to condemn a strip of land at the south end of town to build a new bridge, he immediately went to bat for the residents. The project was dropped, and Holman made a lot of friends in the process, including a few really big developers. In my opinion, plays like that keep him in power.

"On the other hand, a negligent homicide charge, especially with a DWI conviction, would destroy his political career. It would also cost him the backing of powerful people like Mayor Garcia, who's very sensitive to public opinion." In a hard voice, he added, "If my officers at the scene hadn't dropped the ball, Holman would have been hung up to dry."

214

Silence stretched out between them. At long last, Sister Agatha spoke. "We've known each other too long for secrets. There's something else bugging you. I can see it on your face."

He rubbed the back of his neck with one hand. "McKay saved Holman's butt by taking over Bennett's field investigation of the accident—then making sure any additional charges were dropped by not showing up in court. That led me to suspect McKay was dirty. Since Gerry already knew some of what went on that day between his sergeant and Senator Holman, I recruited him to help gather evidence to make an internal affairs case against McKay. Then, as you know, not long afterward we started finding indications—but no proof—that Bennett's responsible for Jane Sanchez's death. It looks like McKay found out what we were doing and went on the offensive to discredit our IA investigation by placing a cloud over Bennett. The problem is that I can't prove any of this, and meanwhile the circumstantial evidence against Gerry keeps piling up."

"Could Bennett explain how unit 73 turned up on Calle de Elena at a time he claims he was elsewhere?"

"He says Sister Jo was either tricked or mistaken. Gerry also swears he's never owned a .22 pistol, though he does have a single-shot rifle of that caliber." Tom paused, then added, "One more interesting thing. McKay was assigned to our K-9 unit when he first joined the department. Though he never worked with Pax, he knows how to deal with an attacking dog. If he was the one who threatened Sister Jo that night, he would have known to wear padding or protection on his arm."

Sister Agatha left the station deep in thought. The suspect list wasn't long—Bennett, McKay, and Holman. Yet instinct told her that she was still missing something—and what she didn't know could end up ruining careers, or maybe costing someone's life.

As she and Pax walked to the Harley, Chuck jogged out of the department doors and hurried to meet them.

"Hey, Sister Agatha. Hey, Pax." Without waiting for an invitation, he scrambled into the sidecar beside Pax. "Sister Agatha, let me ride along with you today. I know you're on the trail of a story. Don't worry, I won't print anything until you give me the go-ahead."

"You're going to be disappointed, Chuck. All I'm doing next is stopping by Smitty's to pick up some things for the monastery. You may have to hold the groceries."

"Just let me tag along. Things happen around you."

She laughed. "Okay, but put on the spare helmet." As a former reporter, she understood that it was always better to be in on a story than to just repeat the news secondhand later. "Maybe we'll do more than shop for groceries," she added, thinking she owed him.

Chuck grinned widely. "So what have you got?"

His enthusiasm was unbounded, and Sister Agatha smiled at him. "Okay, off the record?" Once he nodded, she continued. "What I've got is mostly speculation, nothing solid. That's the problem. I believe Sergeant McKay has been creating and manipulating the existing evidence from the start, hoping to help himself and a politician friend of his. Bribery and payoffs probably figure into this as well. If I'm right about McKay, he's the one who took a photo of me inside Smitty's and used it to threaten the monastery. There's no video available of that day, but I thought I'd ask Smitty which officers stop by regularly and see if McKay's name comes up."

"Smitty's new coffee bar is really popular these days, so he might not be able to be that specific. I'll talk to the clerks, and then we can compare lists."

When they arrived at Smitty's, they found that Chuck's

prediction had been right on target. Too many officers, includ-ing McKay, frequented the coffee bar. Even Tom himself came by once or twice a day.

As they left the supermarket, Chuck's pager went off. He di-aled a number on his cell phone quickly, then spoke in a hurried voice.

Sister Agatha waited, her gaze meandering around the park-ing lot as she tried to figure out her next step. That's when she spotted a truck parked two slots away with a large magnetic sign attached to the driver's side door. What surprised her most was how snugly the sign fit—like a second skin. There was barely an outline, and she was almost sure that from a distance no one would have ever realized it wasn't painted on. As she studied the business telephone number listed on it, another idea occurred to her.

Sister Jo had been sure that she'd seen the number 73 on the deputy's car that day on Calle de Elena—but what if the en-tire incident had been engineered to mislead them? The deputy could have stuck a magnetic sign with the number 73 over the painted number, hoping to pass it off as Bennett's cruiser. Then he made the fake call asking for a Good News lunch delivery. He'd known that the phony address would guarantee that the nun making the delivery would pass right by the car.

Excitement began pounding through her. At that instant, her own cell phone rang. It was Sister Jo.

"I was called to substitute at St. Charles this afternoon and got a ride into town with Father Rick. Now I need a ride back, and Sister Bernarda said I should call you."

"I'm not far from St. Charles. I'll come by and get you."

Chuck joined her again. "Sister, that call I just got was from a source of mine. Deputies have arrested a couple of kids for tag-ging the gym at St. Charles with gang symbols. I'll need to take photos."

"I have to go over there and pick up Sister Jo. Do you want a ride?"

"You bet! Pedal to the metal, Sister Agatha."

"Chuck, you just love riding in this Harley, even at highway speeds, don't you?"

"Yeah, actually. My parents refused to let me have a cycle when I was growing up, and later on it seemed impractical, but it's a lot of fun."

At the school, they saw that the gym had become an advertising poster for an area youth gang. Sister Agatha saw two sheriff's department units parked next to the main building, and there was a prisoner in the backseat of each squad car. The boys were high school age, judging from their size, but she didn't recognize either one.

"See you," Chuck said, taking off his helmet. Getting out quickly, digital camera in hand, he jogged in the direction of the tagged wall.

Sister Agatha didn't give the teens in the vehicles more than a passing glance. She was more interested in the squad cars themselves. She took time to study the height and style of the painted numbers and to confirm their shade of brown, approximately the color of a dead cottonwood leaf, and the white color of the vehicle itself, only a shade darker than the white on her habit. Her thoughts still on the magnetic sign she'd seen outside Smitty's, she hurried inside and found Sister Jo near the main office.

"I need to ask you something," Sister Agatha said without preamble. She told Sister Jo about the magnetic sign and how simple it would have been to apply and remove. "Is it possible that the number 73 you saw wasn't part of the squad car, but rather a magnetic sign overlaid on it?"

Sister Jo considered it for a long time before answering. "I suppose it is. I just took a quick glance, really. At the time, I was looking for a nonexistent house number and not thinking much about anything else."

Sister Agatha nodded. "I suspected as much," she said, leading the way to St. Charles's main office. "We aren't going back to the monastery just yet. There's something else we need to do first."

Borrowing a telephone book from the secretary, Sister Agatha looked in the yellow pages for places that specialized in magnetic signs. Ruling out companies that specialized in billboards or custom-carved signs, she focused on the smaller shops that offered one-day service.

At long last, she found a store in Albuquerque's North Valley that made vehicle magnetic signs exclusively. They assured her they could make numbers as large or small as the client demanded, with hundreds of styles to choose from. Sister Agatha got directions to the shop and hung up.

"The shop I want is in Albuquerque," Sister Agatha told Sister Jo, "maybe thirty minutes from here. We'll go there right after we stop by the *Chronicle* and pick up some newspaper photos of McKay and Bennett."

"You're after the man who tried to drown me, aren't you?" Sister Jo asked, her voice trembling slightly. "Do you think he was the same deputy I saw with Holman?"

"I think so, but don't worry," Sister Agatha said gently. "Our goal is only to find out who he is, not to confront him."

"I'll help you as much as I can," Sister Jo said, taking a deep breath. "That man may have also killed Mrs. Sanchez and shouldn't be walking around free."

"Experience tells me one thing," Sister Agatha answered. "Although the face of evil can disguise itself—and often does—that blackness of the soul always comes to the surface and gives itself away."

ONCE OUTSIDE, SISTER AGATHA LOOKED AROUND, FOUND Chuck, then went to join him.

"Hey, Sister! I need a ride back to the *Chronicle*. Can you drop me off?"

"Funny thing—I was planning to go there next. I need your help finding some photos."

"Get me back there so I can write up this story in time for tomorrow's edition, and you've got yourself a deal."

"You'll have to get on behind me," she said. "Sister Jo will ride in the sidecar with Pax because of her habit. It'll avoid complications."

Twenty minutes after dropping off Chuck and gathering the photos, they arrived at Sign by Design. The business was in a residential area that had been rezoned during the sixties or seventies and ran alongside a major street. The shop itself was a work area inside a single-car detached garage.

As Sister Agatha stepped in with Pax, Sister Jo right behind her, a bell above the door rang.

"How may I help you, Sisters?" the man asked.

Sister Agatha kept Pax close beside her, but the man didn't seem bothered by him. "We were hoping you could talk to us about magnetic signs—small ones listing only two-digit numbers," she added tentatively to see how he would react.

"Like a car designation for a business fleet? I did one of those for a private business recently."

"For whom? Do you mind if I ask? I'd like to see a sample of your work."

"I didn't get a name, or even his company name. He came in, paid cash, and left."

"And you said it was a two-digit number?" Sister Agatha verified.

He nodded. "Seventy-three, if I remember right. Is that the type of sign you're interested in?"

"If it was medium brown lettering on white, I really need to find the person you made the sign for. Will you help us? I wouldn't be asking if it wasn't very important," she added, looking directly at him.

He considered it briefly. "I'll help you. Fact is, I didn't much like him—and I'm partial to nuns. My sister and I both attended St. Pius," he added with a twinkle in his eye. "Like I said, though, I didn't get his name."

"Would you recognize his photo?" Sister Agatha asked.

"He was wearing sunglasses and a cap, but maybe I could."

She brought out photos of Gerry Bennett and Michael McKay. "Do either of these men look familiar?" Chuck had cropped the photos so only their faces showed. She hadn't wanted the shop owner to see that they were sheriff's deputies.

"Both do, since they look so much alike, but I think he's the one," he said, pointing to one of the photos.

Realizing she was now looking at the probable killer, she didn't know whether to be sad or happy. "You sure? Was he short or tall?"

"More toward the tall side. My memory's pretty good when it comes to faces. If I saw him in person again, I'd recognize him for sure."

"And the number he wanted was 73, brown on a small white background, the letters being about five inches high?" Sister Agatha asked.

"That's it, except the letters were five and a half inches tall, to be precise. I was hoping he'd come back for other numbers, maybe 1 to 72, but I never saw him again."

"Thanks very much," Sister Agatha said.

"Where to now?" Sister Jo asked as they walked back to the motorcycle and sidecar.

"Back home to the monastery," Sister Agatha answered. "I need some peace and quiet so I can think things through."

Sister Jo leaned forward in the sidecar to pet Pax, who was sitting on the floor, his head around the side of the small windscreen so he could watch where they were going. It was a cozy fit.

"If the sign maker's right, that means the killer's a law enforcement officer. He probably knows exactly how to cover his tracks." Sister Jo shouted to be heard through their helmets and the rush of the wind. "Maybe he'll keep coming after you or me until he finishes the job."

Sister Agatha's heart went out to the young nun. Stopping by the side of the road, she removed her helmet. "Remember that story in the Bible when Elisha's servant was scared that they'd be defeated? Too many stood against them. Elisha assured him that they weren't in danger despite the way things seemed to be. Then Elisha prayed, and his servant suddenly saw chariots of fire all around them," she said. "God *never* abandons His own."

"I wish my faith was like yours—unshakable."

Sister Agatha blinked in surprise. "You're giving me way too much credit," she said softly. "We all have what St. John of the Cross called 'dark nights of the soul.' During those times we can practically feel ourselves slipping away from God." She was remembering her struggle with guilt and her feelings of inadequacy. "But He always calls us back. That's when we realize that although we left Him, He never left us."

"Sometimes God doesn't answer prayers, though."

"You mean requests. He always answers prayers, but sometimes we're so intent on the answer we want, we miss the other possibilities He brings our way."

Soon they were on their way again. At the lumber store, Sister Agatha pulled in and parked. "We could really use a donation of lumber and materials to build our well house. I'm going to see if I can talk to the owner. We have the new pump, but we need to enclose it before bad weather arrives."

Emilio Rodriguez was behind the counter talking to a yard worker in a hard hat when he saw them come in. "Sisters," he greeted them, waving.

Sister Agatha knew Emilio well. He'd come from Cuba and had worked hard to build his own business here in Bernalillo.

"What can I do for you today, Sisters?"

"Mr. Rodriguez, we could use some lumber to construct a small well house," Sister Agatha said. "Do you have any you could spare? We'd be happy to keep you in our prayers in return for your generosity."

"I'd be happy to help you, Sister," he said with a nod. "You'll need two-by-sixes for framing. You don't want low-grade lumber for something like that. You'll need to make sure you protect that well." He added, "You'll also be needing flooring and roofing, Sisters. I can't afford to give those away, but I'd be happy to let you make small payments if you'd like."

An elderly woman who'd been sitting at a desk at the back of the room came up to join them. "*Que quieren, mijo?*"

Sister Jo smiled. "Just some wood—*madera*," she added.

Emilio looked at her. "You speak Spanish?"

She nodded. "Since I was a kid. That's why the Church had me working at Catholic Charities in Santa Fe, teaching English to new immigrants."

Emilio's eyes lit up. "Sisters, I've got a proposition for you. If Sister Jo helps my mother with English, I'll give you everything you need for your well house free of charge, including the roofing and flooring. Just bring me your construction plans and we'll go from there."

"I'd enjoy teaching her English," Sister Jo said, nodding eagerly, looking at Sister Agatha. "I can help the monastery build the well house, too. I took shop and architectural drawing back in high school. I'm a very good carpenter."

Sister Agatha looked back at Emilio. "It's up to Reverend Mother, of course, but I think she'll be pleased with this arrangement."

"Great!" Emilio said.

"I can whip up a design for the well house in a couple of hours using one of the programs we already have in the scriptorium," Sister Jo added.

"Fax me the design, and I'll deliver everything to the monastery tomorrow," Emilio said, shaking both their hands. He then introduced Sister Jo to Marisol, his mother.

Sister Jo's friendliness immediately put Marisol at ease, and they began chatting in Spanish.

Sister Agatha waited, Pax at her side, then signaled Sister Jo when it was time to leave.

The next day, shortly after Morning Prayers, Sister Agatha went to the parlor. Since Sister Bernarda hadn't arrived, Sister Agatha unlocked the doors, then went to the desk to call the sheriff.

Sister Agatha told Tom what she'd done yesterday afternoon at the sign shop. "The sign maker was pretty sure of his ID. McKay is now your best suspect."

"Suspect, yes, but what you've got doesn't prove murder—or establish a motive. All it proves is that he had a sign made up, *if* the proprietor picked the right man."

"When you're ready, you can have him make the ID in person. I'm sure McKay will try to cook up an excuse for the sign, but it's going to be tough. Why would he want a squad-car-sized sign with the number 73 on it, using the colors and configuration of a department vehicle?"

"I'm sure he'll come up with a plausible reason. For instance, he could say he was planning on playing a practical joke on Bennett."

She swallowed her frustration and forced herself to stay on track. "Have you found out anything new about the pistol?"

"That points more in McKay's direction, but it isn't enough to stand on its own. The lab managed to lift several numbers, and those they did get are consistent with a pistol McKay bought years ago. The problem is that the last three digits couldn't be identified, so McKay's pistol is only one of a thousand possibilities."

"How about those memo pads recovered from the trash bin? Any impressions recovered?" she asked.

"Not a one."

"Jane's the key," she said in a soft, thoughtful tone. "We know that she was more or less stalking Gerry during her lunch hour."

"Yeah, but how does that tie in with McKay?" he asked.

Sister Agatha said nothing for a few seconds, her thoughts racing. "What if she saw another deputy she initially thought was Gerry, caught him doing something that may have been incriminating, then realized she had the wrong man? She wouldn't have necessarily known what to do then. That could explain why she wanted to talk to me."

"That doesn't get us anywhere. We still don't know what she saw. It could have been Holman paying McKay off for falsifying evidence related to a fatal car crash—or not. The problem is, we can't prove a thing now that Jane's dead and the only surviving witness, Carmen Morales, has dropped out of sight. But the theory does make sense and fits in with some facts our internal affairs investigation has turned up. McKay's spending habits don't fit his pay scale."

"So what you're saying is, although McKay was probably responsible for Jane's murder, you still can't take this to court."

"Not with what I've got so far, no."

"Any chance that you could identify the pistol recovered as McKay's weapon by ruling out the other nine hundred and ninety-nine? They should all be registered, right?"

"Thinking outside the box, huh? It's a stretch, but we'll only be able to narrow the list. Some will have been stolen, lost, or sold during gun shows, which makes them nearly impossible to trace."

"What about the actual murder, then? McKay's alibi is that he was playing golf with State Senator Holman, right?" she asked. "Considering what we now suspect, that's awfully convenient."

"Yeah, but two of the senator's aides were part of that four-some. They vouched for him as well."

"Which may just mean they're afraid of losing their jobs. Let me see if I can poke some holes into his alibi," she said.

"I don't like the sound of that," Tom said slowly. "What are you going to do?" Before Sister Agatha could answer, he quickly added. "No, stop! Don't tell me. Sometimes it's better if I don't know."

Hanging up, Sister Agatha began formulating a plan.

Sister Bernarda walked into the parlor. "Will you be off to town again, Your Charity?"

She nodded. "Pray that I'm finally seeing things in the right light and that we'll have a resolution soon."

Sister Agatha stepped outside and whistled for Pax. Seconds passed, but to her surprise, the dog didn't come racing around the corner of the building. Worried, she whistled again as she walked toward the parking area. That's when she spotted him, his tail wagging, standing by the Antichrysler. His panting grin was almost saying, "Where have you been?"

"Okay, furball, have your laugh. I was a little slow this morn-ing." She looked down at her hands. They were more swollen than usual, and her knees ached. She'd taken her medication, but it hadn't kicked in yet.

As a counter to the pain, she began praying. She wouldn't give in to this. She had too much to do. Today, she'd have to find a way to destroy McKay's alibi and an idea about how to do that had come to her.

Twenty minutes later, she parked in front of Louis Sanchez's home. His car was in the driveway, and she could smell the deli-cious scent of barbecue sauce coming from the backyard. Putting Pax on a leash, she walked around the side of the house and found Louis at the grill.

"Sister Agatha, welcome. I bet you caught a whiff of these ribs all the way out at the monastery!" Louis said, waving a long-handled spatula.

She glanced down at the grill, then, puzzled, stepped closer. "Those are salmon fillets, Louis. But they do smell delicious."

He took another look. "Did I say ribs? I meant salmon. I think I've been inhaling too much smoke."

Sensing his confusion was part of the grieving process, Sister Agatha said softly, "We all miss her, Louis."

He nodded and wiped an errant tear from his eye. "So what brings you here, Sister?"

"I've come for your help on something related to Jane. Can you spare a moment?"

"Sure, but for the next three minutes or so I can't leave the salmon unattended. Can we talk out here?"

"Actually, Louis, I wanted to take a look at Jane's prayer book. It was returned to you, along with her purse and other personal items, if I recall."

He nodded. "It's still on her desk in the living room. Why don't you go on in and get it?"

"Okay. Pax, stay." Sister Agatha went through the kitchen door, noting the fresh vegetables and fruits on the counter. There were probably a dozen memos, all pink, still stuck to the refrigerator. Sister Agatha stopped to read one. SUNDAY. PICK UP KALE AND FRESH TOMATOES AT FARMER'S MARKET, it said in Jane's distinctive script.

Jane's handbag was sitting on top of the desk. When Sister Agatha picked it up, she saw the layer of dust beneath it. The desk, however, was spotless. Clearly the purse had been placed on a dusty desk, and later, when the desk's surface had been cleaned, the purse hadn't been touched. She wondered how long Louis would leave Jane's purse exactly where it was.

Sister Agatha found the prayer book with Jane's name written neatly on the front. For a second she wondered if she should pick it up by the edges, but, seeing traces of powder left over from when the police had dusted it for fingerprints, she realized it didn't matter anymore.

Holding it at an angle to the light and close to her eyes, she went through it, page by page. After a moment, she found what she was looking for, the place where Jane had stuck the memo while writing. Hands shaking with excitement, she checked once more to be certain. There were faint impressions there—letters, and words. Thank goodness Jane had used a ballpoint pen instead of a felt-tip marker.

Sister Agatha adjusted the angle several times and finally was able to make out the message. It didn't come as a surprise.

"I've got you now," she whispered aloud, slipping the prayer book into her pocket.

"Got what, Sister?" Louis was standing in the entryway to the kitchen.

"I'll let you know just as soon as I can, Louis. In the meantime, you don't mind if I borrow Jane's prayer book for a bit, do you?"

"Not at all. Do you and Pax want to share my early lunch?"

"No thanks. We've got to get going. But isn't it a bit early for lunch?"

"Jane always told me that several small meals a day are better than a few big ones, so I'm trying it out."

Sister Agatha rushed past him toward the kitchen door. "I'll bring the prayer book back just as soon as I'm done with it, okay?"

"Sure. 'Bye for now, Sister," she heard him say from somewhere behind her.

"Come on, Pax," she called. "We've got business."

Armed with this evidence, and working on the possibility that Holman and McKay had a reason to protect each other's alibis, she decided to go talk to Holman's aides. As a nun, she could get farther with some informal questions than Tom could with his badge. Of course, first she needed their names.

She considered calling Tom and asking, but, all things considered, it would be safer to get the information from Chuck Moody. If she called Tom, she'd have to explain about the prayer book, go by the station, and maybe lose her only chance to follow up without the restraints of police procedures. Her way would guarantee Tom information as well as the prayer book later today.

After a quick visit to the *Chronicle*, she got the two names she needed—John Andrews and Kevin Johnson—and their contact numbers.

"I'd like to come along, Sister," Chuck said, walking her to the door.

"Not this time, Chuck. I've only got one shot with each man, and my only advantage is that they're both Catholics and have been raised to know that they can trust a nun. John Andrews is active in the parish, and I've known his family a long time. I'm hoping he'll find it easy to talk to me in person. If not, I'll try Kevin Johnson."

Sister Agatha went to John Andrews's office, but only his administrative assistant was there.

"I'm sorry, Sister, he's taking the day off. He's been putting in long hours projecting the local impact of regulations and laws passed in the recent legislative session."

"I understand. So I suppose he's over at Las Palomas Golf Course?" It was only a guess, but according to what she'd heard from Chuck in the past, the pueblo's eighteen-hole course was well known and popular with local politicians and business leaders. Lots of deals were cut on the links.

"Yes, that's where he goes to unwind. He'll be there all morning."

"Thanks," Sister Agatha said, then glanced over at Pax as they walked back out to the Antichrysler. "We're going to visit a golf course, Pax. I know the temptation to run around those beautiful grounds will be great, but you'll just have to resist. In particular, stay away from the trees."

Almost as if he'd understood her, he sighed long and loud, then lay down in the backseat.

They arrived at the golf course around twenty minutes later. It was a beautiful New Mexico morning. There wasn't even one cloud in the brilliant blue sky, and the parking lot was nearly filled with luxury cars and SUVs. As she pulled into an open slot several rows from the clubhouse, the Antichrysler backfired loudly. Used to it by now, she didn't give it a thought until she climbed out of the car and saw three golfers standing beside a German-made SUV staring at her. Refusing to feel intimidated, she smiled and waved.

With Pax on leash and at heel, Sister Agatha entered the cool, elegant clubhouse and continued to the front desk. "I'd like to see John Andrews. I'm told he's here on the course."

The tall, slender blonde smiled. "Hi, Sister! Do you remember me? I'm Patti Gómez, now Patti Ortiz," she said. "You taught religion at St. Charles when I was there—though that was a long time ago."

She studied the face, mentally changed the hair color to black, then nodded. "I do remember you. Back then you wanted to become a nun."

She laughed. "That lasted until eighth grade. When I discovered boys, everything changed."

"It happens that way sometimes," she said, then quickly brought the conversation back on track. "About John Andrews . . ."

She checked a list, then looked back at Sister Agatha. "You just missed him. His foursome teed off ten minutes ago. He's probably somewhere between the first and third holes right now." She turned to view the course with a powerful set of binoculars through a big picture window. "Yes, I'm right. They're about to tee off at the second hole."

"Thanks. I'll go and catch up to him on the fairway."

"No, Sister, you can't. Nobody but guests and members of our staff is allowed out on the course. You'll have to wait here until the golfers finish their round."

"How long will that take?"

"They don't have a cart, so it'll be at least a couple of hours."

Sister Agatha didn't argue. This was simply an opportunity to use a little creativity. She thanked Patti and led Pax out of the clubhouse.

Instead of returning to the Antichrysler, though, Sister Agatha walked Pax over to the wooden fence that separated the course from an encircling access road. Following the fence line, she searched for the flags that designated where the greens were located. Once she found the one with a big two on it, she stopped.

"It's time to take a more active approach, Pax," she said.

Looking around to assure herself no one was nearby, she climbed over the low barrier, then called to Pax. He scrunched between the bottom and middle rails and joined her.

"Okay, it's showtime! Keep your head low and run fast. I'll be right behind you, Pax."

Spotting the foursome walking down the fairway about a

hundred yards beyond the tees, she pointed and gave Pax the command to leave.

The dog ran off in the direction of the golfers.

Pretending to chase after a wayward pet, Sister Agatha hoisted up her skirt and went after him.

"Fore!" someone yelled loudly.

Sister Agatha cringed instinctively as a golf ball whizzed by her at waist height. If she'd been playing baseball, it would have been a strike.

22

HEY, CALL OFF YOUR DOG, SISTER!"
Looking up quickly, she saw the man who'd yelled out to her frozen in place. Pax had dropped to a sit directly in front of him as if he were trying to persuade the man to play ball.

Sister Agatha recognized the man as a local heart specialist. They'd consulted him regarding Sister Gertrude's condition.

Sister Agatha ran over and leashed Pax immediately. "I'm so sorry, Dr. Kaplan. He got away from me."

She glanced casually at the faces of the three other golfers. One was the aide she'd come to speak to, the other a real estate developer.

As her gaze drifted to the fourth, the blood froze in her veins. "Archbishop O'Malley."

"Ah, Sister Agatha," the Archbishop said, his blue eyes twinkling. "I should have known. Would you care to explain?"

Despite his soft, pleasant voice, Sister Agatha knew it hadn't been a request. She apologized for interrupting their game, then, speaking rapidly in a hurried voice, continued. "Your Excellency, this was an unfortunate necessity. I've been gathering information that'll help the sheriff find the person who killed a woman from our parish. With your permission, I'd like to speak with John Andrews for just a few moments. I can accompany him during play so it won't slow your round."

He nodded. "I've heard of your success in helping law enforcement officials crack their cases. Archbishop Miera filled me in before he was assigned to Chicago. Just tell me one thing," he said, coming closer and dropping his voice to a conspiratorial whisper. "The dog didn't run away, did he?"

"No, Your Excellency. I gave him the command to leave," she whispered back with a hesitant smile. "I needed a reason to come out onto the course, since time was of the essence."

"I've enjoyed meeting you, Sister Agatha," he said with a chuckle. "I hope we get a chance to talk more in the future."

Her heart was still beating overtime when the Archbishop turned to John and asked him to join her. Sister Agatha could see that although Mr. Andrews certainly didn't look pleased, he wasn't about to refuse the Archbishop's request.

"So what can I do for you, Sister Agatha?" he asked, leading her to where his ball was resting on the far side of the fairway. His voice was as cold as ice.

Sister Agatha kept pace, grateful that the other golfers had to go to three other locations. Once she was satisfied with the distance between them, she began. "I understand that you played golf with Sergeant Michael McKay the morning that Jane Sanchez was murdered."

"Yeah, I did. We were here, in fact."

They reached John's ball. Since he was farthest from the pin, he would be taking the next shot.

It took him almost a minute to decide whether to use a long iron or a wood, and the way he kept fiddling with his golf glove told her that he was ill at ease. A man with nothing to hide wouldn't have been that uneasy around a nun.

Finally he hit the ball, but he must have topped it, because it never got more than five feet off the ground. Fortunately for him, it went to the center of the fairway and rolled quite a ways.

They remained where they were until the others took their shots, then continued down the freeway. She remained close to his side but said nothing. Sometimes people with secrets found long stretches of silence harder to deal with than anything else.

As the minutes ticked by, he grew even more uncomfortable. While they waited for the two others to take their next shots, John pulled a club out of his bag and looked toward the pin. From what she knew of golf, he wouldn't have much of a problem hitting it onto the green from here.

"Sister, I want to finish my round, and to do that well I need to avoid distractions," he said at last, looking at her. "Is there something else I can do for you?"

"Are you and Michael McKay friends?" she asked without preamble.

He nodded. "He's always been there for me when I needed him. I fell off my roof last year trying to fix some shingles and ended up needing knee surgery. Mike took me to work every day and even volunteered to help my wife keep up with the yard work until I was off the crutches."

Sister Agatha was beginning to see the whole picture. "So you owe him."

He nodded. "I guess you can say that."

"But a murder has been committed, and by withholding information, you're muddying the waters," she said quietly. She'd wanted it to sound like a statement of fact, not an accusation. "It's not a blessing to Sergeant McKay either, since it interferes with the process that could clear him."

He didn't answer, but she could see he was considering all his options. John went over to line up his shot, addressing the ball. Finally he shook his head and stepped back, taking a practice swing.

"If he isn't guilty, no one's going to railroad him," she continued. "But if we don't separate the innocent from the guilty quickly, a killer could go free."

He said nothing for a few more seconds, stepped up, then hit a high, arching shot that landed in the center of the green, bounced high, and rolled toward the pin.

Satisfied, he finally spoke. "Michael *did* play golf with us that morning, but he had a stomach virus and had to excuse himself when we were on the third tee. He didn't rejoin us until the sixteenth hole and still looked a little green. You can't fake something like that, Sister Agatha."

She considered it. Judging from the relatively close distance between the monastery and here, his absence would have given him ample time to go kill Jane and return. Murder could have also explained the green cast on his face. An act of that nature, one from which there'd be no turning back, couldn't have been easy for a police officer.

"So Michael asked you not to tell anyone he'd been sick and gone for most of the round?" She wanted things clarified.

"No, actually, Senator Holman did. Mike had pressured some Lobo coaches to score basketball tickets for him, and the senator didn't want internal affairs leaning on McKay. Considering we all knew Michael, we went along with it."

"Thanks for your help. I appreciate it."

"Sister, try to keep my name out of all this, will you? I have a family to support."

"I'll do everything I can."

Sister Agatha hurried with Pax back off the golf course, and made it without incident. She drove back to the sheriff's office, told Tom what she'd learned, and handed over Jane's prayer book.

He held the page at an angle to his desk light and read it aloud. *"Got photo of Gerry's sergeant taking money from stranger. Who and why? Tell sheriff? Ask Sister A."*

Tom set it down on the desk. "Now we have a motive. If this is accurate and McKay's dirty, I want him off my department as soon as possible. That's the *only* reason I'm not yelling at you right now. I'll have this prayer book processed again ASAP and photos taken of the relevant page." He stood and retrieved his holster and firearm from a desk drawer.

"Where are you going?" she asked, following him to the door.

"To the golf course. They have surveillance cameras covering their parking area. Some of their regulars have expensive cars they want looked after. I'll check the day in question, find McKay's truck, watch him leave, and figure out exactly how long it took him to get back."

"Four eyes are better than two," she said in a hopeful voice.

He nodded once. "Follow me there."

Twenty minutes later, Sister Agatha sat with the sheriff in the small clubhouse office. Checking the date and time as he went, Tom rolled the parking lot footage.

"There he is," Sister Agatha said, sitting up quickly. "I'd know that moose of a truck anywhere."

Tom leaned closer to the screen, trying to make out the

details. "There's something in the bed of that truck." He stopped the DVD, ran it back a few frames, froze the image, and adjusted the focus.

"It's red," Sister Agatha said, moving back and forth trying to find the best angle. "I see a wheel. It's a bicycle, Tom—like the one that was stolen from Louis Sanchez!"

Tom let the footage run, and they saw McKay climb out of the tall vehicle cab. When he lowered the tailgate to get the golf clubs out, they caught a glimpse of the bike.

"There's no doubt now what that is," Tom said.

Tom advanced the images forward, keeping his eye on the clock timer at the bottom of the video feed. Shortly thereafter, they saw McKay toss his clubs into the passenger side of the truck, climb inside, and back out of the parking space. The truck disappeared from view as it pulled out into the street.

They continued running the footage, stopping to view things at normal speed anytime a vehicle pulled in. Finally, nearly two hours of video time later, a pickup entered the lot. Slowing to normal play now, they saw McKay park his truck, climb out with his clubs, and hurry into the clubhouse, disappearing from view.

Tom stopped the image and zeroed in on the pickup. "I don't see it anymore."

"It's there," she said, knowing he meant the bicycle. "Run it back for a moment. Now play it at normal speed," she said, then pointed to the screen. "It's closer to the tailgate and partially blocked from view, but you can still see the handlebars, and part of the saddle is sticking up. There's that section of rail or whatever you call that part of a man's bike. See the red?"

Tom studied it, adjusted the focus, then finally nodded. "You've got good eyes."

"Why would McKay need a bicycle to play golf that

Sunday—unless he planned to approach the monastery quietly and kill Jane? Taking the bike out of his truck farther down the ditch road meant nobody inside the chapel would hear him arrive. Silence was part of his plan. After he murdered Jane, he rode the bike back to his truck, returned to the golf course, and finished the last two holes. With the tall bed on that truck, only the high-angle camera could reveal he had a bicycle in there."

"Unfortunately, all we can *prove* is that he had a bike in his pickup. I've got another theory, too, that could explain the events and requires a lot less imagination."

"Go on."

"It could be argued that Bennett hired McKay to murder his mother-in-law. Jane did everything she could to work against Gerry, and he has never reacted well to threats. McKay must have known how obsessed Jane was if she ended up following him by mistake one day. Then, once he knew that she'd taken incriminating photos of him, McKay saw a way to put a quick end to his problems. He'd also have leverage to keep Gerry from nailing him on the IA investigation."

Before she could answer him, Tom's cell phone rang. Tom spoke in single syllables, then hung up and summoned the security man who'd handed over the surveillance disk. "I'm taking this disk in as evidence. I'll give you a receipt."

The golf course employee gave him a hesitant look. "I can't authorize that, Sheriff. I'll need to check with my boss."

"Make sure you let him know that I can get a warrant if he refuses to cooperate. The tribe will save themselves a lot of trouble and embarrassment, not to mention publicity, if you all play nice. You can burn a copy if you want, but I need the original."

While the young man went to get his boss, Sheriff Green looked at Sister Agatha. "The call I took was from our lab. They were finally able to pick up more numbers from the gun, and we got a hit. It looks like the weapon was purchased by a man we'd hauled in on a drug bust earlier this year."

"Who were the arresting officers?" Sister Agatha asked.

"Gerald Bennett and Michael McKay."

She considered the new information. "Maybe you're right. In a warped way, it makes sense that Bennett would hire McKay to kill his mother-in-law. There's a clean, simple motive there. The problem is that we've still got too many loose ends, Tom. Nothing really fits all the way."

Sister Agatha placed a hand on Pax's head, reviewed the possibilities, then looked up at Tom again. "I know how we can get to the truth."

"I'm all ears."

Sister Agatha stood near the monastery gates as Senator Holman and John Andrews pulled up.

"Senator, welcome back to our monastery," Sister Agatha greeted him.

Holman was all smiles, though Andrews appeared pale and nervous, not knowing what to expect but obviously concerned about his own future.

"I'm happy to be here. The sisters at this monastery are part of my constituency, too. I wanted you to know that you have my full support," he said, looking around. "Are we early?"

He'd been led to expect the press, so Sister Agatha wasn't surprised. "A little," she replied. Smiling and nodding to John, she tried to reassure him without words that he wasn't her target this time.

"So when do you plan to have the memorial built for the victim?" Holman asked, looking toward the gates, obviously eager for the press to show up.

"That depends on how soon we can raise the funds. We wanted you to see our plans and hopefully help us find a way to get our project off the ground." Sister Agatha looked around. "I don't see any reporters here yet, so while Sister Bernarda shows Mr. Andrews where we plan to erect the memorial, why don't we step out of the sun? We can talk comfortably inside the parlor."

Sheriff Green arrived just as Andrews walked away with Sister Bernarda. After a brief handshake between the men, Sister Agatha urged Tom and Holman into the privacy of the parlor.

Senator Holman stood by the window, looking outside. "The reporters are bound to arrive soon. You'll want to greet them out on the grounds, won't you?" he asked, obviously ill at ease.

"Unfortunately, the reporters will be a bit delayed," Tom said.

Holman's expression stiffened, and his eyes narrowed. "I'm a busy man. What's really going on, Sheriff?"

"I'm here to make you a onetime offer, Senator Holman. Provide me with enough evidence to bring Jane Sanchez's killer to trial, and we'll give you immunity on manslaughter, bribery, and conspiracy charges."

"Manslaughter? Is this some kind of joke? Surely you don't think I had anything to do with Mrs. Sanchez's death!"

"No, not hers, at least not directly," Sheriff Green answered, "though you might face conspiracy charges. I'm talking about Beatriz Griego. You were drinking that afternoon, and I now have a witness who'll testify to that."

"Then your witness is wrong, or flat-out lying. Your own deputy gave me a field sobriety test."

"No, he didn't, not according to my witness."

243

"Are you calling your own deputy a liar? The fact is, there was only one other person there, and she was in this country illegally. Any court will believe one of your own officers over her, Sheriff. You've got nothing."

"It's difficult to keep a story like this under wraps," Sister Agatha said with a deep sigh. "The press will go wild once they discover the connection between the phony alibi you gave Sergeant McKay, a suspect in a murder investigation, and the fact that he was the officer in charge at the scene of your car accident."

"Even if we never get a conviction, your political career will go down in flames," Sheriff Green added.

"*Murder*? You think Sergeant McKay killed the Sanchez woman?" he asked, his voice rising an octave.

"She saw you two together, didn't she? We finally got the memo," Tom said.

"What memo? What are you talking about?" Holman asked, fear alive in his eyes.

"The one Jane Sanchez wrote, the one McKay *thought* he'd taken care of," Tom said, getting into his face. "It turns out Jane caught you and McKay meeting after the story of the accident came out in the *Chronicle*. A few days after that she was killed. We've now recovered her cell phone photo of the two of you together—with time *and* date."

Sister Agatha knew that wasn't true but kept a neutral expression, recalling her days as a journalist when she'd used deception to loosen tongues.

"Okay, okay. That pain-in-the-ass woman thought McKay was Gerald Bennett when she poked her head in the window. She yelled out, 'Gotcha!' but when she realized it wasn't Gerry with a girlfriend, she crumbled, apologized, and took off. McKay said not to worry, that he'd handle it. But I never thought . . ."

"She was a threat to him. We have evidence to suggest he listened in on the Sanchezes' phone calls. He was afraid she'd spread the tale. And McKay knew *you* wouldn't say a word if Jane ended up dead. You had too much to lose. You'd bribed him to save your butt on those DWI charges. So after he killed Jane Sanchez, he came to you and asked for a big favor in return—an alibi. That would keep both of you out of jail. So now you get to name your poison. Do you want to go to jail for bribery, or conspiracy to commit murder?"

"You can't prove I paid anyone anything. Maybe I just forgot that McKay went back to the clubhouse that morning. People can forget . . . and so do the voters. I've got Mayor Garcia backing me, and he's a powerful ally. All a photo proves is that we were talking together. So what?"

"You still don't *see* that you've been set up, do you?" Tom pressed. "How are you going to explain that other secret meeting with McKay over on Calle de Elena, the one where he changed the vehicle number to make it look like you were meeting with Bennett? Did you know that McKay made a phony meal request using a made-up address on that street so the nun coming by to make the delivery would see you two together? And what *was* inside the envelope you gave him? More bribery money?"

His jaw fell as he realized the truth, but he still tried to recover. "What meeting, Sheriff? I didn't meet McKay, or any of your officers, for that matter. Burden of proof. Ever heard of the concept?"

"The word of a nun still carries weight in this area," Sister Agatha said. "You've got even bigger problems, though. McKay set you up that day, just like the sheriff said. Think about it. He knew about the Good News Meals Program and purposely arranged to have another pair of eyes on that meeting of yours.

That time it was supposed to look like you and Gerry Bennett were meeting." She brought out the photograph of Sister Jo on the Harley and showed it to him. "McKay had a camera with him, remember? And there's more."

She reached behind the parlor desk and brought out a small white magnetic sign with the number 73 on it. The number was the same color as on the sheriff's department vehicles. It wasn't the one originally sold to McKay, but it would do.

The ruse worked. When Holman's eyes widened, she knew he'd recognized it. "I remember the camera and the sign, and I wondered about it at the time," he admitted. "It wasn't the regular number on McKay's police cruiser. But you're wrong about what happened that day. The envelope I gave him didn't have money in it. It was just a copy of our legislative package regarding law enforcement. McKay had asked me for it earlier."

"Maybe it was, maybe it wasn't," Tom said. "Either way, Sergeant McKay was posing as Bennett—at least from a distance—and he wanted a witness while he made it look as if *you* were passing Bennett money, maybe to cover up for that DWI. That gave Sergeant McKay something extra to hold over you. To the nun who'd become his eyewitness, the one who drove by on the motorcycle, *you* were involved."

He paused for several seconds, letting the knowledge sink in. "McKay would give you up in a second if it meant getting a murder charge reduced—or, even better, getting himself off the hook. I want him a lot more than I want you, but it's your call, Senator. Do we go after him, or do I settle for you?"

Holman mulled it over for several long moments. "I'll help you," he said at last, "but I want a few guarantees in return."

"Specify," Tom responded.

"Drop all bribery and conspiracy charges, and don't have any comments for the press when my people put a different spin on things. My story will be that I helped you catch a murderer. By the time I'm finished, I'll come out smelling like a rose."

Tom's eyebrows shot up. "You're quick with a plan."

"I'm used to working under pressure," he answered.

"Deal—if the DA agrees. But you have to get me enough to nail McKay for the murder of Jane Sanchez. And one more thing. You resign as state senator."

Holman thought about it for an agonizing minute. "Okay, but sooner or later I'll be back in the political arena. You know it and I know it."

Tom nodded once, aware that he had no other choice.

Holman suggested he meet with McKay, wearing a wire, and try to get a confession or admission of guilt from him.

"I'm not sure that'll work," Tom said. "He's not a fool. He's been playing you, Officer Bennett, and us for days now."

"How about if instead of setting up a formal meeting you ask him to come here?" Sister Agatha suggested. "Tell him the nuns will be planting a special climbing rose as a memorial to Jane Sanchez and that the local newspapers will be on hand to record the event. Say you think a photo of him and you together will show your support for local law enforcement and also help him careerwise."

"Are you sure you want this to go down here?" Tom asked Sister Agatha.

"Yes. Let the murderer face justice where his victim fell."

23

AFTER GETTING TOM'S OKAY, SISTER AGATHA CALLED Chuck. Although she couldn't give him any details, she asked him to bring his camera and trust her. She owed him that much for all the help he'd given her.

Sister Agatha stood by Sister Bernarda, who was making a show out of digging a hole where the memorial rose would be planted. The rosebush had already been picked up at the nursery.

As Chuck waited for the unfolding story, he helped them make the ruse look good by taking photos while they worked.

Sheriff Green had remained in the parlor, which was off-limits to everyone else right now. From there, he'd listen in and record Holman's conversation with McKay. The off-duty sergeant had come over right away in response to Holman's phone call.

"It's happening," Sister Bernarda said as Holman looked sincere for Chuck's camera and then walked off with Sergeant McKay, who'd arrived in uniform.

Sister Agatha was determined not to look up or even glance in the direction of Holman and McKay, but the temptation was great.

"If you get caught watching them, you'll give yourself away," Sister Bernarda cautioned, guessing her thoughts. "Just keep fiddling with the soil or pretend to be pulling weeds."

Sister Agatha did so, but she could feel the tension thrumming through her body. She was acutely aware of every breath she took and each beat of her heart. She felt like a watch that had been wound too tight.

Her hand shaking now, she reached up and gingerly touched her small earpiece. It was directly beneath her veil, but Tom had assured her that she'd be able to listen in without any problem.

It was then she heard Sister Bernarda's gasp.

"What is it?" she asked her fellow extern quickly, her gaze on the soil.

"I was praying . . . needing assurance, you know, not asking. But I didn't expect . . ." Sister Bernarda stopped talking and pointed.

The sun was filtering through the leaves of the giant cottonwood as it usually did this time of day. On the ground before the massive tree, they could both see the outline of a giant angel. Sister Agatha could almost make out flowing locks of hair around an oval face, and near the waist, light and shadow melded together to form what appeared to be a sword.

"That's your sign, the one you didn't dare ask for but received anyway," Sister Agatha whispered. "You're—we're—being protected."

Sister Bernarda crossed herself.

Following their gazes, Chuck, with a sharp intake of breath, brought his camera up. Suddenly a gust of wind rustled the distant leaves, and the image disappeared. "Rats! That sure looked like an angel, didn't it?"

"Yes, it did," Sister Bernarda responded in a whisper.

"Wish I'd have been quicker with the camera," Chuck replied. He aimed it at the rose, which was still in its peat pot. "Your mark's looking over here. We better make it look good."

Sister Agatha got busy helping Sister Bernarda mix sand and potting soil in a big washbasin. As Holman began speaking to McKay, she heard him clearly.

"You've put me in a tough situation, McKay," Holman said. "Sheriff Green thinks you had something to do with Jane Sanchez's murder and has been pressuring me to poke holes in your story about being on the golf course that day. So you and I are cutting a new deal. I'll protect your alibi and make sure my aides keep their mouths shut. You stop demanding money to keep quiet about my accident. You've got more to lose than me, McKay, so I'd take the deal if I were you."

McKay didn't answer, so Holman continued. "You're already being investigated, McKay, and neither one of us wants to get arrested. And just so you know, Deputy Bennett's been on my tail, too. He's contacted me at least twice, pushing to find out if I bribed you not to give me a Breathalyzer test that afternoon. He's still pissed that you took over the accident scene. If he finds the passenger who was in the car that night and she swears you never gave me a field sobriety test, you're screwed. Bottom line—you've got at least two people gunning for you, and they're motivated, trust me."

When McKay still didn't say a word, Sister Agatha looked up at Sister Bernarda. "Reach for that trowel and sneak a look at McKay and Holman. I want to know what McKay's doing."

While Sister Agatha kept her back to the men, Sister Bernarda walked over to the wheelbarrow they were using to haul the tools and materials and reached for the hand trowel. As

she turned around to head back, she glanced off to the side sur-
reptitiously, not turning her head.

"McKay's not doing much of anything. From what I'm seeing he's just looking around. He glanced over at the deputy
across the street, the one assigned to protect us, and is now looking around the grounds. If you want to take a quick look for
yourself, go right ahead."

As Sister Agatha pretended to brush off her habit, she spotted a piece of amber taillight on the parking lot gravel just behind her, outside the garden ring. Undoubtedly it had been left
there from the time last year when the fugitive had crashed
through their gate in a stolen car.

As she picked it up, she looked to the side, glancing at
McKay. She was sure that something about Holman's attitude or
demeanor must have given him away. McKay smelled a setup.

Holman continued to press. "Bennett was there the day I
had the accident. When you pulled rank on him and took over,
I'm sure he smelled a rat. If nothing else, he must have put
things together when you failed to show up for court and they
had to drop all charges. I think he's looking for payback."

"You talk too much," McKay said at last.

"You told me not to worry about Mrs. Sanchez seeing us in the
car and taking that photo of me handing you that wad of bills.
Now I know why. You killed her, then tried to frame Bennett—the
most believable suspect. He was investigating *you*, and that was
your way of getting him off your back. Wake up, McKay. Bennett
knows and is out for blood."

"Bennett and I are buds. Gerry'd never turn me in for some
bogus charges. We go way back. What have you been smoking,
Holman?"

"You're just going to kiss me off, is that it? Well, don't
expect any more payoffs. You're on your own, and if you go

down, don't think you can take me with you. I've got more clout around here than you realize."

McKay laughed. "With who, that lightweight Mayor Garcia? I'm shaking in my boots."

Continuing to play it cool, McKay walked away, joining the other reporters who'd finally turned up to hear Holman's promised speech.

It was time for plan B. Taking the small piece of amber taillight she'd found, Sister Agatha placed it in her pocket and slipped away. She needed to talk to Tom as quickly as possible.

While everyone's attention was focused on Dwight Holman, who was now making his speech, Sister Agatha found Pax and, with the dog at heel but unleashed, headed to McKay's truck. McKay, off duty despite the uniform, had driven his personal vehicle.

After looking around to verify she and Pax were alone, Sister Agatha pulled down the tailgate and climbed into the pickup. Pax remained at stay on the ground.

With the amber glass still cupped in the hollow of her palm, she began examining the bed of the truck, hoping that some traces of the bicycle's red paint had rubbed off on McKay's new finish. A link like that would go a long way to establishing McKay's involvement in the Sanchez murder. Suddenly she heard soft footsteps behind her, and Pax growled softly.

"What are you doing?" came the deep male voice.

Sister Agatha knew it was McKay without having to turn around. Her heart began beating overtime. Holman had bluffed and gotten nowhere. Maybe there was no substitute for a little courage and the truth.

"Whoever killed Jane rode up on a red bike," Sister Agatha said. "It was stolen the day before from her husband, Louis

Sanchez. A neighbor saw a man in a hooded sweatshirt riding it away. That bike has been recovered and is in the evidence room. I decided to look for telltale scratches that could have been made when you transported the bicycle that morning."

He burst out laughing. "Knock yourself out, Sister."

"The killer knew a lot about evidence and didn't leave much behind. He's human, though, and humans make mistakes."

"Are you saying *I'm* the killer?" It wasn't a question as much as it was a challenge.

Pax growled softly again. In response McKay placed his hand on the dog's head, calming him, and smiled at Sister Agatha. "Love this dog," he added pleasantly.

"Look at it another way, Sergeant. I'm just trying to eliminate you from the list of possible suspects."

He laughed loudly. "Sister, you're something else! You've already made up your mind that I'm the killer, haven't you? Well, you go right ahead and snoop all you want. But I should tell you I was playing golf over at the pueblo's course Sunday for about three hours during the time of the murder, I believe."

"Las Palomas," she said with a nod, then continued to search. "Funny thing. I've been talking to people here and there and discovered that you left as your foursome was teeing off at the third hole, and you didn't return until the sixteenth hole. That leaves a big gap in your alibi."

His eyes darkened. "Satisfied now that no paint rubbed off onto my truck?" he asked after a beat.

"No paint smudges, but I think I've just spotted the link I was looking for. The stolen bike was missing a piece off the reflector, and they couldn't find it in that trash bin anywhere. I guess the reflector broke when you tossed the bike into the back of this pickup. You were undoubtedly in a rush to get back to the golf course before they finished the round. A partial alibi is better than none."

She crawled over the hard surface of the bed, the metal ridges digging painfully into her knees. Then she put her hand into the left corner, the spot closest to the driver's door, and pretended to retrieve the small piece of taillight she'd palmed earlier.

Sister Agatha held it out and showed it to him. "Interesting, don't you think? I wonder if this'll fit into the broken spot on the reflector."

He sat on the tailgate, blocking her exit. "Give me what you've found," he said, holding out his hand and keeping his voice soft for Pax's benefit. "You and I both know that there's no way that could be part of the bicycle's reflector. I used a power washer and hosed this truck down completely last Sunday afternoon."

Sister Agatha saw the rage in his eyes. He didn't really want the small piece of worthless plastic. He wanted her to be afraid. Every one of his threats to the externs had been designed to generate fear and uncertainty.

"You don't scare me," she said flatly. "My life is in God's hands, not yours."

"Who says we're talking about *your* life? There's a saying that a running man with a knife can slice a thousand throats in one night. You have no defenses here, except that dog, and I've already shown how I can take him out in the blink of an eye— or a little spark. If you value the lives of the nuns who live here, you'll hand that over and keep your mouth shut. I make a *very* bad enemy, Sister Agatha. Believe that."

This time Pax's growl was much more pronounced, but McKay placed his hand on the dog and gave him the command to settle. Pax obeyed. McKay's years of working with police dogs were paying off for him now.

"If you do *anything* to me now, the dog will attack you no matter how many commands you know."

"I wouldn't be that stupid. My move would come when you

least expected it—in a week, a month. Or maybe I'd strike out at one of the other nuns when she's out alone making a meal delivery."

Sister Agatha handed him the amber plastic. "You win this round."

He offered her a hand and helped her down, a show of courtesy for the benefit of anyone watching from a distance. "Just remember that I'll be keeping a real close watch on you and the other sisters. None of you are ever out of my reach."

Sister Agatha looked off into the distance and added, "Did you get all that, Sheriff?"

McKay turned his head just as Sheriff Tom Green stepped out of the shadows. He'd come around from the far side of the monastery, hidden by the wall. Tom quickly moved between McKay and the driver's door, effectively blocking his escape. Several other deputies also converged on them, including the one who'd stayed in plain sight across the road.

Sister Agatha kept a tight hold on Pax's collar as she reached into her pocket and pulled out a digital recorder. It was still running. "Here you go, Sheriff," she said, handing it to Tom.

"Your own words, along with all the evidence we already have against you, will be enough to make sure you serve hard time. You and Senator Holman are going down," Tom told McKay.

Sister Agatha looked at McKay and smiled. "As it says in Job, He 'catches the wise in their own craftiness, and disappoints the counsel of the wicked.'"

Reverend Mother and Sister Agatha sat outside on a *banco*, watching the team of nuns building the small well house. Sister Jo was at the top of her form, directing the construction of a solid structure that would serve them for many years. The framing was almost complete around the sturdy foundation, and an insulated wooden floor was already in place around the pump. Some electrical work would come next—but outside help would be needed for that part.

"Did Chuck say anything else about seeing the angel?" Reverend Mother asked Sister Agatha as Sister Ignatius joined them.

Sister Agatha nodded. "He's still trying to decide if it was just the power of suggestion and a trick of the light, Mother. Without a photo, I'm guessing he'll remain a skeptic."

"Tzuriel was sent to *us*, not to the world," Sister Ignatius said, now as familiar with the incident as the rest of the sisters. "Our Lord must have asked Tzuriel to show himself to us so we wouldn't be afraid. The rest of the world didn't need to see him."

"I just wish we all could have had a chance to say thank you directly," Reverend Mother added with a wistful smile.

Sister Ignatius suddenly crossed herself and pointed ahead. "You were heard," she whispered. "Do you see it, Mother?"

Sister Agatha searched the ground ahead, but she couldn't see what Sister Ignatius was talking about.

Mother glanced at Sister Agatha, questions filling her eyes, but Sister Agatha shook her head, mystified.

"The leaf," Sister Ignatius said in a whisper. "The *gold* leaf."

Although they were surrounded by many varieties of green, all part of the new spring growth, there was one perfectly formed gold leaf on the ground directly in front of them. The breeze suddenly caught it, and as it lifted up off the ground, Reverend Mother and Sister Agatha saw that it was in the shape of an angel, wings and all.

Reverend Mother gasped, then whispered a heartfelt "Thank you."

Before she'd even finished the words, the leaf floated upward into the trees and out of their sight.

"It wasn't meant to stay here. God demands faith most of all," Sister Ignatius whispered.

As the bells for Compline rang, a hush fell over all of them. With bowed heads, the Brides of Christ put down their tools and answered their Lord's gentle summons.